The Dating Policy

Suzanne Eglington

Reading a good book in silence is like eating chocolate for the rest of your life and never getting fat.

—BECCA FITZPATRICK

The Dating Policy Copyright © 2019 by Suzanne Eglington. All Rights Reserved.

All rights reserved. No part of this book may be reproduced in any form or by any electronic or mechanical means including information storage and retrieval systems, without permission in writing from the author. The only exception is by a reviewer, who may quote short excerpts in a review.

Cover designed by Cover Creator

This book is a work of fiction. Names, characters, places, and incidents either are products of the author's imagination or are used fictitiously. Any resemblance to actual persons, living or dead, events, or locales is entirely coincidental.

Suzanne Eglington
Visit my website at www.suzanneeglington.com

Printed in the United States of America

First Printing: July 2018
Independently Published

ISBN-9781086802276

Acknowledgments

I would like to thank my kids for their independence that gives me the time to write.

To my fans with your endless compliments and feedback on how much you enjoy my storytelling.

To my man, who encourages me, compliments me, and is my think tank when I run into an issue. I know my life would not be this full without your love.

To my friend and family with all of your unconditional support.

And to my writing community that presents endless opportunities to help me grow.

Thank You

The Dating Policy

Chapter One

I glanced down at the silver and ivory invitation sitting on the table next to my handbag. This elegantly crafted postcard displayed two raised doves, each clamping onto a ribbon to form a heart shape, symbolizing the love and unity of Jessica and Brian.

I picked up the note and laughed. *Who in their right mind hosts a dry wedding reception?* I opened my purse and tucked the card on top of my stash of nip bottles. This was Jessica's wedding. If I had to suffer through this afternoon, then tequila was going with me.

No sooner had I parked, and Angela was making her way toward me. I grabbed my bag and pulled. The commotion from the tiny bottles shifting inside made me smile. "Shh, you weren't invited; you have to be quiet in there, okay?" I exited my Honda. "Mallory! You look gorgeous, but sweetie, black? I knew I should have coordinated our outfits. This is a wedding, not a funeral."

"That is strictly a matter of opinion, Angela." I immediately noticed she too was carrying a much larger bag than she usually does. I pointed, "Which poison did you bring to mix?"

"What are you talking about?"

I tapped my bag, "Tequila."

"Vodka. We just might find you a man here this afternoon."

I managed to answer in a playfully sarcastic tone. "We didn't bring enough booze for that, aside from the fact of there being too many co-workers here, and none of them worthy." I scanned over the majority of wedding guests lingering in the parking lot. I adjusted my sunglasses as I confessed, "There is only one man I would consider dating at SBS, and he wouldn't be caught dead at Jessica's wedding, which makes him even more appealing in my eyes."

She did not even inquire as to whom I was referring, "Well, you are one man up from me. There is no one that appeals to me there."

I placed my hand on her bare shoulder. "Well, remember, I am supposed to be working on finding love, and I very much doubt it's going to happen at this wedding."

She linked our arms, giving me a sassy grin with hopeful encouragement as I further stated: "Besides, I have you and tequila; my dance card is full."

Angela laughed as we both secured our bags over our shoulders and made our way in. I watched the exchange of wedding vows, Jessica repeating hers to Brian. I quickly glanced over to Erin, her eight-year-old daughter and flower girl who looked completely out of place. I knew that look all too well as I flashed back to the last three of my mother's five weddings. I, too, had to endure standing there at the altar with everyone looking on, knowing my life was going to change once again, adjusting to my mother's new decision.

Just as I suspected, Jessica placed all the SBS employees at two large tables in the back of the hall. Looking at our attendance, I was fairly certain we were invited to fill the empty chairs on the bride's side. I doubt she even had any friends.

Nevertheless, we made it through the afternoon, and I even had the pleasure of meeting Brian's older brother Thomas, who insisted I take his phone number. He was pretty funny, but I wasn't sure if my hand-packed wet bar had helped him out with that.

Tuesday afternoon, I had had it. Even though that wedding was lame as could be, Thomas reminded me I had not been in the company of a man alone for over a year. It was a calling for me to break back into dating, and I decided Thomas was going to be my starter date. I dialed his number without hesitation. I was feeling confident. He seemed pleased to hear from me as we secured Saturday night for dinner.

My next thought was that I needed to get back into better shape. I found a gym a few miles from work and signed up online. Tomorrow, I was going to make another fresh start at getting this extra weight off.

Wednesday morning, my "fantasy man" paid a visit. It only took a glimpse of his stride crossing by my workstation for Todd Duvall to distract me and remind me that I have not been touched by a man for over a year.

I wanted sex, and I wanted it with him. I had his physical movements programmed to memory. As if on cue, my stomach fluttered, my brain started to sizzle, and my body temperature rose a few degrees as a gentle hint of his cologne hit my nose, awakening my aura, completely making me lose concentration on the order I was presently taking. My eyes fixated on his hair, the only thing I could still see over the rim of my cubicle.

Embarrassed suddenly by my lack of attention, having to clear my throat, I asked my client to repeat his order.

Today's Todd sightings were up; twice this morning he has been down here. Something must have gone wrong.

Todd is one of our quality control managers; he has a few other titles, but this is the only one I care about because it brings him down to my department. The only times he makes an appearance in our sales department is when the company is about to lose money.

Todd does not like anything that disrupts the flow of success here. He was hired a year ago, specifically to solve a hiccup between the sales department and the distributers. He was still working it through.

Deep down, I also believe Todd was sent here to work at this particular company for our paths to cross. This is fate, something that I never really believed in before last year. It was working with my life coach that opened my mind to the possibilities.

My life coach, um, ya... didn't see that one coming either, but I have to admit, she has been exactly what I needed.

Todd Duvall was that single, hardworking man I set my chance at finding love with, though I am not sure he even knew my name yet.

There are times I am convinced he purposely glances at me.

In my mind, I have been working on a plan to introduce myself and start that conversation between us. In my mind, I see it playing out beautifully; there I am walking right up to him, commenting that I admire his work style, fluttering my eyes as he tells me he has been waiting for this opportunity. We exchange information, and he texts me before the end of the day, asking to meet me for drinks.... Yeah, then reality takes over as my heart pounds in my throat every time I see him, making me unable to speak.

Never have I been shy around men but there was something about him. Something about him threw me off balance, making everything go haywire.

My life coach commented that it was time to take control, to trust myself and my instincts. If I allowed myself to fail at love, then it would just snowball into my old reckless pattern.

This is why I needed to practice with Thomas first. Get the kinks out before I could get the courage to give it a go with Todd.

My office sister poked her head in. "It is seventy-three degrees outside. Let's go sit in the park and eat our lunch today. I'm sure we will be well entertained; besides, it's a full moon tonight, and all the crazies are out."

"I'm game." I grinned, twisting to grab my bag, and following her out.

People-watching was a minor sport with us. Angela leaned in, giving my left arm a sharp nudge. "Incoming four o'clock."

She pointed. "Ouch!" I grabbed and rubbed the throbbing area while simultaneously scolding her with my fixed stare.

She raised an eyebrow to challenge me. "You're gonna miss him, Mallory."

I turned my head to see who was so important to cause such a big reaction from her. Instantly, my lips parted as the currents of electricity misfired a few brain cells. There he was in this park, rewarding me for the third time today.

I could watch this powerhouse of a man forever. My pulse raced as my face began to flush. We were away from the office right now, and there could be an opportunity presenting itself.

Only Todd was walking with purpose through this crowd. He was clearly preoccupied. Something was definitely going on with him, and now I wanted to know what it was. Angela laughed. "Are you okay, Mallory?"

I cleared my throat, battling to break free from the intoxicating rush seizing my brain. I would not look away to save my life. Todd was approaching, getting closer, and I was sizing up this moment to break the ice and say hello.

My brain shifted into panic mode, Red Alert! Red Alert! It scrambled as my feet suddenly felt like cement blocks attached to the dirt under our park bench.

Angela continued talking for the both of us as I managed to exhale a long slow breath that I just realized I was holding.

"Damn, he looks delicious in blue. That color radiates his strong outline, right? Wow. Is Todd single? Do we even know this about him?"

I could feel Angela looking at me, waiting for my reply, but I was too busy dealing with my brain and body in panic mode.

I watched Todd making his way closer. I knew we were within eye-sight range now. He glanced down at his phone in his hand and sharply brought it back to his ear. His pace was slowing as he began talking.

Angela was rambling and flipping her opinion now, "Too bad he can be such an arrogant ass, though. I mean who treats people the way he does AND gets away with it?"

She shook her finger in his direction, "Besides, that condescending side to him, not attractive at all. I bet he is single."

I sat straighter because he stopped abruptly, causing the crowd behind him to quickly veer their forward motion to avoid bumping into him.

He stood there, talking away with his chin angled slightly upward, clearly not caring about anything else going on around him.

The people walking past us became completely annoying as I shifted my upper body back and forth for better angles.

Angela pointed, "Look at him. I mean there, right there, proves everything I just said about him. Look at the way he's standing right now like he owns this park. Todd can't even move to the side for people walking. He's making them move, disrupting the natural flow of traffic."

Straightaway, my heart raced as his chiseled face gave way to a confident, almost mischievous grin. That was it; I was a goner. This was the first time I had ever seen him smile, which was causing me to smile along with him.

My body took over, releasing the heavy feeling that was grounding my feet, now making my sitting position more forward as my hands started to numb while gripping the seat bench on each side of my legs.

Angela laughed. "Well, would you look at that, Mallory? We should take a picture. Todd is genuinely smiling. Who would have thought he was even capable? Mr. Business, Business, Business can express other human emotions besides being a dick."

I watched intently, sketching that grin to a memory. This man took my breath away, and just like that, Mother Nature rewarded me with a gentle breeze whispering through his dirty-blond Scandinavian-kissed hair, causing him to angle slightly into the same direction of the wind.

That same breeze washed over me, blowing my hair across my vision, making me pull the strands from my face and tuck them securely behind my ear.

Todd stood confidently, owning the space around him, while walkers gave him a generous margin as they passed. Suddenly, that grin was gone just as quickly as it had appeared.

I wanted to stand for a better angle, but the sound of Angela's voice reminded me I was not alone.

She sighed at first, then lifted her arm to rest on top of the park bench. "I will never get tired of looking at him, though. Too bad his personality doesn't match his looks. Otherwise, he could be a catch."

I softly nodded to her last words. Todd was a catch, but Angela didn't need to know how I felt about him right now.

She continued, "I often wonder what happened to make him the way he is." Finally, I turned my head away from Todd, giving Angela my attention now. "What do you mean?" I inquired curiously.

She flipped her chin toward him again as if I already knew. "Oh, come on, Mal. Don't you ever wonder why the universe created such a fine specimen on the outside, then made him an insensitive jerk on the inside? You, of all people, have seen him in action and how badly he can treat our team managers."

I couldn't help but defend him. "His job is not easy. You know that. Besides, he is under Samantha's thumb. I can't even imagine what it's like working for that woman."

Angela straightened up, now challenging me. "Neither is your job or mine, Mallory, but we are not rude to the level he is when something goes wrong. He has such a bitter, vicious streak in him. What about when that condescending mannerism comes out? Normal managers do not talk to people the way he does."

The Dating Policy

There was no defending him there. She was right. He could be extremely ruthless toward people. I turned back in Todd's direction. He was still talking on his phone, and now he turned his head, scanning his surroundings.

There was one moment that our eyes met. I felt time stop, and my heart skipped a beat as his features softened. His glance was a validation that he noticed me, giving me hope. Then, in an instant, he dismissed our connection, stripping away that sudden hope, leaving me with an instant feeling of void that almost hurt.

I took another deep breath, slowly refocusing and breathing how Barbara, my life coach taught me, as I watched on, restoring calm to my emotions.

An empty pocket from the steady stream of people allowed him to turn left, away from us. Within seconds, he was out of sight. Angela and I followed him to the last moment as she flip-flopped her thoughts over him.

"He is like when you are on a diet, and he's that last perfect piece of cheesecake sealed behind the glass counter. You want it, but you know you will regret every bite when it is gone."

I raised an eyebrow. "Cheesecake?"

She nodded. "Death by cheesecake, Mallory."

I now confessed to Angela. "I made a date with Thomas for Saturday."

Angela flipped her palm up. "Who the hell is Thomas?"

I reminded her, "Jessica's new husband's brother? The stockbroker I was talking to at the end of the night?"

She narrowed her eyes at me, "The divorced stockbroker with two young children?"

"Yup," I replied.

She sighed, "Well, it's a start, and he certainly isn't the typical man you settle for. Where are you meeting him?"

"I told him I would call on Thursday to decide on a place."

Angela contemplated a moment, "Have him meet you at Martini's; that way, I'm ten minutes away if you need back up."

I laughed, "Martini's it is then."

We arrived back at work with a few minutes to spare. Shelborn Building Supply Company, or SBS as everyone calls it, is our state's leading building supplier for the past seven years.

Rumors have been circulating that we were merging, but so far, they remained rumors. Angela and I worked in sales. Our department is a fast-paced atmosphere, and the staff is big. We had thirty-nine full-time employees, and all of us were busy.

Our sales department here was on the first floor with a door separating our department from the main lobby. Each one of us had our own cubicle, and the outside perimeter supported six enclosed offices, one large boardroom that could accommodate a good fifteen people, and an ass-chewing room for when something went wrong. That was mostly Todd's room where he became judge and jury before his boss Samantha stepped in.

Todd was hired here eleven months and two days ago. I kept track because he had his first anniversary coming up, and I planned to use it so I could sneak in my congratulations to break the ice between us.

I have been planning this since the day he walked into our department. At first, my plan seemed easy and casual, but as the year went on, and I worked out my issues, I became more anxious about the idea and was now petrified to execute it. He made me nervous. I felt like an immature girl around him, not the grown woman that I am. I don't ever recall feeling this way toward any man.

Angela sighed as she reached her cubicle. "Back to the reason we collect a check every week." She eased into her chair and picked up her headset as it blinked with a call. I walked past her and made my way down to the opposite end of the room where my cubicle sat.

I was the last one to the right, just outside Ned's office. He was on the phone, but he managed to give me a little acknowledgment.

Ned got me this job, starting as an intern when I was in college full time. I was hired after the summer and dropped to part-time classes. I liked making money. It gave me a new sense of freedom as it finally allowed my mother to ignore me guilt-free.

I genuinely liked Ned. I have known him for years personally, despite our age differences. He and my brother were good friends. They were in the service together right after high school.

Ned came back and married, while my brother made the military his career. Ned sometimes shared my brother's stories that I would never hear otherwise.

My position in the company is under the top managers' jurisdiction. I was next in line for one of those offices. They restructured new titles here over a year ago, and I ranked as a senior sales advisor, just waiting to make the jump to become a manager.

I placed my bag on my desk and noticed Ned was straightening up. I thought he was getting up to ask me something when I noticed his alarmed look. Still fixated on Ned, I quickly moved away from my desk, stepping right into the path of a collision.

Hands seized the sides of my arms, making me shriek while controlling my body to spin in the opposite direction. He placed me right back in my cubicle as if I were weightless. Todd examined the state I was in for an awkward moment, then he verbally acknowledged me, "Miss Kennedy."

He dropped his tone in a commanding voice as I regained my steadiness. He held onto me, waiting to make sure I had my footing.

I felt the intensity of his hold, the heat radiating through his hands instantly warming my arms to complete relaxation. Todd scanned over me again, quickly, then released his grip, leaving an immediate chill where he had held. Emptiness washed through me for the second time, not even an hour apart.

I stood there, startled, as he observed me. I was busy catching my breath after what just happened. My brain was stuck on his hands touching me, the warmth I felt... my gosh... his grip... the power. Todd's power was not only in his words but also in his physical strength.

He looked into my eyes once more... I read conflict in his regard.

He took a step back and turned toward Ned's office, leaving me in a state of bewilderment as he shut Ned's door behind him.

I watched the front of the steel door, confused and momentarily dumbfounded as to what had just happened.

I was in Todd's hold. He took complete control as if in well-rehearsed dance steps. I think I floated back in my cubicle. And what was with that look he gave me?

I strained to see Todd in Ned's office; he must be standing behind the door.

My headset was blinking, and now my phone was ringing, pulling me back to where I needed to be. I fumbled for it, pushing the button on my phone to connect. No one liked hearing a phone ring. It meant you were not picking up, not being active, and that raised a caution flag to anyone within earshot.

I was now relying on autopilot. I knew this job better than anyone here, except Todd had just scrambled some of my circuits, and I was not functioning at full capacity yet. "Good afternoon, SBS."

I barely managed to get that out. I needed to clear my throat a few times to get my breathing back under control. On the other end of my call, saying my name for the third time now was one of my favorite, most challenging customers, Randall Mack. "Mallory, are you there? Mallory, I don't have all day!"

I apologized, trying to stay focused. I heard Todd's voice speaking to Ned as I glanced up.

"I will let her know it was production. She'll understand with the floods down there." Todd turned in my direction and walked with purpose right past me.

I caught his glance from the corner of my eye. It was brief, but he definitely looked at me.

I exhaled softly, closing my eyes for a few seconds, letting go of the thoughts that were formulating about Todd Duvall.

Before I knew it, Angela was next to my cubicle as I finished up my last order of the day. She waved to Ned as he called her in.

I heard their laughter. I can only imagine what they were discussing. With everything in order and my computer off, my day was done as I packed my belongings. Angela made her way back to me.

"Ned said Todd nearly ran you over this afternoon. He told me the look on your face was priceless."

I scowled at Ned while he smirked, leaning back in his chair with his hands clasped behind his head.

"Come on. Let's get out of here, Ange," I requested. We walked through the doors, then made our way to the employee parking lot. While evaluating my life choices, one of the things I thought would benefit me the most was getting my butt back in the gym.

I had control over my body shape and fitness. I was carrying an extra twenty pounds out of my comfort zone, and I wanted to fit back into my clothes from three years ago. It was Wednesday afternoon and time to test out my brand-new fitness center.

Angela had a commitment every Wednesday night, so I was solo this evening.

In her spectacular Italian family, it was mandatory to spend Wednesdays with her parents and siblings for family dinner night. Without fail, her big Italian family would get together to cook, clean, play card games, talk, laugh, argue, and spend the evening together.

I have been to my fair share of Wednesday family dinners over at Angela's. It's incredibly nice. No matter who is fighting with whom or who is celebrating, they all come together every Wednesday evening without fail.

Angela politely invited me again, but I declined apologetically, wanting to stick to my new goal. This year, I was going to get off my ass to make things happen for the better. My goal included Todd, and now I was convinced it just might happen.

I headed to my new gym. By six, this was a busy place. I was lucky; as soon as I surfaced from the ladies' locker room, a treadmill had opened up. I plugged my ear jacks into my phone and went straight to my playlist.

A half an hour into my workout, the gym was busier now than when I first arrived. I jogged for another ten minutes, then cooled down.

I moved to the thirty-minute workout station. I completed it and called it quits. At this moment, I doubted my ability to be able to walk tomorrow morning.

As I made my way back to the locker room, I passed the free weights, enjoying the view with some of the men working out. There was some serious eye candy here, pushing the weights hard and heavy.

Maybe Todd wasn't my only choice. Maybe I was already settling when I should be more open. Maybe Thomas was going to straighten all this out for me.

I was jerked to a stop as my nose was an inch from some guy's chest. My feet fumbled to balance while hands held both sides of my arms. Just as his scent hit my nose, I looked up — it was the same guy I had already done this to earlier. Oh, geez, it was Todd right here, holding me still.

My lips parted as a grin ripped across my face, and I began to giggle nervously. I had no idea he was a member here. He kept his grip on my arms, with my whole body willing to move in any direction he wanted to place me.

His hands held skin to skin this time, and the heat radiating from them felt more intense than when he held me earlier.

He looked right into my eyes, and his features softened with a look of amusement skirting his gaze. "Well, Miss. Kennedy, this seems to be a pattern with you today. Either you are not paying attention to your surroundings enough or the universe is telling me that I need to catch you."

I lost the nervous laugh as my facial expression went as blank as my brain. My arms felt heavenly, melting in his touch; the heat radiated to my tired muscles. All I could articulate was a soft, "Ahhhhh."

I did not know what to say to him now. Everything I had practiced saying turned to white noise. Nothing was working in my head. I was simply mesmerized. I wanted his return look to turn into so much more. It did.

Todd ever so slightly, with an eyebrow raised, internally questioned my reaction. He read my signal loud and clear. I swallowed hard and managed to look down, breaking our eye contact as I glanced at his grip on my arm.

Todd let go and grunted.

Without another word, he moved around me and deeper into the gym. That was it. He disappeared from my sight.

What was that? I stood there, jaw dropped, while the gym traffic now had to veer around me as I tried to remember his comment. A chill shot through my body, making me shiver with a twitch... ugh... what the hell is going on with me?

I took a deep breath; I must be tired from my intense workout. Besides, he definitely caught me off guard.

Finally, I made it to the locker room. I decided to shower here and take a little extra time. Maybe, if my plan worked, I would bump into Todd again before I left, and I could start that normal conversation and not be caught off guard like he keeps doing to me.

I extended as much time as I could, and then made my way out. I scanned the weight area and found no sign of Todd.

Expelling a disappointing sigh, I conceded to the fact that this universe was messing with me as I headed toward the exit. Todd was all I could think about on my drive home. So much so that I arrived outside my gate, not remembering the drive at all.

I worked in a suburb of the city where I live. It's always nice to go against the traffic on my commutes. I also lived in a gated condo complex. There were forty semidetached units, which was a fancy description of a duplex.

I shared my duplex with an airline pilot. He's always gone. Nice guy, kept to himself just like me. I pulled into my garage, and two things were happening right now simultaneously.

I was starving, and I completely forgot to go grocery shopping on the way back here. I bumped my head to the steering wheel, realizing that I was a complete idiot for being so preoccupied and thinking about Todd.

Damn it! He needed to get out of my head! It was breakfast for supper tonight because I was not going back out. At some point, I fell asleep with the television on, and several messages were on my phone.

My mother called; my brother called. Sean made it a tradition always to call me when he was deploying.

I had an obnoxious alarm set up for his ringtone, and I didn't even wake up for that call. What was going on with me? I listened to his message, and his last few sentences were always the same. "Oh, and, Mal, you are the biggest pain in my ass, always have been since the day you were born. I love you, kid. Talk to you when I can." I held the phone to my heart and smiled.

Chapter Two

Morning came quickly, and I realized I was in much better shape than I thought. Not as sore and achy as I expected I would be. I arrived back to work over forty minutes early and had a premium parking spot. I waited in my car for a half-hour to see if I could catch what kind of vehicle Todd drove. I figured the advantage to me knowing would be that I could scan the gym parking lot to see if he was there or not when I arrived to work out. Angela knocked on my driver's door window as I jumped out of my skin.

She bent down, looked in, and then opened my door. "What are you doing, Mallory?" Calming myself down, I picked up my phone, and I lied to her. "Sean is going on deployment, and we were just talking."

"Where are they sending him this time and for how long? Does he know?" she asked out of concern. I shrugged. "You know he can't tell me nor say a length of time." She groaned in empathy to my complete lie.

"He'll be fine. Come on. Let's get this party started." Angela opened my door wider for me to get out, signaling the end of my stakeout.

I collected my bags and followed her lead. No Todd today. As a matter of fact, I didn't see him at all today. Usually, this is the normal cycle of how little we interact. I don't know why I was hoping to see him, but I was, and it was completely stupid and an irrational way of thinking for me. Todd Duvall had no business being in my head. Now, I had to kick him out of there and move forward, no matter how much I wanted him to stay.

Good. Now that my brain and I were on the same page, my life's mission could get back on track. That did not include obsessing over a man. A strange confirmation backed this up as I was receiving a text from Thomas asking about possible places to meet on Saturday.

Perfect; this was exactly what I needed. I suggested Martini's, and he quickly agreed. I now decided that my first date in the future with Todd was going to be treated as an interview.

I hoped he would pass, but I must keep an open mind. Open my mind to all possibilities. It may be Todd or it might not. Open mind. Open mind. Open mind, I chanted to myself.

Angela was at my desk at five minutes after five. Our day was closing. "So, what's the plan?"

I smiled. "I'm going to the gym; do you want to join me?"

That was not a subtle sigh. She was giving me a clear protesting huff. "Fine!" she stated, not happy about more work after work. I actually loved it when she joined me.

As crabby as Angela is about the idea, she makes up for it when she starts. I have a hard time keeping up with her, and that brings on pure motivation for me.

At first, all I could think about was Todd and whether he would show up today. She noticed my distraction and started asking a lot of questions. That was it; she busted me. Time to focus on why we were here.

This was all girl power… no room for men as we worked out hard. It ended up being a very productive session as we talked about setting a schedule that we would love to follow through on, but life always seemed to get in the way.

We no sooner set up tomorrow when she remembered she was babysitting her two nieces.

My point exactly — it started before it started. Then the invite to babysit with her followed. That was not on my agenda, as I told her I was right back here for round three tomorrow. She understood and went over what my exercise goal for Friday should be.

Friday started as a typical day. Life was back on track. My day could not have gone more smoothly, and it was already three o'clock. I just ended an order, and I removed my headset, having to use the bathroom. I signaled to Ned where I was going. He gave me a nod and instantly sat forward.

I curiously looked at him for a second and exited my cubicle. Seven strides away was Todd, clearly heading right to me with determination.

He commented, "If that elevator hadn't stopped for the second floor, you would be in my hold again." Todd now halted before me, wearing his white dress shirt with a simple gray and blue print tie, his sleeves rolled a few turns, and his scent was filling my nostrils.

He took hold of my right arm securely, keeping me right here. I licked my lips as my mouth began to dry, my heart already pounding against my chest.

"I, I was just on my way…" He didn't need to know I was going to the bathroom! I didn't finish the sentence but started over. "Do you need me for something, Mr. Duvall?"

He studied me for a second. I searched for any hints in his expression… He spoke. "Mallory Kennedy, what are you doing tomorrow night?"

WHAT? Did he just ask me on a date? I could barely breathe. I could barely speak. Is this happening here at work right now? I quickly pulled it together and squeaked out, "I'm not sure, why?"

Yes, there was a slight grin gracing his lips as he continued holding me in place. "Do you like baseball?"

The Dating Policy

He was asking if I like baseball. Oh, we are going to a game together. I glanced around for a moment, trying to see if anyone was watching us. I know Ned was. I could feel his eyes on me.

I quickly answered, "Yes, I like baseball."

He softened his grip, then asked, "Do you want to go to the game tomorrow?"

He was asking me to go! I think I could do cartwheels right now!

"Yes." I accepted before he could speak another word.

My head was in the clouds as my heartbeat echoed in my ears, and now I was slightly trembling.

He let go of me. "Good. I have two tickets, and I have other plans this weekend. I'll have my secretary drop them down to you."

What? What did he just say? I stared wide-eyed as my eyebrow flexed. I didn't know what to do... What? What just happened? Now, he walked around me and right into Ned's office, closing the door behind him.

I followed him with my eyes until he shut Ned's door. Ned looked over to me, then back at Todd.

I practically ran to the bathroom. I was not sure which emotion was battling to the surface first. Anger — that was the baby that hit me first... I was sweating as I heard myself breathing. My whole head was pounding to the beats of my heart. I looked at my reflection in the mirror, and the lights showed off my pale complexion.

At least my face wasn't bright red. I cannot believe that just happened. He was an ass, and I just fell right into it. How dare him!

I needed to splash water on my face. It took me ten minutes to leave that bathroom. Jackass was gone, and Ned watched me with concern.

He got up from behind his desk and came over to me. "You okay, Mal?"

I nodded. "Yeah, I'm fine, girl things."

He held up both hands. "Okay, got it, all good, not another word."

Ned retreated.

By four-thirty, a woman whom I have never seen before stopped at my cubicle. "Miss Kennedy?"

I looked up, confused. "Yes, can I help you?"

"This is for you." She extended her hand and passed over an envelope that I took and opened. Crap! It was those damn tickets! I shoved them back in the envelope, thanking her as I waved her along.

This was the perfect cure to get over Todd. The only way I was thinking about Todd Duvall was the many ways I wanted him to die.

Angela arrived at my desk at five past five. She immediately noticed the envelope with my name penned across it.

"What have you got there?"

I was still fuming while I snapped at her. "Baseball tickets for tomorrow's game."

She tilted her head at me, wondering why I was so cranky. Then, she grinned. "Really? How many?"

I replied coldly, "Two."

She smiled brighter, ignoring my ill-mannered mood. "Are you going?"

I was still miffed. "NO!"

She studied my reaction. "Where did you get them?"

"Todd."

Now, she was very curious. "Mr. Personality? Why did he give you tickets to a baseball game?"

She reached over and picked up the tickets and opened the envelope to see where the seats were located.

"He has other plans and asked if I wanted to go."

Well, that came out more bitter than I intended.

She laughed. "They're on the party deck. Wow, you scored. I'll go with you if you want?" She was suddenly really happy about our potential Saturday afternoon entertainment. "But what about the divorced stockbroker with two young children?" She reminded me of my other option.

Damn it! I completely forgot about him. I picked up my phone and texted him to see if we could make it Sunday afternoon instead.

He texted right back that Sunday worked better for him too.

I rubbed at my temples as the pounding seemed to calm for a moment. I never thought to see what section they were in, and the party deck meant premium seats.

I was clearing my head about how I acquired my new weekend arrangement as I began to calm down. Maybe I took this all wrong. Maybe he was trying to do something charming, I thought as I heard her enthusiasm and how nice it was for him to give the tickets to me.

It took me a few minutes to wrap my head around this. Why not? Maybe he was trying to be genuine about offering them to me.

Maybe I read the whole situation wrong. He was a tough guy to decode. Maybe this was him making a step to reach out.

I became hopeful. I looked at Angela, who was waiting for my answer with a wide, encouraging grin on her face. "Sure, let's go see the game and drink some beers."

She clapped and gave a hearty, "Yes."

I took the envelope back and looked at the tickets. This had potential, even though Todd was confusing the heck out of me at this moment.

The Dating Policy

Ned was wrapping things up at his desk while I was doing the same at mine. He finished before me and came over to us. "You two troublemakers have any plans over the weekend?"

Angela announced our plans with excitement. "We're going to the game tomorrow. Party-deck style," she bragged.

Ned shook his head curiously. "I'll be sure to watch the game then, to make sure you two are behaving yourselves."

I rolled my eyes as Angela answered, "We make no promises. Anything goes on the party deck." He watched me put the envelope in my bag. "Just watch yourselves."

Every time Sean deployed, Ned stepped up his game by asking more questions and keeping an eye on me. That was his warning playing guardian.

I was now ready to get out of here, so Angela and I headed for the gym. Her sister's date night canceled, so we could hang out this evening as well. There was no sign of Todd tonight, and I was a little relieved.

That whole approach on how he offered me the tickets was bothering me. I was analyzing it to bits. I dissected that encounter and rebuilt it again, moment by moment, and I still couldn't figure it out.

I just needed to let it go for now. By the end of our workout, Todd became a faded memory.

Angela and I hit the showers and decided we had burned enough calories to go out to our favorite Mexican restaurant in town.

Tonight, it was a little more crowded than usual. The warm streak of weather must have had an influence. We had a thirty-minute wait, so we went straight to the standing-room-only bar. I snagged one of the wait staff and put in our margaritas order. We loved this month's special blueberry-pomegranate margarita. It was becoming a favorite on our drink list.

Angela spotted a well-known couple friend of ours before I did. Her radar was impeccable as she waved her hand in the air, getting their attention.

Peter and his girlfriend Kelly were making their way over. I grinned. I loved seeing Peter, especially seeing him with someone else. He was part of my life for a while, but I was glad he was with Kelly.

He leaned in for the hug, and there was zero awkwardness, same when Kelly followed suit. This was where I thought my relationship skills were less than average. Peter and I had been a couple during our college years. We even lived together off-campus for the last year, and we were nearly best buddies now. I loved bumping into him. I loved his girlfriend. I loved them being a couple.

There should be something to make my attitude toward him different. This was a clear point that made me feel I don't know what love is, or what it actually feels like.

Angela was already sharing our plans for the game tomorrow while more comments for us to behave were made.

Two margaritas each and we were finally sitting down to our meal. That was it for me. I switched to water as did my partner in crime.

Both of us were driving, and we had a baseball game to attend tomorrow. Winding down to the end of our apparent Mexican eating fest, we split the bill and started to make our way toward the door.

Angela's radar was as sharp as ever as she poked my side, muttering, "Look, look, look... ha, ha, ha. Ten o'clock. Should we go over and thank him for the tickets?"

I stopped dead in my tracks, looking toward her coordinates. There he was as my mouth fell open.

I could see several people at his table — two guys who I didn't have a clue whom they were and this extremely attractive young brunette who was sitting next to him.

She looked stunning, olive complexion, deep brown hair with red highlights casting from the low recessed lighting above. Her hair shined with the lighting overhead. I almost could not take my eyes from following the motion. She was tossing her head back and laughing as I witnessed her placing her hand on Todd's shoulder, clearly making him snap his shoulder into a hands-off roll while she removed it with indifference in her expression.

I wanted to hide right now so I could get a better look. I scurried, looking around at my options. Angela was watching me. Then she tilted her head. "What are you doing?"

I was already crouched behind the four-foot wall, trying to sneak a better look.

I shushed her. She stood straight now with her arms folded. "Why are you shushing me? What's going on?"

She looked at me, then over to Todd. I could see the wheels turning as she was piecing it together. Then that ah-ha moment hit her. "You cannot be serious! You have a thing for Mr. Business, Business, Business?"

She adjusted in the open to get a better look at him. "Although, he looks more relaxed in this low light; I have to admit. I wonder who that woman is next to him. She looks very familiar."

I straightened back up. I needed to abort my mission on checking the female out. Angela was that bold type who would drag me right over there to thank him for the tickets and find out who exactly she was.

"Come on," I grabbed her hand and pulled her toward the door. She had a smug grin as we cleared the entrance. "Well, well, wasn't that display quite interesting?"

I ignored her and dropped her hand when we were near my car. "I'll see you tomorrow. We can take the subway in, so we don't have to drive."

She stood there, hand on her hip, pointing at me with her free hand. "This does not get you out of my questions that you have coming."

I waved a hand in the air and slid into my driver's seat. I looked in the rearview mirror to see her giving up for now and walking to her car. Phew, but all I did was buy some time.

I woke up Saturday morning, ready to hit the gym. I had goals to meet and felt anxious to keep on track.

After last night's indulgence, which I was still feeling dehydrated from, I packed up, slid into my driver's seat, then immediately pulled the visor down, adjusting my sunglasses in place because the sun was already bright, and it was going to bother me until I hit the highway to change directions heading west.

It was still early on a Saturday morning, and I had my choice of equipment. An hour later, the guilt had vanished, and I was done.

Angela texted me; she wanted to meet at the subway station at three o'clock.

The game started at five, and this would give us plenty of time to get in and enjoy some of the street shows. I had an easy afternoon.

All my domestic duties were done before noon on a Saturday... this was clearly a new record. I even had time to read, nap, or do my nails. Hmmm... getting up early on a Saturday had its benefits. I must take this into consideration.

The next few hours breezed by, and I was ready for the game. I grabbed my keys, ID, small back sack, and, oh, yeah... the tickets.

I briefly stared at the envelope with my name on it. Was this his writing or the secretary's? Nice penmanship... whoever wrote it.

I examined my name. I think this was his writing. I brushed my fingers lightly across the letters. Does that make this more personal if it is?

Then my brain switched to last night. Who was that damn brunette with him? My phone rang in my hand. It was Angela. "Hi, Mal. You on your way?"

Oh, geez. "Keys in hand and walking out the door."

Angela called to inform me there was a car accident on Wilson Avenue and to go around it. That was my friend who thought ahead by keeping up and watching traffic delays, what the weather conditions were going to be, and upcoming events in town. Angela redefined the word detailing. I drove around the pile-up just as she told me to, and I ended up four minutes early.

I spotted her immediately at the ticket counter. She looked adorable — baseball cap, long black hair pulled through the back of it, full makeup, jeans, and a T-shirt. Angela was two years younger than me, Italian by heritage, and a very pretty girl.

She had that exotic look about her, even though she was born in this city. She was not skinny by any means; she was average weight.

This girl loved to eat, but all her curves were in the right places. I met her at the ticket counter, and she started right away.

"This guy over here," she pointed right at him, "said we get complimentary food credit if we are in the first three rows. Can you pull out the tickets so I can see?"

I swung my back sack around to pull out the tickets. Angela waved him over, and he approached. She was smiling and introduced us, making him say his name because she already forgot it.

We looked, and yes, they were in row one. He inspected the ticket. "You girls scored. You're right in the middle. You have your own table and the good chairs. That is a corporate table."

Angela asked if that was better. He chuckled. "Um, yeah... have fun, ladies. You are in for a treat."

I thanked him, looked down at my tickets again, and thought... this was starting to really take a turn. Maybe Todd was reaching out to me.

The guy continued to make small talk with us. Only now we were done with him, and Angela was done with his usefulness. It was time for him to leave us alone, and he wasn't getting the hint.

Another talent my dearest friend Angela possesses is that she can slap on a bitch face quicker than a blink, and there it was. He got the hint, backing away as I thanked him again for the information.

Angela had this Italian flaring temper that I have personally experienced, and it took me quite a long time to learn that she can blow up in one second, get it out and over with, and then be perfectly fine the next second.

She did not hold onto any grudges. It was like boom... and done.

As for myself, I tend to hold onto anger; a grudge is my specialty. Over the past few years, from hanging out with Angela, she has taught me to let go a little, and it's been a slow practice and habit to turn around, but I am improving. At least now I'm starting to talk to my mother.

Husband number five, I couldn't give a crap about, but the past year with my life coach has shown me that all my adult decisions have been my own, and the only one stopping me now is me.

The tram was arriving as we chatted, waiting for the doors to open. There were a lot of baseball fans on this vessel, so the energy was exciting. Twenty minutes later, we all unloaded at the ballpark.

Street vendors were lining the gates, peddling memorabilia, trying to catch our attention. We confidently walked past everyone and right to the gate. Breezing right through security and having two special wristbands slapped on us, we were in.

Angela grabbed my hand, not daring to be sidetracked by any street vendors now and headed right toward the deck.

She was too excited about all the hype that came with these tickets. And if that guy was right, there was nothing down here worth hanging around for now.

The first thing we discovered was a separate entrance to get up there. Three flights of stairs later, and we were here.

This section was its own entity. I took a moment to look around. It was amazing. It was a perfect view from here, and there was a guy checking wristbands and tickets.

I pulled my tickets out. He looked at them.

Then with a smart grin, he said, "Miss Mallory Kennedy?" I was taken aback that he already knew my name.

I lost my "in the moment grin" on a slight verge of panic.

"Yes, that's me." I was about to ask how he knew my name when he called over a waiter.

This older woman greeted us as he relayed her my name with, "Duvall Table," echoing his last words.

She smiled pleasantly, giving us her full attention. "Very nice, ladies, is this the first time up on deck?"

Now, I was wondering if we seemed out of place as I consciously observed people around us. Angela took over answering all the pleasantries.

She had no worries if she fit in or not and gushed that it was our first time.

Our server was named Holly, we learned, as she introduced herself again with a more personal tone, guiding us over to our — "Holy mother of God! This is our table?"

Angela screeched, clapping her hands. "This is magnificent!" she boasted. We were in front of a real wood table covered with a linen tablecloth and napkins, with real wood and leather chairs.

Holly pulled out my chair as Angela told her she was all set and pulled out her own chair.

She withdrew two menus from her long apron and handed them to us, announcing she would be right back.

Angela looked at me. I looked right back at her, and we both squealed. This was incredible. She leaned in. "How the hell did Todd score these tickets?"

I shrugged. I felt completely baffled myself. Our server, Holly, was coming back to us with another waitperson following her, carrying an ice tub.

She signaled for the fella to put it on the table. Angela and I both watched as Holly went into her welcome introduction.

She smiled. "Welcome to the Duvall table, ladies. As Mr. Duvall's honored guest, please feel free to order anything on the menu. This beverage tub is his traditional beverage choice and is always offered first. Should you have a particular request, I will be happy to accommodate anything on the menu. All our alcohol and nonalcoholic choices are listed on the inside cover of your menus."

She folded the menu and placed it back in front of me. She smiled again. "I'll be back in a few moments to take your orders. Ladies, enjoy this afternoon." Holly smiled genuinely, tapped the table, and walked away.

Angela and I had the stupidest star-struck smiles on our faces. We both scanned over everything offered in the ice tub — two different brands of beer, two bottles of water, two different types of soda, and a full carafe of what looked like lemonade. We both just took a moment, looking at all the possibilities.

Angela motioned to the lemonade carafe. "This looks like a good place to start. What do you think?"

I laughed. "Umm... sure. I wonder if this is lemonade."

Angela pulled the two chilled glasses wrapped in plastic from the tub. "Go ahead, Mal. Let's see what it is." And there was no asking me twice.

I poured a little into each glass. We each sniffed. There was alcohol in this, so we clinked pint glasses and sipped. Wow. This was refreshing and delicious.

We had about three hours here, and this stuff would need to be sipped gently.

I filled each of our glasses halfway and stuck the carafe back in the ice, then sat back, taking in our surroundings.

This was a good decision on Angela's behalf. I would have been home, fuming, alone, and would have missed out on all this. So, I thanked her, "Hey, thanks for talking me into this."

She laughed. "Ya, you owe me. Did you catch what our waitress said in the speech? She said, 'Welcome to the Duvall table.' Do you think this is Todd's? Or maybe his family's? Who is Todd Duvall? Now, I'm wondering what he drives and where he lives and who is he connected to. Or is this his parent's and he is showing off?"

I was thinking of those same questions: Who was Todd Duvall, and why did he give me these tickets? Was he trying to tell me something?

I reached over to my sack and pulled the envelope out. I studied the writing again. I think this was his handwriting. I brushed over the penmanship, thinking about Todd.

Angela was commenting on what a spectacular view of the park we had and what a gorgeous day this was.

She must have talked to me for two minutes straight, and I barely heard a word as I replayed yesterday over and over in my head: that moment he held me in place going over in my mind, with him asking me about this afternoon. Who was Todd Duvall?

Angela was clearly asking me a question as she snapped her fingers in my direction. "Mal... Hey, Mal... Hello? Earth to Mallory."

The Dating Policy

I looked up from the envelope. "What?" She tilted her head. "What's on your mind, lady? I've been talking for the last five minutes, and you haven't said a word. Are you even listening to me?"

I laughed. "I heard you... spectacular view, beautiful day." Then I grinned as she leaned in.

"So, who do you think Todd is? Do you think he comes from money?"

I sat back, sighing. I was so attracted to this guy, and now there was another layer I needed to sort out. "I don't really know. He is just so difficult to figure out."

She laughed. "Yeah, that's one way to put it." Oh, good. Confirmation... that made me smile as I took a sip of my new favorite spiked lemonade beverage.

Honestly, we feasted like royalty and used every perk those tickets had come with, which was unlimited.

There was even a photographer coming around from table to table, asking if we wanted a keepsake photo. Of course, we did. He snapped our photo several times then took a few of just me.

He explained the process to us. They would be ready via e-mail within an hour as he placed two cards on the table with instructions to a website and where to go to download them.

This was such a fun evening, and as the game was winding down and the players were changing innings, photos from the photographer lit up the big screen. There were pictures from all over the stadium.

The crowd cheered as new pictures faded in and out of the fun people were having throughout the game. This was complete enjoyment. One of our photos made it on the big screen as we laughed and pointed, along with several other pictures of people from this deck.

Holly came over and started to clear the table. I asked her how this all works. Do we pay a balance on the extras, or do we leave her a tip? She smiled big and replied, "You are all set, ladies. Your evening is completely taken care of. We thank you for joining us and hope you enjoyed yourselves."

Angela and I gushed at the same time, thanking her and commenting that this was a fabulous evening. She smiled big and winked, turning with a big tray of our dirty dishes.

We left before the end of the game to make a smooth getaway. The ride back was easy, and when we reached our cars at nine, we concluded the evening with a hug and a goodbye as we went our separate ways.

I was in my condo and plunked down on my couch with my phone in my hand, scrolling through all the photos I took.

I pulled the envelope from my sack and placed it on my lap, looking at it once again. I smiled. This was a great evening. How was I going to thank him? I knew how I wanted to thank him... with my lips kissing him.

Maybe I should send him an e-mail. I thought some more. I only had the company's e-mail to contact him, and it probably wasn't the correct way to send a thank you.

This required some thinking, but I was tired. Tomorrow was a new day. I shut everything down, taking my tickets and envelope up to bed and tucking them under my pillow as I got settled for the night.

Chapter Three

Sunday morning, I was hopeful as I drove to the gym. No Todd here today. I was a little disappointed, but I had the afternoon to meet with Thomas.

I must say, meeting Thomas in a more casual atmosphere was an unexpected delight. This stockbroker had some potential that I had not paid attention to at the wedding. He may have been divorced with two children, but his wife had left him for another man because he was working all the time.

I wanted to find love, but I didn't want the extra kid issues right now. I knew all too well their perspective, and to deal with another woman on top of that... he was going to have to be placed in the friend zone.

I was straight up with him, and he thanked me for being honest. He also mentioned this took a lot of pressure off the relationship part and just looked forward to hanging out with me. I liked that thought as well.

Monday came and went. No sign of Todd, who was back on top of my list of potentials. The week pretty much reflected this over and over.

My emotions were all over the map, and I had to keep reminding myself this was the norm. I rarely saw him, and if I did, it was because of a problem. This week was smooth sailing, and I hated it.

Thomas was a good distraction on Thursday as he met up with both Angela and me this time. He handled Angela rather nicely, and she had fun interrogating him. He was a good sport about it, and that gained respect in my eyes.

I accepted the way it was by Friday and kicked Todd out of my head once again. Angela was babysitting for her sister, so I hit the gym solo.

I was proud of my workout — one class completed and thirty minutes on the treadmill. I was chugging the last of my water as Todd walked in front of my machine with a group of guys.

He stopped and hopped up on the platform, holding my handrails. I was now choking on my water.

He quickly turned down the speed as I jumped my feet to the sides on the stationary ground. I recovered as he said, "Are you okay?"

I nodded, wiping my mouth from any droplets that escaped. "Just swallowed wrong; that's all."

"Well, we can't have you doing that now."

I was a hot mess, and he was grinning at me. "The look suits you — one ponytail wearing, sweat-soaked Mallory Kennedy. I must say you wear it well."

Suddenly, I felt conscious of what I must have looked like. Yes, we were at a gym, and I now knew he worked out here as well, but I didn't want him to see me like this.

He leaned in over the treadmill bar closer toward me. "Personally, I think you never looked so good."

That was it. He jumped back down and resumed walking through the doors. Did that really just happen? Did he say that to me? He sounded like a regular guy for a moment, but Todd was not a regular guy.

He was a mystery. He was the air of authority, not a jump up on this platform type of guy.

That was a curveball, and that just messed with my head on a whole different level. I didn't know what to do... except follow him with my eyes.

My brain started working again... leave... I needed to get out of here. It was way safer to get the hell out of here right now.

I showered at home to avoid the risk of bumping into him again. My emotions were all over the place after seeing Todd. I could not understand why I was so shy and tongue-tied around him.

I thought more about the gym as I had to adjust for the sunlight beaming in my windshield. Damn it; my sunglasses were in my gym bag behind me. I finally stretched up, so my vision was more comfortable, alleviating an extra stop to fetch my glasses from the back seat as I began to drift my thoughts back to the gym.

That was a clear ambush that I had not prepared for. I pulled out the envelope that was now traveling with me everywhere I went, trying to think about what he said a little while ago.

I struggled with thinking about e-mailing him through the company again. I knew there was a strict policy about using the company computers for personal use. They probably check our e-mails, so I would just have to wait until I saw him again.

Patience was not my virtue as I dismissed the e-mail idea altogether. I would have to think about this. Sunday morning arrived, and I started my busy day ahead; I woke up at six in the morning, fully refreshed, and I packed for the gym again. I was on a mission. Two hours I was there, and no sign of Todd.

I met Angela and her family for brunch. They all commented that it's been too long between our visits and that I was looking beautiful. Her mother remarked about how radiant I looked, and then the conversation turned to the ballgame a weekend ago and who this Mr. Duvall was.

I must have blushed because Mrs. Deprima stopped talking and slowly smiled, watching my reaction.

"Aha!" She nodded her head as she read me like a book. "We will speak later." She casually tapped her finger in the air toward me. She could see it; she had my number.

Gratitude flooded my mind. Thank goodness for this big, loud Italian family carrying on about four different conversations at the same time because none of them caught on to what Angela's mother just did.

The last two hours of my workout canceled out what I just devoured at brunch. No gain, no loss.

I said goodbye to my adopted Italian family and headed home. I used the Internet again to find any information I could on Todd Duvall. I was in stalker mode.

I don't know why I thought new information would pop up from only a day ago. Todd was pretty much still off the grid — no social media that I could find.

He had a couple of professional links with a really nice photo of him looking serious with only minimum information on the links.

Suddenly, I realized I could leave him a private message on this site, and it would not be traced back to work. Did I dare do that? Now, the conflict started again. I came up with a plan to wait and see if I saw him tomorrow.

Monday came, and Monday went. So did Tuesday, Wednesday, and Thursday without any sign of Todd. I gave up. This was never going to go anywhere. Thomas had become my texting buddy and was fishing for another get-together. I didn't want to lead him on, so I told him I hadn't decided what I was doing this weekend and I would get back to him before the end of tomorrow.

I must have sounded like a complete jerk, I thought when I read the text I sent. He must have felt like he was on standby, so I called him to explain.

I blabbered. There was no other word for it, so I tried to be as honest as I could. He expressed that he completely understood and looked forward to the next time when I was available.

Wow, Thomas alone was teaching me what I have been missing all along. Friday afternoon was slower than usual.

Ned came out of his office and leaned an arm on the top of my cubicle. "How goes the battle, Mal? Any plans for the weekend?"

I sat back in my chair. "Nothing too pressing, gym, laundry, grocery shopping... I think Angela and I might catch a movie. How about you... any exciting plans?"

"Kids are in sports, full weekend ahead."

I grinned. "Nice. I'm going to hit the bathroom while I have a minute."

Ned nodded with a hang-on-a-second finger as Greg called to him. I stood and looked over at Greg as I exited my cubicle.

"Be right back, Ned." I turned as Ned turned back to me, watching me nearly slam into Todd. "Mallory, look out!" he warned.

Todd grinned, stopping in front of me and gently placing his hands on my arms in what had become the standard meeting between us.

Todd steadied me in place as he always did, while Ned apparently was talking to me. I looked up at Todd, admiring the spark in his eyes as his hand released the soothing warmth comforting my arm.

Todd sported a slight grin. Yes, that was a grin, a genuine grin at that; it was adorable.

He answered Ned's question for me, "I've got her. She's fine," and as he relayed that, my weight unexpectedly shifted; he had cupped his hand to pull me a step closer to him.

Oh, he pulled me all right because I shifted away from his touch for a second. He stared straight into my eyes with that alluring smile still in place. "Hello," he greeted.

We were nearly kissing-distance apart. Even I knew this distance. He was saying hello to me, and I just stood there, becoming inarticulate, trying to register this simple exchange. His lips were so inviting... Ned said my name, and I snapped to... pulling my head out of the clouds as Todd's cologne permeated my nostrils. His scent was delicious, intoxicating, and wow.

"Mallory, are you okay?"

I cleared my throat, answering Ned softly, "I'm fine."

Ned seemed agitated. "Duvall, do you need me for anything?"

Todd shifted to look at Ned. "No, I have what I need right here. You can go." He was dismissing Ned. Oh, Mr. Military was not keen on that.

"Mallory, I'll be with Greg for a bit. Call me if you need me." I was still well aware of the close distance between us.

I managed to squeak out an, "Okay. Thank you," to Ned.

Todd studied me, softening from his exchange with Ned, and started over. "Hello, Miss Kennedy."

I cleared my throat. "Hi... is there something I can do for you?"

The expression in his eyes smoldered as his grin disappeared. "That is a loaded question, and I will leave that one alone for now. The reason I came down here was to see if you could help us out with Randall Mack's account."

I awakened, abruptly freeing myself from his intoxication, and cleared my throat slightly. I tossed my head, causing my hair to flip around. He was talking to me, asking for my help.

Todd let his hand slide a few inches down, almost in a caress on my arm that never lost contact.

"Mallory, I know this isn't your department, but you seem to have a way with him, and his account has fallen behind."

Now, his left thumb moved a little. I cleared my throat again, quickly glancing down at his thumb out of pure shock because this was clearly intentional.

I glanced back up at him. "What can I do to help?"

Todd nodded. "We need you to call him and give him a friendly reminder that his account has fallen behind. He has an order that is ready to be delivered, but we need him to bring his past-due balance up-to-date, so his shipment won't be delayed."

I sighed, fully aware of what he was asking me to do now. "You're right. That is not my department. Why do you want me to do this?"

Todd turned up a grin. "You have a gift with the way you speak to people, and he likes you. Look, I know this is above and beyond your duties. If you try this approach, you will be rewarded. I will personally see to it."

"Rewarded? How?"

"Let me worry about that. I want to conduct an informal experiment. He's a good customer, and we feel a reminder coming from you will be the best path taken."

This was too weird. Todd Duvall was softly asking me to do something and not just demanding that it be done. He was actually being charismatic, and he was smiling. Wow, he had a nice smile.

His hands relaxed a little more, and if I wanted to, I could break free at this point, but I didn't want to. I wanted him to pull me in closer and kiss me right here, right now. I think he felt my energy. "Mallory, will you do this for us?"

And now, I was back in the here and now. I focused better and answered, "Yes. Do you want me to do it right now?"

"If you don't mind. That would be best." Todd was looking me over.

"Umm, okay."

I stepped back away from his hold and went to turn back to my desk. He grabbed my hand and hooked it into his as I stopped in my tracks. The pressure of his hold was enough for me to follow wherever he was moving.

I glanced at the new connection and followed with my eyes up to his face. He pulled me toward him. "Let's go to my office and do this."

Now, he was in control. He let go as soon as my momentum put me side by side with him, and he placed his hand on my lower back to guide me.

I loved how he positioned me where he wanted me. I was light-headed and floating along. Actually, I started to heat up a bit. I hoped my face wasn't red, but I felt like my skin just had a hot flash. What the hell was this?

It had better not be some cruel joke from the universe. I was reacting to his touch, and my body was ratting me out. We entered the smaller office, his ass-chewing room as I referred to it.

He closed the door behind him. Wow... if he tackled me right now, I would welcome it. He motioned for me to sit as he sat on the corner of the desk and pulled the phone over.

He had Randall's phone number already.

I dialed. "How much is he behind? Am I allowed to know this information?" I shyly glanced up at him with my knees tightly pressed together and my hand going numb from trying to grip the phone.

Todd tapped the top of the desk. "I am not to disclose the exact amount, but I can tell you above a hundred thousand."

I hung up. I was not accounting receivable/payable. "Are you sure this should come from me? I'm not trained to deal with collecting money. I take orders and keep the customer happy."

Todd turned slightly more into me. "You are the perfect choice for this. I am right here if you get stuck."

He handed me the phone as I tried not to shake. Okay, I dialed the number again. Now, it was ringing. Randall answered, "What the hell do you want? I'm busy. Make it quick!" he barked on the other end. I just went for it. "Hi, Randall. It's Mallory from SBS."

He went from barking to pleasant right away. "Mallory, how are you, sweetheart? Now, you're calling me. You know, beautiful, this is how rumors are going to start. Is everything okay with my order?"

I cleared my throat. "That is why I'm calling, Randall. It seems to have a red flag attached to your next delivery, and I thought I should call you and give you the heads up. I know how busy you are and how much you do."

He huffed, "Red flag... what does that mean?"

"They're delaying the shipment because your account has fallen behind in payments."

"Oh, is that all?"

"Yes, Randall. I just wanted to make sure you knew."

"I will call that damn kid of mine. He's supposed to be keeping up with this. How much do you need?"

I looked up at Todd as he mouthed, "Two-hundred-thousand dollars."

My eyes widened as I watched Todd speak the number with the serious executive look in his eyes.

I cleared my throat quickly, and I repeated it into the phone.

Randall was a little mad. "Oh, looks like I need to be back in the office some more; don't worry, Mallory. I will have that overnighted by the end of the day. Thanks for the heads up, kid."

"Thank you, Randall. I look forward to talking with you soon."

And I hung up. Todd had a half-grin on his face now. "Well done."

Then he continued looking at me for another moment. He asked like this was a normal conversation, "What are you doing tomorrow morning?"

This was not normal Todd, and I remembered the last time he asked me what I was doing. "Is there another ball game in town?"

He shook his head with a slight grin and looked down, then tilted it back up, looking me right in the eyes more seriously now. "Did you enjoy yourself? Because it looked like you did."

How could he have known that?

I told him I took Angela, and we had a nice time, and then I thanked him.

He replied, "You're welcome," in a serious manner. Okay, that's all I was saying about that.

He edged off the desk and extended his hand in my direction. This was very out of character, and it was too much too soon.

I was completely unfamiliar with this Todd Duvall. I hesitated, but I put my hand in his, letting him guide me. "May I take you out for coffee in the morning?"

WHAT? This man was so confusing! I made my mental checklist. I had nothing but a movie planned with Angela within the next fifty-two hours.

"What time?" I asked like I had a busy day.

He observed, then continued, "My schedule is open until 10:00 a.m. Does that work for you?" Another confident grin slowly crept into place as he held the door shut, waiting for my answer.

Okay, I decided this was going to be okay. "I can do eight-thirty. Where do you want to meet?"

He inquired, "Is there a reason why I can't pick you up at your house?" Whoa... that wasn't even on the table. He wanted to pick me up at my place. Nothing could have prepared me for that chain of events, and my hesitation was becoming awkward with a long silence.

He added, "I would really like to pick you up if that is all right."

I conceded, "Umm... okay."

"Good. Now that that is settled, I have a telephone conference in fifteen minutes. I will send my secretary down shortly. Just write your contact information for me."

He opened the door a few inches, then stopped and looked deep into my eyes. "You did very well with Randall."

Then he proceeded to open the door all the way as he led me through, then dropped his hand and exited to the left, leaving our department.

I stood there, watching him walk away. Ned was observing from Paul's station, now making his way toward my cubicle. I pulled myself together and also walked back.

We reached it at the same time. I looked at Ned, then sat, replaying everything that just happened in my brain.

Ned started right in. "What the hell was that all about?"

"He wanted me to address a past-due balance with Randall."

"What? That's not your department! I'm going to talk to HR about this!"

"No, don't! It was really nothing, Ned. He just asked me to remind Randall that he is overdue and his next order won't ship until he brings his balance up-to-date."

"Again, Mallory, this is not your job." I reached up and put my hand on Ned's forearm because he was ready to storm away. I managed to stop him, explaining in detail further. "Ned, really, it made a lot of sense. Just listen a second."

He settled down by the end of the whole story because it did make sense. There was a long pause, and then he said, "You do interact with our clients very well. He's right. You are gifted at dealing with customer service. Randall is one of our more challenging clients, and you have a great rapport with him. Todd was right to take a chance and see if you could resolve this through you making a simple phone call."

I lifted my hand and did the Italian twist with my finger that I learned from Angela's family. "No big deal. Believe me; I was just as taken aback, but it all worked out."

Ned had more to say, but he hesitated. We sat there in a standoff. I had known this man for many years, and he was still my brother's best friend.

I started, "What is it you want to say? I know there's more to this."

He struggled, then squared his shoulders and just addressed his issue. "SBS has a strict dating restriction policy between workers. It's in our handbook."

What? If I could have guessed what he was going to say, I would have been so off the map, it would be ridiculous. Now, I had to recover and pretend like this wasn't even a worthy conversation.

Chapter Four

I know for a fact that the nonsense coming vocally from me was not matching what was going on visually with my expressions. He didn't say another word, and I was going to have to dig this up on my contract. Ned left me and went back to his office.

Ten minutes passed, and there was Todd's secretary stopping at the end of my desk. She was looking to pick up my information in the envelope.

Suddenly, I wasn't sure I was allowed to give it. Oh, geez. What do I do now? I decided to play it safe until I could get ahold of that employee handbook.

I wrote, "Gym tomorrow 8:00 a.m. if you dare."

There, that was a safe deterrent. I sealed the envelope, scribbled his name across the front, then handed it back to her.

Ned was watching from his desk.

She smiled and thanked me. I wondered what it was like working for him. Could Todd be nice like he was with me an hour ago? Or was he always like stern Todd, who I witnessed when he dealt with the bad side of the business?

Tonight, I had this employee-dating policy to deal with.

Angela tried to coax me out, but I had my mission to sort through this stupid employee handbook's policy about dating, and I had to do this alone ASAP.

Five minutes before I shut down, Todd's secretary was at my desk with a reply.

Startled at first, I reached over and accepted it.

She nodded and left right away. There was my name across the front. I opened it immediately and read his response: "Working out together? What will the bystanders speculate... one condition... you follow my lead, Kennedy? I will be there at 8:00 if you make it or not."

Ohhhhh... this was going bad fast.

I did not mean this as a challenge for him, and clearly, he did not care for my response. Darn it, why didn't I just give him my contact information and let him pick me up for coffee?

Now I put myself right back on the other "no go" side of him.

I had some serious reading to do, and I couldn't wait to get home. It figured that my normally easy ride home was taking twice as long today.

This was killing me with all the breakdowns and an accident. There was no reason for my flow of traffic to be delayed because of an accident on the outbound side of the highway. I hated nosy people who had to see what was going on.

Thomas was texting me, asking if I had free time this weekend. I felt horrible about my answer, but I replied that this weekend was out.

An hour and twenty minutes later, I was inside my condo, searching for that fist in cuffs handbook. I found it and slapped it on the coffee table.

I sighed and decided to change into more comfortable clothing, and then I poured myself a glass of red wine. Now, I was ready. I picked up the handbook I'd signed when I was hired over ten years ago and turned to the pages containing the policy on employee dating.

I read line by line, and I had not realized the strict code they had outlined. Ten years ago, I would never have even considered dating someone at work.

However, since the week that Todd Duvall had held me by my arms and ended up giving me those baseball tickets, I wanted to date him. I wanted to mount him, kiss him, and ravage him.

This stupid outdated book says I could lose my job if we dated while employed by the same company. Now, what do I do? Not show up at the gym? This sucked.

This was the first time I had been interested in anyone for a very long time, and my job says, "Nope, no can do, not at this company."

I open-handedly dropped the manual on my coffee table and reached for my glass of wine, taking a big sip and sinking into the back of my couch, while the cushion molded around me, easing my body.

I felt restless as I scrubbed my hands over my face. This was a very cruel joke the universe was playing on me. Leaning forward, picking up my glass again, I took several more sips, feeling the wine raising my internal temperature.

Sighing heavily, I leaned my head back and closed my eyes. What to do? What to do? After thinking through several debates going on in my head, I decided to meet Todd at the gym tomorrow.

It was neutral ground. We both had memberships there of our own doing, and it definitely was not a date.

One glass of wine, and that was it. I was all done. I cleaned my house and headed to bed for an early night's sleep.

By six in the morning, I was ready to get things going. This was not a date. I was meeting Todd at the gym to work out, and that's exactly how I approached this.

I dressed like that was my only intention — no makeup, hair in a ponytail, and plain, regular gym clothes. I totally blended. Nothing about me drew any attention, and this would show that this was not a date.

I had no idea what to expect with Todd this morning. I turned down his invitation to pick me up at my house, and I sent back the change of plans written on the paper where he was expecting my contact information.

I was getting myself worked up for no reason. Our company had very strict policies about dating other employees, no matter what department, so this was the correct choice, and I was doing this so I wouldn't jeopardize his and my job. I sort of saved the day, and now working out would be something very safe, and I still got to hang out with him.

I arrived at the gym, and there was already a nearly full parking lot. I was ten minutes early, hoping to have the upper hand. I still did not know what he drove, so he could be here or not. I crossed my fingers for the not part.

I swiped my member's card, and a greeter slightly acknowledged me. Scanning the room, there was no sign of him. Good. I pulled it off. I made my way toward the women's locker room. I passed a small office on the left, and just as I cleared it, I heard, "Mallory."

Whoa... I didn't know anyone who worked here. Taking a few steps back, I caught a movement from the corner of my eye of a person standing from a chair as he repeated my name.

Now, I recognized the voice as I stopped and turned. It was Todd, who was now standing in the doorway, looking a little full of himself.

He positioned his self-assured posture to lean up against the doorframe. I was confused. Why was he in there to begin with? That was a staff-only office.

I needed to ask, "Do you work here too?"

He let a slight cocky chuckle turn up the right side of his mouth and answered, "No." That was it; that's all I got. Okay, then... I was about to tell him I was going to put my stuff in the locker room when he gave directions for me to follow. "Mallory, go put your bag in the locker room, then we can get started."

Yes, he was telling me what to do, even though that's what I was about ready to do, only now he was telling me. Yeah, that didn't sit well.

Work is one thing. I get why he needs to take control and get questions answered and issues resolved, but this is not work.

This was downtime, and this was definitely not a date. He had already managed to raise my body temperature. I replied fairly confidently because, at this moment, I was not caught off-guard; he was not holding me in place, and I had a year of working on my issues not to build a wall around me backing me up. I was confident, and I was a new me. Narrowing my eyes, I said, "Actually, I was just about to tell you those exact words. Wait here until I come back out. I'll just be a few minutes."

How do you like me now, Mr. Duvall? I accepted his command and raised him with my own, and I told him when I was returning.

The ball was back in my court, and there was that look in his eyes, recognizing the challenge, and he was ready to play. I turned and continued to the locker room. I found a spot against the wall and just tossed my bag there.

I had nothing worth taking, and this was a hardworking crowd, so the risk level of someone snooping through my bag was very low to nonexistent. I checked myself in the mirror and fixed my ponytail tighter while clenching my teeth, and I was ready. "Okay, Todd Duvall. Let's see what you got," I told myself with my game face on.

Todd was talking to a very attractive younger woman, much younger than me — that was for sure. As soon as he saw me, he excused himself, telling her his next appointment was here. Was I an appointment? Did he work here on the side?

She was all smiles and gave him a little wave, and then she glanced at me for a moment, dropping that stupid grin and giving me a cold stare.

I flexed an eyebrow, wondering what the hell her problem was. She turned with a bit of an attitude, walking away.

Todd waited for me to close the distance between us. I stopped about five feet from him "I'm an appointment?" I questioned as he now made the moves to close the gap between us.

"Are you ready for me to make you breathless, Kennedy?"

That statement was unfair, in my opinion, and the region south of my belly button was reacting to it. I cleared my throat, focusing on that reaction from the girl to distract me. I announced, "Show me what you got, Duvall."

He was very amused with my reply and made a step even closer, invading my personal space, bringing my self-control down another notch. I wanted to seize his smooth, lush lips and kiss him for everything I had. He was so close to me that I was becoming intoxicated with his scent.

Oh, my... he smelled freshly showered with a hint of masculine body cologne, and I could feel the heat radiating from his body. I wanted to touch him. I concentrated my breathing through my mouth, nearly tasting what I was becoming high on.

His return gaze was confusing me on so many levels. His intense eye contact looked like he had a mission, and those were definitely bedroom eyes.

I went to step back, feeling that this was too much for me to handle. His hands, one placed on my right bicep and the other on my left, quickly caught my motion, keeping me in the place where I stood.

He searched my eyes and softly started, "Don't pull away from me, Mallory. Don't ever pull away from me."

Right then, I thought he was going to kiss me right in the middle of this gym. My heart was hammering so hard, so fast as our eyes locked.

Just as soon as that feeling appeared, it disappeared as he dropped one of his arms. "Woman, you are going to bring me to my knees."

What did he just say? Was I going to bring him to his knees? That didn't even make any sense, but my next breath was his other hand following down my arm until my hand was hooked with his, now pulling me along slightly behind him. I stared at our joined hands. How did that happen and why was he holding my hand?

This was a gym. We were supposed to be working out together, and the only thing working out was my brain, and how could this be happening? And what did he mean... Don't ever pull away from him? He towed me all the way across the gym and through the doors of the basketball court and through another set of doors, not once releasing the skin-to-skin contact of our hands. I could feel his energy as I tried to feed on our connection.

There was one last set of doors, and this led to an area in the back that was outside. I never knew this place existed. The cool morning air felt welcoming but made me shiver for a moment with the adjustment. Todd still had his hand in mine as he led me deeper into this training course.

We were the only ones out here. As we reached the middle, he released my hand, breaking the bond, and I suddenly felt extremely self-conscious, wrapping my arms around myself, rubbing to keep warm in the cool morning air.

I said it because I was very confused and my brain couldn't take it anymore. "What was that? What's going on here?" and I quickly pointed one finger at him to me and back again. He turned to me with an odd look.

"I am just as confused as you, Kennedy. The only thing I know is if we don't start working out soon, I am going to take you over there and do exactly what my lower head is telling me to do, and somehow, I know you will not resist."

WHAT? Did he really just say that? My body reacted, ready to take him on. And then my brain kicked in with reason when it should have been overruled by the passion and emotion I was feeling.

I stated, "We are not allowed to date." He cocked his head to the side, surprised I just said that.

Then amusement sparked in his eyes. "Why do you say that, Mallory?"

I took in a sharp breath. "It's in the employee handbook. We both signed it when we were hired, and there are strict rules on dating between SBS employees."

Todd grinned now, very amused. "Well, it's a good thing we're not dating. Come on, Kennedy, I like looking at you when you're breathing hard; let me work you before you can catch your breath."

I wasn't sure how to respond, but he reached for my hand again, and I gave right in. It was not long, and I was breathing heavy with sweat running down my forehead, watching him and following his lead.

He had such a strong core. Todd was not the big muscular type, but he was solid. Watching him perspire right now made me want to wipe his sweat off with my panties. Every so often, I was rewarded with a gentle breeze wafting his scent in my direction.

We were still the only ones out on this project challenge course. I needed a break before flipping that huge tractor tire up the incline. He was walking back to me after finishing his tire, and I plunked myself down on mine. He grinned. "Don't give up on me now, Kennedy. We have ten more minutes."

He stopped in front of me, his wet T-shirt clinging to his body with sweat that I wanted to feel under my touch. I slowly looked up at his face. That blend of dark and sun-kissed golden hair was matted down, forming clumps of wet strands and soft spikes. That was the second place I wanted to thread my fingers through.

He reached his hand out to lift me to my feet. I extended mine, accepting his gesture.

Todd pulled me up; only this time, it was right to his mouth. With his other hand cupping the back of my head, he started kissing me, and I was willing. His tongue skimmed and swirled with mine.

My heartbeat pounded against my chest as this dizzy feeling took over my brain, drowning any emotion other than the desire to surface. His mouth covered mine in hunger as he dipped and devoured, entwining our tongues.

Nothing else mattered right now except us. We were finally together. He kissed better than I could imagine. After almost a year of dreaming about this moment, no one I have ever been with could kiss me this way.

His hands were melting their way down my back and around my ass while I pressed my body into his. He did a quick squat, not once leaving my mouth as he guided my legs to wrap around him. He lifted me around his waist. We were moving, but I wasn't sure in which direction because of the effects of his tongue assaulting mine. The next thing I felt was my head slightly spinning as gravity took over, and my back was laid gently against the ground.

I was ready. I didn't care about anything but wanting us together right now. We rode the moment for another few seconds, and then he broke free, separating the connection, leaving me breathing heavily. I watched him mimic my reaction. We stayed there, just staring at each other.

It was clear that this was all that was going to happen right now. Suddenly, I began to feel too exposed and readjusted my position, so I was sitting up properly.

Todd stood, running his fingers through his hair. And now he started to pace. He was clearly pacing. I collected my thoughts and also stood.

He kept at a safe distance, now looking at me. I broke the ice, trying to make light of what just happened. "So... yeah, anytime you want to work out together, just let me know."

Oh, no, he was closing the distance between us again. This wasn't good. Todd lifted me to my feet, put his arm around my waist, then caressed his fingers and thumb on my face. "You have been my biggest distraction for a good part of my year with SBS. I have tried to dismiss you on many accounts, but I can't, and now that I know what you taste like, it's going to make me crazy every time I see you."

He leaned down and kissed me softer, but I wanted that lip-mashing, tongue-hungry first kiss back. I attempted to turn up the heat, but he broke free, leaning his head back. "I'm barely able to contain myself right now, Mallory, and I'm sure you'd like to come back here without the memory of someone walking through, seeing me pumping you hard."

Ohhhh. Suddenly, the realization hit me that we were in a public place, and we were in an open area, even though we were still the only ones back here at the moment. Needless to say, he'd admitted that he wanted me. Todd wanted me, and I was a distraction to him. Why did we wait so long for this?

Then, right on cue, the doors opened, and a group stepped through. He grinned as I tried to break free, but he held me to him, trying to soothe me with gentle shushes. I stopped struggling when he softly lingered a kiss on my forehead. "I will figure this out, Mallory." He let go.

I was level five confused right now. I also let go of him, only to walk away, then in a circle, walk back to him with my body needing him to hold me again that way. I turned again and walked further away, hoping the distance now between us would solve the problem.

"Todd, how is this ever going to work? We can't date. Bottom line."

He narrowed his eyes. "Why not?"

"Once again... work policy!"

He snickered. "That is the least of my problems, Kennedy."

"Well, it's the biggest of mine right now," I reminded him.

That concluded our workout, and this time, he did not hold my hand as we walked back. Instead, he had his hand resting on my lower back. When we reached the locker rooms, we stopped.

I was about to say something witty about the workout again when Todd announced he had a busy rest of the weekend.

He looked into my eyes and promised he would see me soon. He pulled me in, taking ahold of my waist, then leaned down and kissed me right on my lips right in front of everyone in this gym and added, "We will be together soon, Kennedy." He caressed my cheek with one stroke of his thumb, and then he left.

That was it... I looked around, and definitely, a few people were staring at me. My arms wrapped to hug the empty feeling I was left with while watching him disappear.

Just then, Jessica's new husband walked in front of me. "I'll tell Thomas you have someone else."

I threw my hands out in a defensive reaction, being completely taken by surprise. "Brian! Brian, I am not leading Thomas on. He is a great guy, but I don't want the drama. I know all about that kind of a family mess. I was in it until I reached college. Your brother is a great guy, and I made it clear to him that he could only be a friend. So, if you were led to believe that we were more, then it's not by my doing."

Brian grunted, "Whatever, he's too good for you anyway."

I stood there feeling reduced for no logical reason other than allowing Brian to do that to me. What did he just say to me? Why did I let that happen!

This is what I have been fighting for the last year.

I exhaled, darting for the security of the women's locker room to gain control of my spinning head while softly rubbing my sides. I had a headache coming on. This was too much to deal with on a Saturday morning.

I expected a workout, not a total life changer as well as being accused of something I was not responsible for. I could not get out of here quick enough.

Now, I had a whole new set of concerns. Brian was a member here. Was Jessica? Was Thomas? Oh, good grief. What was I opening up?

I calmed down enough to keep my eye on the prize. Had I missed the hints or subtle gestures that Todd Duvall was interested in me? That maybe even Todd wanted me?

He kissed me. I mean full-on assault kissed me. I have never been kissed like that in my life, and if his kisses were a prelude of what to expect, then I needed Todd Duvall to be in my bed. My fantasies about him were sadly underrated compared to anything I experienced in that outdoor challenge course.

I tapped my fingers on my steering wheel the whole ride home. I really hoped this would all work out. The hot water rained down my back as I turned slowly in my shower, touching my lips, remembering how his mouth felt on mine, then the last kiss in front of the locker rooms, in front of everyone at the gym before he left.

Oh, my God! I panicked, thinking there could have been more people we knew even from work. Brian was there, and I never noticed him. No dating; no dating! How was I going to deal with this?

There was no way I was ever forgetting that kiss. How was I going to ignore him at work now or, better yet, not want him to kiss me there? I had to figure this out and quick. I remembered Todd still did not have my contact information. I wasn't sure if that was a blessing or a curse right now. I knew this was going to bother me all weekend.

I was right. That was all I thought about the entire weekend. I even canceled Angela and the movies because I could not stop thinking about Todd, Brian, and what Monday was going to bring.

Angela would pick up on my distraction so easily, and I didn't need the questioning right now. I had too many of my own questions to work through with no clear answers as of yet. Sunday, I stayed home and deep cleaned my already clean house. There was no way I was going to the gym to risk bumping into Todd.

I had not worked this out in my head yet. I couldn't get past the kiss as that employee handbook taunted me from my coffee table. I went to it as if it were cursed with an evil spell as I slapped my hand down on the top before I picked it up. I hated this binder. I flipped right to the pages and, once again, studied the dating policy word for word, over and over. I physically growled out angrily. This was just cruelty, and I wanted to throw it against the wall.

This damn manual was keeping me from my happily ever after. I glared at it, slammed it shut, and then slapped it down on the coffee table, which seemed just as satisfactory as throwing it against the wall. I growled out loud. Why did they have this dating policy?

Did something happen at my company that made them initiate this? Great, more homework, and how could I bring this up without attracting attention to myself? Ned... I would ask Ned. He was the one who pointed it out, and he has been there longer than I have.

Okay, I worked that out in my head. I will go to Ned and resolve this. Now, to focus on what I was going to do about Todd... The drive to work consumed my thoughts with wondering if I would even see Todd today. I let go of a heavy sigh. I was yearning to see him as my hands gripped tighter on the steering wheel and a muscle quivered in my jaw.

I really wished this was a rough week in quality control. I did not care if I saw him angry while yelling at someone or a casual glance as he walked by. I just wanted to see him. Every thought focused on Todd as I walked into my building, my mind now flip-flopping. Half of me hoped I didn't run into him, and the other half hoped I saw him all day long as I approached my building's entrance.

Great, the person just back from her honeymoon thought it was a good idea to confront me about what her new husband witnessed this past Saturday. "So, I hear you have been leading Thomas on when you obviously have a boyfriend at the gym. That's pretty low, Mallory. I thought better of you, but clearly, my intuition failed me. Seriously, I wish I'd never wasted the invitation."

Then she abruptly turned, walking away. I stood stunned for a moment; this was another attack that was completely uncalled for. Then my first emotion surfaced, anger. I was pissed. "Hey, Jessica! When you need to fill seats for your next wedding, make sure you include an open bar for an actual incentive to go!"

She narrowed her eyes for a sharp look over her shoulder, dripping with haughty disdain. I knew I had achieved my point, and it felt damn good as I made my way to my top dog senior sales cubical with quite a few surprised looks from the fellow staff.

Jimmy high fived me, walking by and muttering, "Isn't that the truth, sister," in a hushed tone that made me crack a slight grin.

No Todd all morning. Angela was suspicious of me today, though. I could see her thinking but not quite ready to ask yet.

At our first break, I bee-lined into Ned's office, closing the door and asking everything I wanted to know specifically about the dating policy. Why was it as strict as it was outlined? He slanted his brows in a frown, not happy about my curiosity.

There was clear disapproval on his face and in his tone as he explained the lawsuit that occurred a few years before I was hired. "The company was sued for over a million dollars from a supervisor and a lower stationed employee dating in the same department. When he broke it off, she sued for sexual harassment. Our company paid her off to make her go away. Then, they fired him."

I stood as my mind was swirling, and I paced. "Yeah, but that was like fifteen years ago, right?" I stopped and stood with my right hand on my hip, waiting for his answer.

Ned watched me and lowered his voice. "What's going on, Mallory?" He asked this, playing concerned big brother now, and Ned was actually close enough to me to play that role.

I blew out a slow breath, holding onto the back of the chair I had been sitting in as I confessed that I wanted to date someone here. He ordered me to sit.

He sounded just like my brother, as a matter of fact. I sat, but I was ready for the challenge. Then the military came out in him, making a big mistake with me. Ned ordered me, "Stay away from Todd Duvall. You do not need that mess in your life."

"What do you know about Todd?" Ned was now clearly interfering. There was something he knew, and he was not sharing.

Ned changed tactics, deciding to approach it like a warning instead. "Look, Mal. He comes with a lot of baggage. You don't need that in your life."

"Baggage, what baggage? Does he have kids?"

Wow, I never pictured him as a father. Ned sighed. "No, he does not have kids but just stay clear. Trust me." That was not convincing at all.

I needed more information, and Ned was done sharing. My break was not long enough, and it was time to return to my desk. Ned stood aligned with me. "Mal, he is no good for you. Forget about him."

"Why are you being so tight-lipped about him? Ned, you obviously know more about him than I do."

"I am not at liberty to give you employee information, Mal. Just trust me." This made me angry. I did not like my employer at this moment. I finally found a guy I wanted to date, and this company and my "fill in" brother were squashing the relationship before it started. It turned out to be a good thing that I didn't see Todd all day, but I didn't see him Tuesday or Wednesday either.

Now, I was missing him in my heart. Then on the flip side, Thomas called me three times and sent several text messages, wanting to meet up when I was available. It bothered me that I hadn't given Todd my contact information.

The one guy who I now didn't want to have it was abusing the power. The other guy I wanted to have it... I haven't been able to see so far this week. This was torture. No Todd today as well.

I had to convince myself this was completely normal with Todd's working schedule, though it didn't help my ego as the little voice in my head told me that I was an idiot for kissing him and this was the consequence for being so stupid. The only time Todd would be down here usually was when a problem came up. I'm pretty sure I resolved the issue with Randall, so it must have been an easy week for the sales department.

Chapter Five

Thursday afternoon, Angela had had it with me not sharing what was going with my change in moods. She knew something was up, and now she wanted to know. It was mostly because she was worried about me, but that Italian-family instinct was getting the best of her since I was part of the family, whether I wanted to be or not.

On the one hand, I really needed to tell her because Ned was no help at all. Then, on the other, I knew the price of telling her and what she was going to make me reveal. This Thursday, I needed her more than my pride.

So, we went to the gym together, and I proceeded to tell her everything. At first, I thought she was going to smack me, then she softened, then she got mad again, then she softened, and then she laughed.

Lastly, she told me she knew by the way he carried himself that sex was going to be amazing. I tried to bring it back to the SBS dating policy and Ned's warning. She dismissed both without concern.

She wanted me to hook up with him, and what the company didn't know wasn't going to hurt them. I was not prepared for her layer of acceptance.

This made my situation even more complicated. Here I had my best friend and substitute brother, both who looked out for me, on opposite sides of the great Todd debate.

I had to find out what Ned knew and was not allowed to share with me. Friday was here, and the morning madness was finally winding down. It was a much slower afternoon, and I was between calls, watching my orders.

I started applying my own quality control, following up on my customers' orders and seeing if there were delays coming up. A motion caught my eye, and I turned to see Todd's secretary was now at the end of my desk.

I jumped in my seat, letting out a gasp while holding a hand to my chest. She handed an envelope to me, trying not to react to my startled surprise. I removed my headset. She stated that she was to stay here for my reply. Oh... I leaned in and snatched the envelope from her with a little more force than I anticipated.

My heart was pounding in my chest as I tried not to rip it open. My hands were shaking, but I managed to keep the envelope intact and read his handwritten message: "Gym tomorrow at 8:00 a.m.?" I flipped it over; that was it. After a week since his last kissing assault, he wanted to meet me back at the gym. Back to where I knew other people were members now. What game are you playing, Mr. Duvall?

I looked up at his secretary, and she informed me she was not leaving until she had my reply. I peeked over at Ned's office. He was away for a moment. I scanned my surroundings, then picked up my pen and quickly wrote my reply, resealing the envelope, crossing my name out, and writing his name on the front. Then, I handed it back to her.

The moment she left, Ned spotted her and came right over to me. "What was that about, Mal?" He was suspicious. And there was no way of lying to him. He knew me, so I answered with the best truth I could give. "Todd needed an answer. I gave it to him."

Ned shook his head. "Forget that I asked." He turned in disappointment and went to his office. I tried not to take offense, but I knew deep down, I had just messed that up with him.

The next two hours crawled by, but I tried to fill them with watching more of my customers' orders. This was a whole new level of customer service with me. I made a few phone calls, making sure they knew what was going on with the delays, and they appreciated my new involvement.

Angela had babysitting duty tonight for her sister, so she and her husband could go out on that previously canceled date. She tried her best to persuade me to join her, but I needed to be alone tonight. I hit the gym with no expectation of seeing him, and I was in the clear. Tomorrow morning was going to bring a different can of worms. It was a given he was going to be there.

I made it home, had a relaxing bath, and walked around in my bathrobe and slippers. I made my way to the fridge to pour a glass of wine because I was feeling a little anxious.

Everything about Todd played like a movie in my mind. I went over every encounter that I'd already dissected for the hundredth time. There really was nothing more I could work through.

This was the most bizarre relationship situation I have ever been in, and why wasn't Ned forthcoming with the information he had about Todd? I was perplexed, but this wine tasted good, so I wrote down the brand.

I fell asleep on my couch with the television on. My bladder woke me at three in the morning. I shut everything down and went up to my bedroom to catch a few more hours of sleep.

My alarm rang at six in the morning, and I was now thinking that third glass of wine was a mistake. I was dehydrated, and there was a little bit of a headache there. I decided my sleep number should be two glasses of wine, not three. The third was too much, and now I had to work out with a guy who made my head spin without any alcohol present. I tossed my blankets off and immediately changed the dragging attitude around, getting myself ready, and trying to be more positive.

I decided to skip the shower. I was only going to the gym anyway. I simply brushed my teeth and washed my face. I arrived and grabbed my bag from the back seat and made my way to the entrance with my sunglasses on. No sooner had I made my way inside the doors than there was Todd, talking with the girl behind the counter as she over laughed about something he was saying. He spotted me and excused himself from her as he moved toward me.

He plowed right through my personal space and leaned down, greeting me as he went right for the kiss, pulling me against his body, kissing me like I had been away on some trip, just returning, and this was the first time he had seen me.

It was like this was a natural act, and we had been doing this for years. He released me, and I was very unsteady. He brushed the back of his fingers across my cheekbone while he said good morning to me.

Then he confessed he had been waiting all week to do that again. I couldn't even tell you my name right now if you asked. I just exploded inside with every emotion hitting me at once, and he grinned, going in for another kiss. This time, he made a little pleasure hum that accompanied his lips against mine.

Surprisingly, my body knew what to do. It was following the program just fine. He released me again. "Did you go out last night, gorgeous?"

I answered with a soft, "No," as I was on autopilot from his greeting.

He gave me some distance as he stepped back and gave the hmmm sound, followed by, "Did you have friends over last night?"

He was taking my bag from me and placing his hand in mine now. "No!"

He chuckled. "So, you were drinking at home alone last night?"

I stopped for a second. "I had a couple of glasses of wine. Why?"

He grinned, quite amused because I was getting defensive. Todd Duvall tested the waters. "You're not a closet drinker, are you? I mean, should I be worried about this?"

Oh, I was getting very, very defensive now. "You're questioning me about having a couple of glasses of wine on a Friday night, after work, in my own home?"

Todd Duvall was trying to keep a straight face. "I'm just saying, Mallory. I don't know you well enough yet."

I was irritated now. "Me? What about you? I know nothing about you!" I had not realized I was talking a little louder as other gym members were starting to observe us.

He was amused as he grinned, pulling me into the side of him, kissing the side of my forehead. I was internally battling, wanting to put my arm around him but trying to resist this affectionate action he was making. I was doomed.

"You know a little about me." He was having great fun riling me up, now handing my bag over because we were in front of the women's locker room.

Todd gave me instructions to put my bag inside and not to keep him waiting. I was annoyed, but my feet were obeying his command. I walked slower coming out, just to prove a point, and there he was, arms resting against a machine, talking to the same girl from last week.

The Dating Policy

I started to go to him, then hesitated because I wasn't sure who she was, and I didn't want to interrupt their conversation.

He noticed I was there and came at me, reaching for my hand. He asked if I was ready. This man was impossible to figure out! I nodded as the girl turned to leave, and he guided me to another part of the gym that I had never been to.

We were upstairs with a variety of free weights, ropes, and machines. There were a few guys up here, but that was it. He turned to me and asked, "How did you feel the next day after our workout?"

Confused was the answer that popped into my head, but I knew he was asking about my body recovery. "I was a little sore, but it wasn't bad."

He looked me over. "Today, I want to make you a little sorer."

"Todd, hang on. Before we go any further, I have to tell you. Last week here, when you kissed me in front of the lockers, there was a husband of one of the SBS sales employees here." I now looked around, realizing Brian could be here.

He shrugged, "Yeah, so?"

I couldn't believe his reaction "He saw you kiss me and reported it back to his wife, who confronted me on Monday."

Again, he looked unaffected. "Does that bother you, Kennedy?"

"Umm?" I didn't know where to go with this but, "What if work finds out?"

He chuckled. "Stop worrying about this. The gym is safe."

It was apparent that I was making way too big of a deal about this. What could Jessica do if she found out it was Todd? I let it go and focused on my workout partner. "Okay, enough said about that. So, what's on deck for today?"

He grinned as he said my last name formally. "Miss Kennedy, always a good warm-up to prevent injury." There were a few treadmills up here. As he reached for my hand, my body was reacting to him of its own free will again. My hand gravitated into his.

He set me up on one treadmill. He kissed me, sending my brain into overdrive. "Ready, Kennedy?" I nodded.

We did not start slow. I think he did it that way so I had no chance to ask questions. I did everything I could just to keep up with the pace. He kept telling me to drop it down to this level, then, a few minutes later, to increase to another level. It was a long twelve minutes, and I was glad this part of the workout was over.

I was warmed up all right and now feeling the effects from that third glass of wine that I wished I never poured. I had to give Todd credit. He certainly knew what he was doing as far as a good workout.

I didn't know what his game was with all this confusing affection he was giving. It was like we were together as a couple here, with no questioning that we were together, only there were thousands of questions going on inside my head, and it was time he answered a few.

I started to ask as I took a break. "You do know we have that strict dating policy at work, right?

He stopped and grinned. "Well, Kennedy, it's a good thing we're not dating, so that policy is moot." He went back to his workout.

What? That was the Todd I knew — arrogant, harsh, frustrating to judge. This was all wrong. Every bit of me being here with him was a mistake. Ned told me to stay away, and now I knew why. My brain snapped too and was fully functioning without the side-effects Todd had left me with before. "What's with all the goddamn kissing then?"

Yes, I was riled up because he put me there. He stopped trying not to be amused as he stood in front of me. He was breathing a little heavily from what he was doing, and he was too close again. I stepped back, and as his hand slipped around my waist, he caught me, pulling me into him, losing the smirk, and widening his stance.

"Don't you like me kissing you? I mean, I think this is enjoyed on both our ends." Todd was much too close, and I was losing my sudden attitude, feeling the heat coming on from his palms holding onto my waist. His scent was squelching into my every pore, hot, heavy... no... no... no. I had to get answers.

"Why are you kissing me was my question!" He leaned in, softly kissed my forehead, then slowly took a breath, and continued kissing a pattern across it.

He replied softly with tenderness, "I crave kissing you. I am very attracted to you, Mallory. I have not wanted anyone for a long, long time... if ever at this level from my own free will. Being around you has taken my self-control to a level I don't even understand. I cannot overstep my boundaries with you just yet. There are some loose ends I need to take care of before I take you on. Just be patient, Kennedy. I promise I will be worth your wait. But in the meantime... is this so horrible?"

He tilted my chin even further upward while his lips pressed into mine, separating them as his tongue rolled and savored slowly, passionately reinforcing every word just spoken. Up in this loft area, he acted as if I was the only one here. He showed me he didn't care who was watching.

I managed to break free from the passionate intoxication to take a step back. I was panting as my chest heaved to slow myself down. "Do you know how confusing this is for me?"

He tried to close the distance again, but this time what he said needed to be explained before I let my body take back over. "What do you mean about a loose end? Are we dating or not? I feel like you're messing with me, and there's a lot not right with this whole setup."

He stopped advancing on me and sat on the bench, then motioned for me to sit. I wanted to sit, but my stubborn side wanted control over this whole nonsense, so I moved closer and leaned against a workout machine.

The Dating Policy

He smirked at my resistance and sat back in a sexy pose. I was sure he didn't realize what he was doing, but it was working on me. He started calmly, yet his tone was a little lower than it should have been right now.

"I'm working on changing the dating policy at work. I found out why it was initiated, and the times have changed from fifteen years ago when it was put into action. I'm actively working on making it possible for the dating ban to be lifted as long as the employees are not in the same department and at fairly equal levels as far as status in the company. There are six happy couples at SBS that were married right around the time the sexual harassment lawsuit happened. It has never interfered with the work they produce, nor has their relationship been strained by working for the same company. Every couple has been married fifteen plus years. I think that sets a good counterargument.

I am also researching the girl who filed the lawsuit. I want to see if this has been a pattern of behavior for her. I know she settled for a half million, which is a drop in the bucket, and most likely, all that money is gone, and she is working-class again. Besides the office issue, there are some other matters that interfere with us coming together right now... I have some personal obstacles that I need to resolve on my own. I will not drag you into them. You do not need that on your plate. I want you, Mallory. Just be patient. I am making the steps, so we are free to be together no matter where we are — work, socially, anywhere."

I was not expecting that boatload of information. I went to him as he guided me to sit on the bench. He took my hand in his. "What do you say, woman? You going to give me what I need so I can give you what you need?"

He was now being playful, and that made me smile. Then I stated, "Right now, I need my job, Todd. I cannot risk being fired until you get work to change that dating policy."

He still found amusement in what I was worried about. He put his arm around me, pulling me in to kiss the top of my head. Why did being with him just feel right?

He rested his chin on top of my head and repeated, "You won't get fired, and I will not make you wait too long. I will hurry this along as quickly as I can. I'm good at dealing with this kind of stuff under pressure."

He let go and let me straighten back up. "Todd, why are you doing all this now? I mean, why didn't you take care of what you need to before this point?" I asked, very curiously. His answer was decisive as he shrugged a little. He looked into my eyes. "Mallory, I didn't have a reason to. Recently, you gave me that reason."

I was feeling pretty good right now. His confirmation and validation were huge pride builders for my ego. We wrapped up our gym session. I finally felt we were getting somewhere for the first time.

Today, Todd even waited to walk me out to my car. He carried both our bags as if this were something he did all the time.

He apparently knew my car as he reached it first, then patiently stood waiting for me to open the back door. He tossed my bag in and kissed me goodbye. I asked him if he wanted my phone number, but he surprised me by saying that he had my number in a sarcastic tone.

This was my opportunity to see what he drove, so I waited and watched as he made his way over to his car. Oh, my... I had not expected that class of vehicle... or had I? No, I really didn't. Todd Duvall drove a sleek looking full-size BMW sedan. It was black with heavily tinted windows.

This was a car that I could never afford in my lifetime. That car payment was like a mortgage payment. This was a car clearly from an upper management's salary. Todd was management. I wasn't exactly sure of his level, and as far as I knew, he was single. There was a lot I didn't know about this man, and now that was starting to bother me.

By noon on this overcast day, I was ready for a nap. All my chores were done, and I needed to shut my brain down from overthinking about what was said and mostly what was not said this morning at the gym.

Todd Duvall came with issues, and from the sound of his proclamations, we were going to be dating in the future. I was becoming anxious. Just as I was allowing myself to nod off, I shot upright in my bed, remembering the exotic-looking girl who was next to him in the Mexican restaurant. Who was she? Was she the loose end?

I quickly scooted out of bed and paced. Sometimes, not enough information was worse than too much information. This was going to kill me. There was no way I could sleep now.

Thomas was texting right on cue. *Hey, Mallory want to meet me for a drink?*

Why, yes, I do, Thomas?

I met him an hour later near Angela's as I texted her that I was meeting up with Thomas for a drink. The first thing I told him was that I had invited Angela along too.

I could see the surprised look on his face, but when Angela walked in and found us, he seemed good with both our company. Angela being Angela and having family as a huge priority, pried more about Thomas's children.

He seemed reluctant to talk about them and just answered her that he doesn't get to see them nearly enough. He gave us some detail that his ex-wife was crazy and was constantly trying to put them against him. He said she used them as pawns, creating friction. Angela was very angry that his ex-wife would do that. He admitted to us that, after three years, he just gave up. The court fees were unjust, and it was like throwing tens of thousands of dollars away on top of what he had to pay in child support.

I felt bad for him after hearing all of that. Angela's sister was calling her as she excused herself.

This gave me an opportunity to clear the air about Brian and the gym. "Thomas, I want to bring up seeing your brother at the gym last weekend."

For the first time in my life, I could not read a man's reaction as he waved his hand slightly from the grip on his beer. "Mallory, you were very clear when I met you the first time that we were only in the friend zone. I just don't want to lose you. I know where I stand, and I want to build on this friendship."

I wanted to hug him. How awesome was he for taking this for exactly what it was? This was the kind of guy I dated in the past and became friends with after we broke up. Maybe I was making progress in my life for once. I was on the right track, and my track was headed to Todd Duvall.

I left Thomas and drove home, feeling a little tipsier than I should from the amount I drank. I had two drinks in two and a half hours, and right now, I was feeling increasingly drunk as the moments ticked on. Maybe it was my workout or my mood.

Thomas was texting me because he did offer to escort me home. *Let me know if...* That's all I could read. Shit, I was drunk. I tossed the phone down on my passenger seat and noticed I was less than a minute from home. I knew that much. I opened my gate and pulled into my driveway. I didn't have the depth perception to pull into my garage, so I shut my car off, and everything went black.

My head felt like it was being squeezed between two wooden blocks. I opened my eyes, and the streetlight alerted me that it was nighttime. I looked around, and I was in my driveway, the garage door open, and my keys were in my hand as my head was pounding.

I started my car and finished pulling in. I leaned over to grab my purse, and Angela was calling me. I picked the phone up off the passenger seat and said, "Hey."

She started talking too loudly, "Mallory, are you okay?"

"Shh, don't talk so loud; I have the worst headache."

"I'm not talking loud. Where are you?"

"I just pulled into my garage."

I looked at the time on my dashboard; it was nine-thirty. "Where have you been? I've been trying to reach you for seven hours," she asked, upset and worried.

"I passed out in my driveway. Those two drinks hit me hard." I was now inserting my key into the front door and turning on lights.

"You had two margaritas in two hours; I'm not sure that's possible," she retaliated.

"Maybe it's my new routine, a chemical change in my body?"

"Bullshit! I don't buy that."

I filled up a glass of water and chugged it. Oh, that felt good. "I don't know, but I have been stressed out, and I'm dealing with some issues."

There was a long pause as she conceded, "Well, if you need someone to talk to, you know I'm always here for you."

I sighed. "I know you are. I just have to figure this out on my own right now."

"Okay, Mallory, I'll see you tomorrow. I'm glad you're safe and get some rest."

"Thanks, and I will see you tomorrow." I tapped to end the call, and the screen switched to all the missed calls and texts from both her and Thomas.

Thomas seemed very concerned and wanted to know where I was and then kept asking for my address and said he wanted to check on me.

I didn't want to deal with him right now because this headache was getting the better of me. I took a few Ibuprofens and chased them down with orange juice, then headed to bed. I slept until ten o'clock on Sunday morning. I have not done that forever.

There was definitely something going on with me.

I met Angela for coffee, and she commented that I looked a wreck and we agreed that I must be coming down with something.

I finally texted Thomas back that I was fine, but I was coming down with a bug, and I hoped I didn't contaminate him at our meeting yesterday.

He replied for me to get better soon and get lots of rest. Then he offered to bring me anything if I needed something from the store. That was so nice, but I told him I was all set, then thanked him.

The rest of the afternoon, my mind was on Todd. In my eyes, he was working on changing the rules in a big way so that we could date. He said he was initiating the steps and doing proper procedure, which I believed and admired. It seemed like he was ready to take on the world just so we could be together.

Yes, I was impressed. I knew his work ethic firsthand. He did his job very well at SBS, and there was no doubt in my mind that he was the only one who could challenge and change our company's dating policy to bring us together. I tried again to bring up Todd Duvall on my computer.

Still, nothing came up as I released a frustrated heavy sigh. Pulling into my work parking lot, I was thinking this was going to be another torturous workweek. It started with Ned, greeting me at my cubicle... no, that's too nice of a way to state what Monday-morning Ned was doing. He was fishing for information about what I did over the weekend. Yes, this was an interrogation done very smoothly, I might add.

I started to catch on when he mentioned specific times of days. First, he said, "Oh, I was at the ball field around ten. What were you doing then?"

The Dating Policy

Internally, I laughed, chanting in my mind, "You have to be quicker than that, Ned."

For him, the answers I gave eased his mood for some reason. I had five more minutes before the official start of my day. I leaned into him as he sat at the corner of my desk. "Heard from Sean yet?"

Ned nodded and brought me up to date about Big Brother. I knew Sean would call Ned long before he would call me, and that was okay.

My family was nothing like Angela's. My mother was self-centered and cared more about her husbands or boyfriends than she cared for Sean and me.

My dad had taken off long ago when I was little. He just disappeared one night. I don't even remember him anymore.

Ned was distracted by whoever was approaching. He stood as I turned to see. I grasped ahold of my desk, steadying myself. Oh, good Lord, it was Todd... in a black suit with a white shirt that showed off his exquisite features. His chiseled face looked more regal than I had ever noticed. The many shades of blond in his hair and his blue-gray eyes stood out against the solid dark blazer. The blue-gray tie matched his eyes. It was the most attractive tie I had ever seen, and I wanted to pull it from being tucked against him snugly. He looked every bit the modern-day corporate Viking, able to sell any product you stuck in front of him.

He was the perfect poster model you could fantasize over. He stopped, smelling amazing as his cologne hit my nasal passage. First, he glanced at me, then at Ned with an air of confidence and authority. I was breathing between my now separated lips, still gripping the edge of my desk and pressing my thumbs up the underside edge to keep myself still.

He glanced down at me again, making eye contact for a moment as I registered his aura of power. It sizzled; Todd was clearly on a mission. He now looked right into Ned's eyes, informing him that he, along with all our sales department managers, was to be in the boardroom, and then he glanced down at me. My palms were sweating as I focused on his mouth, "Along with Miss Kennedy."

Todd continued, "Ms. Gary and I will be down in one hour. The meeting will start when we arrive." What? Was I included? I am not a department head. I searched Todd's eyes that were focused on Ned as he gave no expression away, and then he shifted his gaze directly to me, and I twitched like I was just caught doing something wrong. "One hour, Miss Kennedy." He turned and strode away.

Ned shot a sharp annoying look at me. "Okay, then... I'll gather the others. You heard him. Make sure you are in there." Ned now mimicked Todd in the opposite direction.

My phone lit up. It was time for me to start taking my calls. That hour felt like only twenty minutes. Ned walked by, giving me a five-minute warning to get my ass in that boardroom.

Everyone else was in there, waiting, talking among themselves. That was until I walked in. They all looked at me, and Richard smiled. "Do you need something, Mallory?" Frowning, Ned answered for me, "No, she does not. She is here per a request from quality control."

He said that as if he too could not believe I was asked to participate. Now, they all stared at me, making me feel like I did not belong here. There were seven seats open. Ned ordered me, "Mallory, come sit here."

Ned motioned to the chair next to him. In the order of the boardroom, there is a hierarchy in seating placement. Even I knew that much. Whoever was directing the meeting sat left side head seat. Then the next would be the department head, such as in sales.

Our department head, Richard Cross, sat at the opposite end of the head position. I was smack in the middle with my back to the door, which was the lowest seat in this room. The door opened wider as the focus moved from me to Todd entering the room, followed by Samantha Gary, Allen Flynn — who was management in accounting — and Paula, Samantha's secretary.

I had known Allen for years, and I smiled, nodding to him. About six years ago, Allen and I seemed to arrive at the same time nearly every morning. It became a joke between us, and eventually, we waited for each other so we could walk and talk. It wasn't until a few years back, when he started dating and married that the timing just never seemed to work again. I liked Allen, and I was very happy for him. Life changes, and that's how it goes.

Samantha sat, and then Todd sat to the left of her, and the secretary next to him. Allen sat to the right of her, and the meeting opened as Todd stood. He went right in on why we were all here.

"A few weeks ago, Mr. Flynn approached us about a more creative method of collecting money with some of our more difficult clients. We went over a few ideas, then held onto them. In our second meeting, through some more research, it was brought to our attention that Miss Kennedy seemed to have the brunt of the dealings with this type of client. By the end of our meeting, we decided to conduct our own sample experiment. I approached Miss Kennedy and asked her to give a 'friendly reminder' to one of her customers who had fallen behind on payments. Lo and behold, our experiment worked. The customer paid up to date, and it was a success."

Ned raised his hand slightly to speak, but Todd dismissed him. Todd went on, "With our experiment and the approval from the owner, Mr. Gary himself, along with accounting, we are creating a new position for Miss Kennedy. She will be moved to a management position. She will take over the office next to us. She is still part of this sales team, but her job duties will change. Miss Kennedy will be working with accounting as part of this new position. She will mostly be dealing with the clients

Allen sees fit for her new position, and we believe this will benefit all our departments."

I was gob smacked, and I believe the expression on my face reflected this after I heard myself gasp. Todd sat, looking right at me, as Samantha Gary now spoke, "Miss Kennedy, welcome to the next level of management with SBS. Your record and employment with us are honorable. With great confidence, we move you to this position. Mr. Duvall will be in charge of settling you in, and he will bring you down to HR to go over your new title, salary, and benefits. Allen will meet with you this afternoon to go over his ideas, and then IT and Maintenance will get your office set up."

I squeaked out a, "Thank you," as Samantha continued.

"If there are any questions or comments, please speak with me directly. I will be available after lunch. Paula will schedule an appointment."

That was it. This meeting was over. No one had the authority to speak about it in this boardroom. Ned stood and sternly offered his congratulations.

Something was going on that I was not catching onto right now. All the other department heads offered me flat congratulations as well.

Allen smiled and told me he looked forward to working with me. Samantha stood to the side of the table; she had scared the hell out of me since my start at SBS, and now she was telling me personally to e-mail her directly or to call Paula, her secretary if there was anything I needed. Then she added that this was a new position in the company, and there were bound to be some learning curves. The quicker those were addressed, the sooner we would see my new position as the right choice among the three departments.

The first sentence was the first time I had witnessed Samantha Gary close to having some sort of an understanding that people could make a mistake.

The next sentence was her underlying threat and the example of how she ruled with an iron fist. Todd came over to me and put his hand on my shoulder with a faint grin. "Congratulations, Miss. Kennedy. Please walk with me to HR, so we can make this official."

Before following him, I spoke to Samantha Gary and mentioned I was still taking all this in, and I would do my very best to fulfill the role they had created. Then I thanked her for the opportunity. I left it at that. I didn't want to grovel too much because it was a sign of weakness, and I was starting to ramble.

She nodded respectfully, and Todd guided me out, and we went right to HR. I had so many questions and wanted to explode or jump for joy. I wanted to jump in his arms and kiss him until my lips bruised.

We entered the elevator, and I had to ask as he stood silent, "Did you have anything to do with this?" He cleared his throat slightly. He looked so goddamn good in that suit. I wanted to climb him.

He replied, "This was all your work ethic, Miss. Kennedy. They recognized your talents and will utilize them to benefit the company." He turned, looking into my eyes. "This was all you."

A sudden heat hit me everywhere. I wanted this man, and he felt it. "Not now, Mallory. Soon... just not right now."

I had to get back in control... fast. The doors opened, and he put his hand on the small of my back, guiding me out. I melted into his touch, and I knew he felt it.

We made our way to HR, and Carole was ready and waiting. I liked Carole and had known her for years. She was a wife to one of the married couples who met at work that Todd was going to use for his argument. Carole was all smiles, reaching her hands to clasp mine as she said, "I am so proud of you, Mallory. You are going to be wonderful in this new position. If you need anything from me, don't be afraid to ask."

Todd let us know he would be back in an hour, and he turned and left. Carole grinned. "Come on, Mallory. Let me explain your new benefits and let you sign your life away again."

She was jovial, making me feel more at ease with all this as I followed her. She went over my extras. Honestly, I didn't hear a thing. I was stuck on my new pay level.

Even though I was next in line for starting management, they did not give me the starting manager's salary. I was pretty sure I matched Ned's income now. If I wanted to upgrade my car, I could on the way home. I could also actually go on great vacations and not worry about the money.

She went through the whole program, and I tried to absorb as much as she was explaining, but I was still stuck on my new pay. Carole pointed out, under her breath, "Mallory, use your sick days first. Leave your personal days for when or if your sick days are limited."

I was confused. "But what if I'm not sick and it's personal?" She looked at me. "Did you not understand where I'm going with this, dear?"

I thought for a moment, then realized she was guiding me on how this would benefit me the most. I thought for a second, mulling it over in my brain. "Oh... oh... okay... got it." Carole was satisfied and checked that off.

She looked up, grinning again. "Mallory, it's very refreshing when someone like you comes across my desk in a positive way."

I answered, "I am stunned, grateful, and very anxious about all this, and I will make sure they know I was the right decision."

Carole smiled. "Mallory, you are our breath of fresh air. I know you will succeed. Once again, if you need anything from me, including a shoulder to cry on, I am in your corner. Don't hesitate to reach out to me, even when it's not HR related. You, my dear, are an asset to SBS, and they are recognizing it."

Her smile was so confident that she made me tear up a little. The overwhelming first announcement was finally hitting me. Carole handed me a tissue and walked around her desk, sitting on my armrest, and throwing an arm around me, holding me to her just as a good mother would do. "Mallory, we have your back. Enjoy this moment."

I let out a shy laugh as I blinked rapidly, willing the tears to stop, and she let go. I wiped the last teardrop, and she patted my arm. "Come now, Miss. Kennedy — manager specialist. Let's get your autograph and make this official."

She was right. I had about fifteen papers to sign. My title was "Communication Specialist Manager, Sales Division." Todd arrived back, knocking on the door and poking his head in. "Is it my turn, Carole?"

She grinned. "All set, Todd. She's all yours." Oh, my God! That statement packed a punch. He opened the door wider, extending his hand. "Miss. Kennedy, if you would follow me..."

I slipped my hand into his while Carole reiterated, "Mallory, any questions, large or small, do not hesitate to reach out to me. If I can't answer it, we will find someone who can."

Overwhelming positive emotion filled me as I thanked this amazing woman again. Todd and I were off to my old cubicle. He informed me that maintenance was done, and IT was setting up my two computers... I had two computers?

Ned didn't even have two computers, and I was basing my position on his position. This was learning from scratch at its finest. Todd had organized maintenance to come down and move my file cabinets. My cubicle looked so bare. They left me to clean out my desk. Todd went to my new office to check on things. I was supplied with two boxes to fill with what I needed to move.

I looked over at Ned's office. He was on the phone, not looking in my direction. I felt a little off with the atmosphere around me. Was everyone upset with me and my new position?

I finished loading my boxes, and I was about to go to Ned and see what was going on when Todd arrived back, asking if I was ready.

The way he said that to me, capturing my gaze with a slight lingering pause before he annunciated the word ready, left me thinking. With Todd and his confusing signals that really could just be my overactive imagination working to find a meaning that wasn't there, I supposed I should just take it for the word it was.

I tried to send him the same feeling of the message back. "Ready," I said, and I added a cocksure grin that made him grab for one of the boxes, then he commented, with one brow now raised, that he was sure I could handle the other.

Oh, he said that a little flirtatiously. I had to step over and face Ned's office, picking up the other box, while Todd was in route to my new office.

Ned glanced over at me for a split second, then immediately looked away. What the hell was his problem? I arrived at my new office. IT was wrapping things up as I took in all the equipment on my desk.

Reality still had not set in about what had happened this morning. I just played along, focusing on the moving events at this time. Everything else, I was going to have help with adjusting to this new position. Allen was going to get me through this, as well as Todd.

I looked at him as he unpacked the contents of my box. He spoke with a gentle warning. "Miss Kennedy, if there is anything I can answer, you are going to have to ask it verbally, not stand there staring."

Oh, good Lord. I must look like an idiot right now. I tried to recover. "I am a little overwhelmed with this sudden change. Sorry about that."

A slight grin appeared and disappeared. He answered, "We can't slow down progress for you to keep up. Keep focusing and see the future, Mallory."

Well, that was a message. He didn't have to slap me up the head for me to know that. IT was done. They went over a few things with me on both systems while Todd watched over us.

I made my notes, and they left, leaving me with their direct number should I have an issue. Todd announced, looking at his watch, "We have a meeting scheduled for two. Don't be late."

I nodded, accepting the instructions. I could see he really wanted to say something else, and he was having an internal battle about whether to say it. Just as I was about to ask, he turned and walked out. I wasn't sure how to handle that, and I just stood there for an awkward moment.

I turned back and scanned my new office. Reaching forward, I touched the edge of the desk and let my fingers trace along the edge as I walked along, taking it in.

I mentally pictured our department's layout. The most important thing to my left was the boardroom, then to my right was Richard. Everyone else fell in line from there.

If this was true about how the hierarchy of this department was set up, then right now, mine was the most important office. I grabbed onto that analogy for a moment, then laughed and completely dismissed the idea because this was the only space available and this was the ass-chewing room — Todd's room, in fact, his particular ass-chewing room.

There was a knock on my door as I quickly turned. Angela walked in, stunned, taking it all in. "There have been rumors flying since ten this morning. My girl got a promotion so fast, they had to adjust a space for her."

I nodded, not believing it myself. "Yeah, it's still not real to me," was all I could answer.

She grabbed my arms like Todd does, celebrating with, "Congratulations, congratulations, and congratulations!" She released my arms and took hold of both my hands as we spun like schoolgirls, rejoicing in this former ass-chewing room.

Angela, right here and right now, slapped reality in my face, and I welcomed it head-on. "Something is going on here, Mal. I mean, you deserve this one hundred percent with how many problem customers they dump on you. And you handle everything like a champ. But there is something else we're not seeing. They don't just call a meeting and pull rank like this. I heard all the department heads down here are fuming."

She had three minutes. We made a plan to work out after work so we could talk and go over today's events.

Yes, good plan. I needed to go through this with her. She gave me a huge grin with two thumbs up and told me I was going to rock this. Then she opened my new office door and left.

I couldn't stop looking at the clock. I now had nineteen minutes before I had to walk out of here to make it to my meeting in Samantha's office.

I set my phone alarm because I was acting ridiculous, and I went at those last minutes like everything was normal, and I patched in, taking calls. I was on the phone with Cal Nelson when my timer went off, and we were only a third of the way through his order.

I panicked, then explained about my new position and the meeting I had and asked if I could please call him back in an hour. I felt horrible as he gave me a hearty congratulations and said it was about time they moved me up. Cal was proud that I had finally made rank, and he told me to take my time calling him. There was no rush.

I hung up and darted out the door, looking down at my notepad and my pen and... What the heck else would I need? I started to turn back to my office because I left my phone. I swiped it off my desk and turned to collide with the only man I was really good at doing this with.

He closed the door slightly with his foot. Still holding me in place, he said, "Ready, babe?" That's how he addressed me. I was not prepared for that at all as he followed with a covert quick kiss on my lips. I was breathless.

He winked. "Come on, Kennedy. Let's not keep them waiting." He took hold of my shoulder and guided me out. He just kissed me in his ass-chewing room. This was slowly registering as we entered the elevators.

Once we did, he had his hands resting in front of him, clasped neatly, and he began to go over the general feel of what this meeting was about. I was grateful, but he blew me away with the sneak-attack kiss, and he was acting like he had not just done that.

This was new to me. My mind was going in twelve directions, reaching multitasking overload, even for a female. I cleared my throat and politely thanked him for the fifth time today.

As we walked down the hall toward his department, nearly reaching the door, he asked if he could see me tonight. I stumbled back a step, making me anxious and confused again. He caught me and began speaking low. "Mallory, may I see you at your place around seven tonight?"

I could not handle this right now, but I have to admit, it took my mind off what I was feeling about the meeting and catapulted it into: I don't understand you, Todd Duvall.

I looked at him and looked away, then looked at him again because he was waiting for an answer. "Okay," I answered him quietly. He transformed from business to get down to business. He bent slightly as we arrived at the quality control suite in front of the heavy wooden door. He said, "I will call you by six."

Everything he just said melted into the background as I took in my new surroundings. Once again, I had never been up here, and this was much nicer than my work department. I think their plants were actually real, unlike our fake ficus trees that had year-round Christmas lights on them. The waiting-area chairs were more expensive than both the computers sitting on my new desk, and the artwork was simple wood patterns that represented structure. I stared at the wall-covering pattern, and it was beautiful. I wanted to remember the artist because I was intrigued by the design.

Todd touched my lower back, getting my attention as he guided me over to sit and wait. We were still a few minutes early. Paula checked me in, and walking in behind us was Allen.

I realized I had forgotten my laptop as I saw him holding his, checking in with Paula. He smiled, greeting me on a more casual note as we caught up on the past few years with a minute to spare.

It was nice to hear that he and his wife had their first child a year ago as he brought up pictures on his phone. She was the cutest baby I had ever seen. Paula called us in. He tucked his phone away, and we headed toward her.

Chapter Six

This meeting was different. I feverishly took notes, but then Samantha pointed out that I was going to receive copies of the meeting's minutes. I excused myself about what I was doing and thanked her, explaining that sometimes I understand my own explanations on what they were covering better. She allowed me to continue.

When they went over my whole new job's criteria, I myself had some questions. Samantha half-listened at first. I registered loud and clear that I was boring her with trying to understand. I found that was uncalled for, especially since they had created a new management position.

I understood how she was, and I was going to let this slide for now. After all, I had my one moment of her understanding when she said there would be some learning curves back in the boardroom.

Todd took over as a supporter of how impressed he was with my thinking process. He pointed out that my troubleshooting ability would benefit this new position and was happy to hear I came up with these intelligent, creative examples. Allen even commented that I had thought through a few key points that needed to be addressed. Samantha had enough and closed the meeting with a final statement: "This was a good start."

I knew what was expected of me, and now it was ready to launch into action. Allen requested that he and I meet at four in my new office. I jotted that down. The meeting was adjourned with Samantha mentioning for me not to forget my notes. I wasn't sure if that was a dig, but I thanked her regardless.

Allen walked me out, and that was it. Todd stayed behind in Samantha's office. When we reached the hall, Allen commented again that he was impressed with what I had presented, given the fact that I had only learned a few hours ago that they created a new position and I had been filling out HR paperwork all morning. Then he said he would see me in an hour as he took the staircase and allowed me to ride the elevator alone.

I walked into my department and got a few more congratulations from fellow sales staff. I walked into Todd's old ass-chewing office, sat at my new desk, and breathed for the first time since this morning. Wow, this was mine... all mine. That was it. I allowed myself two minutes, then fired up my computers, starting a new list of different strategies.

My headset lit up and reminded me that I was still in sales, so I answered it. Allen knocked as I was just finishing up an order. He was grinning and closing the door behind him, then he waited, looking around. I was done in less than a minute.

He pulled over a chair and sat next to me because he had to use one of my computers to go over what he wanted me to know about my new job.

I grabbed my notepad and started taking notes. We went a little past five, and he said we could finish in the morning. I was good with that. He left, and I wrapped up my first afternoon as a manager. Angela peeked her head in. "Instead of the gym, can I take you for a drink to celebrate?" I looked at my phone to check the time. "I have so much to do before tomorrow. Can I get a rain check until the weekend?"

She smiled, understanding, and walked through the door to hug me. "Sure thing, lady. I am so proud of you. I can't wait to tell my family." I thanked her, and off she went.

I still had a few minutes to wrap some things up, and my next visit was from my date for later tonight. He walked in like he owned the office still and sat right on the corner of my desk. "Good first day, Mallory, and great first meeting. You were strong in there. Samantha took notice."

I sighed. "I hope I didn't overstep my bounds." He sat back with a look of superiority while sporting a slight smirk. "No worries, Kennedy, like I said, good first meeting. Why don't you wrap it up here and call it a day? You've had a lot to juggle today."

I wasn't sure if he was sending me home because he was still coming over or sending me home because he forgot he said he was coming over. Then, I wasn't sure if he really did have my phone number. I wanted to ask but wasn't sure, considering the company policy, if that was safe to ask.

Just to make sure, I asked him if he was going to the gym tonight, in case people were listening. He grinned and replied, rather seductively, "I have other plans." Well, that was my confirmation as I looked at my phone again and raised an eyebrow. "Well, I better get home then and look over these notes."

That made him grin wider. "Yes, your notes. Good idea. Maybe you'll learn something new tonight."

Oh, my... oh, my... now, I had a silly girlish smile on my face. "Okay, Mr. Duvall. I will get home and study. By the way, thank you for all your help today."

He lost the smile because he heard some men talking nearby. He leaned forward and stood, winking at me. "My pleasure, Miss Kennedy. Go home and study. I hope you have a productive evening."

I stood as he was leaving. I replied, "Thank you." And he was gone. I shut everything down and realized the first thing I was going to buy was an office briefcase-type bag with my next check.

I collected my pile, realizing my lunch was still in my bag. I had not eaten yet, and this was the first time I had noticed. Well, I was going to throw that out when I got home, and it looked like I was stopping at some fast-food place because I was starving now, realizing my stomach was empty.

The Dating Policy

I arrived home, brushed my teeth, and freshened up. I didn't know what to expect, but my office Viking was due in about half an hour. I was a little nervous, so I poured some liquid courage, a half glass of wine.

I heard my cell phone as I snatched it off the kitchen table. I answered, not knowing the phone number, and it was Todd, here at my gate, waiting for me to let him in. I watched out the window, and this sleek white Audi pulled into my driveway.

I was confused. I thought he had a black BMW. He was carrying in a bag, making his way to my door, still dressed in today's clothing.

Damn. I was fantasizing about him coming home to me like this all the time as my hands began to moisten. He didn't have to ring the bell. I had the door open, and I was leaning against the frame, trying to look cool and calm.

I watched him approach as I fumbled my words at first, cleared my throat, and then straightened my body. "I see you had no problem finding the place," I hinted at a little sarcasm because I never told him my phone number or address. He was way calmer and more collected as he answered, "I have people."

I laughed, thinking he was able to get it through HR. "Whatcha got in the bag, Mr. Duvall?" I inquired, trying to take a peek.

He leaned in and kissed me, just like this was an everyday normal thing to do. I stood there, surprised, while flutters rippled through my stomach.

He balanced the bag in one hand as his free hand slipped around my waist, pulling me in a little closer. "Well, let's go inside and have a look, shall we, Miss. Kennedy?"

He dropped his hand, now stepping inside, and continued to walk further into my duplex as I followed, closing the door.

Todd stopped for a quick moment, getting the layout of my floor plan. I chuckled. "What? 'Your people' don't know the inside setup of my condo? The kitchen is to your right."

He grinned like I had found out his secret. I could tell he liked that comment. He walked ahead and set the bag on my counter.

First, he removed his suit coat and handed it to me. I asked if he wanted me to hang it up. He said no, just to drape it over a chair. While I was doing that, he removed his tie and unbuttoned a few of his shirt buttons as I took his tie and placed it over his suit coat.

Wow, he looked even more delicious. Then he pulled me in and really kissed me. When he let go, I lost my balance, causing him to grin, and then said, "I was proud of you today. You handled the day beautifully from start to finish."

I thought about that and had a couple of questions for him... but now was not the time to get into it. He went to the bag and pulled out a chilled bottle of champagne with two velvet-wrapped glasses. The bottle looked expensive; I was very impressed.

He unwrapped the glasses; they had dipped gold rims. "Wow, nice touch," I commented. He opened the champagne and poured a half glass each. He handed one to me.

He held his toward me, then made a toast. "To our newest ranking manager; success comes from what you put into it. Here's to you, Mallory Kennedy, well-deserved today. Congratulations." He clinked my glass, and we drank.

My eyes were still closed as I swallowed my sip and slowly opened them. I looked down at my glass, then over to the bottle. It was really delicious bubbly. I smiled, thanking him as my nerve ends shivered, making my body jump with a little jolt.

He reached into the bag again and pulled two phones out. I cocked my head slightly to the side, wondering what this was all about.

He went right into it as he explained, giving me one and his was the other. He said this was how we would call each other so neither of our numbers would show up on our regular phones.

I instantly had mixed emotions, wondering why. I scrolled through mine, and it was already preprogrammed. I searched the contacts before I asked him how I would know his number. My only contact listed said, "personal trainer." I laughed as he grinned, letting me know his said the same.

I started thinking more about why the secret phone, and then it hit me. "So, this phone is because we can't date yet for multiple reasons with work and your 'unresolved' issues?"

He nodded, and I continued, "But this phone means I can call or text you any time, day or night?"

He nodded again. "So, this is like the bat phone?"

He chuckled. He liked that and stepped in toward me. "Yes, Mallory, this is our bat phone. Even though our situation is a little tricky right now, I made it so you can always contact me."

Wow, this was nothing I could even think was possible at this moment. That was until he took the phone out of my hand, placed it on the counter, and then took me in his arms and started kissing me.

Todd had clearly mastered the skill of kissing. That was apparent from the uncontrollable soft groans that I hadn't realized I was making until he pulled himself away.

With the heat smoldering from his eyes, he held me at arm's length and demanded, "I want you... right now." I felt the same way. Screw it. He gave me 24-7 access when he presented the phone thing. I decided that I could handle the work issue as I gave him the sign that I was on board: "My bedroom is upstairs."

He shook his head side to side, groaning in protest. He assured me that would take too long while he began stripping my clothes one article at a time. I mimicked

The Dating Policy

his actions until there was a mixed mesh of our garments thrown into a heap on the floor.

Todd ogled me for a second and pulled me into him. I barely had any time to look and take in what I have been dreaming about for the last year. But I knew his body would be incredible when I saw him naked.

His hands touched my shoulders, trailing around my back, easing my body to press into the heat radiating from his torso; his body scent mixed with masculine perfumes permeated my breathing, activating every sensory neuron in my body.

His lips touched mine as my fingers found the perfect patch of his chest hairs and I playfully combed them over. His hands smoothed over my buttocks, traveling up my frame. He released our kiss while my head lazily reclined back. I felt Todd adjust his stance.

"Mallory, open your eyes." As I did, he looked right through them. His look smoldered. "You are incredible; I want you."

His arousal was pressed between us as we mish-mashed into each other, entwining our holds. He felt of power under my touch, and now he was backing me against the counter.

He released our kiss only to declare, "I noticed you the first day I started working for SBS. I have wanted you from that day forward, and here you are, incredibly sexy, making me ache for you, naked, standing before me, and I can't stop touching you, kissing you…"

I made the next move and took ahold of his erection, feeling his soft, smooth skin in my grip. He groaned out loud in relief as I stroked him slowly. I haven't touched a man in a long time, and right now, I wanted to guide him into me.

It was not even a moment, and his words came out in a throaty whisper. "Babe, how do you feel about oral sex?" I looked into his eyes as he looked close to becoming unglued.

I tried to sound more confident than I was, but the pitch of my voice was a little too high from what I thought my delivery should have been. "It's been a while," was my answer as I was ready to lower myself, thinking this was a request from him.

It happened so fast. He dropped to his knees and spread my legs. His tongue extended, touching my flesh, swirling and dipping, skimming over my nub, stimulating uncontrolled reactions from me. The sounds Todd was making were pure starvation groans as he lapped at my sex, gorging himself on my core.

Never had I experienced anything remotely like this, influencing my vocals to moan in vowels as my body took over involuntarily. Contracting my vaginal muscles, simultaneously causing my heart rate to speed, I panted, groaning in sheer pleasure. He supported my body upright because all I wanted to do was collapse over him, and I think he felt it. Todd quickly searched, retrieving a condom from his coat pocket, then he stood. He guided both my arms around his neck and pinned my body against the counter because I was near ready to collapse.

Todd was entering me. "Ready, gorgeous?" he whispered with victory in my ear. This was happening right now. After months of fantasizing about him, here he was in the flesh, consummating the future of our relationship.

I wanted him to continue and claim him as mine. I wanted this more than anything... I nodded yes as he slowly penetrated me, adjusting himself as he delved deeper. He was being careful and checking all my reactions.

He stopped at full entry, kissing the top of my head. "Still good, beautiful?" I nodded, breathing in his scent as my nose took in everything above his pecs. He started with a simple rhythm while moving his hand to cup my butt and positioning us better. Right here, right now, standing in my kitchen was the best sexual experience I've ever had in my life.

Todd Duvall was better than any fantasy I could dream up. Not only did the shape of him give me pleasure upon initial penetration, but his cock was also doing a fine job of rubbing everything that needed to be touched along the way.

I was in a new realm that was utterly unfamiliar to me. My strength was coming back fast, and my hands found their way, feeling his strong upper frame, then pausing for a moment and making my way into his hair. I wanted to feel those strands between my fingers.

This man was everything I wanted. Lifting my chin upward, our lips mashed. He kissed me hard as he pulled completely out, stopping all the action. He announced, "Mallory, I have wanted this to happen for a long time."

He lined himself back against my sex; his fullness made me gasp with this angle change, and he halted, asking if I was okay. I tilted my head, feeling a passion and arousal I had never experienced and answered, "Yes."

At one point, he was groaning and talking through his teeth because I was now trying to participate, and he clearly liked it. That was all he could take as he filled the condom while gritting out how beautiful and sexy I am.

He separated us as he took care of his clean-up. He kissed me, and with a playful grin, he announced, "Let's get dressed. I would like to hear your version of how today played out."

Okay, sex climax over. But being able to stare at his Viking-like outline in my kitchen after we had just committed a forbidden act, according to company rules, was totally worth it.

We needed to get dressed now, right now. Putting ourselves back together, he poured more bubbly. He handed me another glass of champagne. I welcomed the alcohol as I took it and sipped. My eyes fell right on the gold-dipped rim that my lips were just touching.

I thought how beautiful this glass was as Todd leaned in to kiss me again, then picked up his glass. The look in his eyes radiated complete victory as he pulled a chair out to motion for me to sit. Yes, sitting was another good idea. He took the chair across from me, then sat back fully relaxed as I started my story.

I came to the "Ned part," making Todd lean in toward me. My story had stopped while Todd began asking question after question about Ned. I told him about my relationship with him and said that he was a longtime family friend who got me my job at SBS.

Todd sat back and said, "I'm grateful that he found you a position there, but he could be an issue. We both need to be aware of him more carefully from now on. I'm glad to hear that you don't do anything socially with his family. If he asks about us or me, don't tell him anything. This is more out of protection for you, not me."

What? This was odd. I got that we needed to keep a low profile, but Todd was being a little... then I thought more clearly. This was the Todd I knew, and this was him handling the office and looking out for me as well. He waited for my response, and I simply said, "Okay," only that kind of put a kink in the rest of my storytelling.

I switched topics. "How long can you stay? Want to go out and get something to eat?"

He looked at his watch. "I would love to, but we can't just yet."

Then I remembered we couldn't be seen together in public because of work. "I can cook here if you want to stay."

He leaned back, finishing his drink, then checking his watch again. "Another time perhaps; thank you, though. I have to go, Mallory."

What? Now he's leaving just like that. "Oh."

"You have studying to do, babe, and we both have work in the morning, but my day still isn't quite over yet." It was only Monday. Damn. This was going to be a tough week.

Todd kissed me goodbye as he grabbed his tie and jacket. He kissed me once more, pulling me to my feet, and, with his hand cupping my neck, he softly spoke, "It's going to be very difficult not being able to touch you during the day, especially now that I know what you taste like."

Every word he just spoke went straight to my crotch, and now I was throbbing inside. "I'll see you in the morning, Kennedy." He gave me one final kiss and walked out.

I stood there for a moment and watched until he drove away. I needed to fan myself or do something like that. I've never had a man have this kind of effect on me.

It was eight o'clock, and I poured the rest of my celebration champagne. I picked up my new bat phone and went right to my only contact. If I texted him right now, did that mean I was a little needy? I tossed the idea around some, then decided against it, even though I wanted to test the waters. My other phone vibrated with an incoming text. I picked it up, and it was Thomas asking how I was feeling. I replied that I was fine, and I got a promotion today. He answered that we needed to celebrate. I texted back — maybe over the weekend. He replied with a smiley face and texted that he would pay.

* * *

Tuesday was the first full day of my new position. I worked out my duties on a spreadsheet, and despite the coldness still from the other managers, I marched right along as if nothing had happened outside of my office relocation.

I thoroughly enjoyed seeing Allen's welcoming face and Todd stopping in and sitting on the corner of my desk for ten minutes today. That was quite a treat.

Before I knew it, the day was over. I pulled out the bat phone because I hadn't seen Todd again for the rest of the afternoon, so I texted to see if he wanted to work out with me.

His response was immediate that he couldn't tonight and commented about what a good job I did today. I thanked him, and he told me he would see me in the morning.

Angela and I went to the gym instead. She wanted to hear all about yesterday, so I told her everything about my day but left out my evening. I did not want her to know about the intimacy I'd consummated with Todd just yet. My kiss-and-tell moment would have to come later.

Chapter Seven

As we walked in, Angela spotted Thomas sitting in a waiting area. "Hey, there's Thomas," she called out to him. He looked up from his magazine and broke into a grin.

We walked over to him, and my biggest fear was confirmed. He was a member here. Angela did all the talking, "I didn't know you were a member?"

Thomas grinned shyly. "That's my brother's fault; he made me sign up because Jessica is busy during the week with Erin and homework."

Oh, that made sense. "Hey, Mallory, congratulations on your promotion." He was focusing on me to answer.

"Thanks again, Thomas." Why, oh, why did he have to belong to my gym? It was only a matter of time before he would see me with Todd. I know I'd made it clear he was in the friend zone, but this was going to be strange. Now I knew that seeing him out socially was never going to work.

"Angela, how about we take our girl out this weekend to celebrate? My treat, of course." Angela thought that was a great idea and glanced at me. She read my expression perfectly.

"Umm, I'll get back to you on that, okay?"

He smiled, "Absolutely."

Then, she excused us, and we headed toward the ladies' locker room. "What's going on, Mal?"

"I don't like it that he's a member here."

"Why?"

I was about to say *because I was with Todd* and I couldn't. I couldn't tell her yet... or anyone for that matter. This really sucked!

"I can't stand Brian for starters, and I don't want to pal around with Thomas when I'm working out."

That's all I could give her for now.

Angela grew suspicious, "Mallory, you need to stop bullshitting me. It doesn't work. When are you going to learn?"

Her famous hand on her hip pose made me cave. "Okay... because Todd works out here; that's who I'm working on, and Thomas isn't going to help that at all."

"Mr. Business?"

"Yes, okay! Not another word about this; let's go work out."

Angela grinned while thinking it over.

By the end of the week, I clearly understood my new job duties. This was a great position; the only problem I was having is that sometimes there were not enough hours in the day. A few days, I was here till six; and half the week, I skipped my lunch hour to eat at my desk.

Angela was not a fan of my new position. I would have to make it up to her. The bat phone rang. It was my personal trainer calling. I laughed as I answered the call, shutting down my workstation.

"Hi, babe," greeted Todd.

"Hi, yourself."

I was going to need to come up with an endearing nickname for him. "Can I come over for a bit this evening?"

"Sure. What time?"

"Seven work again?"

"Yup. Oh, and my code for the gate is 123456."

He laughed. "Seriously?"

"Yes, seriously?"

"Okay. I think I can remember that. I'll see you at seven."

"Want me to cook anything?"

"I just want to eat you, gorgeous."

All right then. Booty call it was. If I hadn't felt the same way, I would have had a problem, but I wanted him just as much.

Ned approached my office. "Okay, that sounds like a plan. I'll be there at seven." I didn't even wait for him to reply as I hung up.

Ned was poking his head in. "Hey, Mal. How are you settling in?"

"Just fine, Ned. Thanks for asking."

I slid the bat phone into my purse and collected my other bags. He stepped further into my office.

"Look, I know I've been busy this past week, but I wanted to let you know that I am proud of you, kid."

If he wasn't considered part of my odd extended family, then I would have just said thank you, but he was part of the family, so he was going to get an earful because this ass-chewing room was now my office.

I pulled him in and shut the door. "You were a downright dick this week. I had no clue about my promotion, and all you could do was offer a flat congratulations, then fucking ignore me all week! Thanks for the support like I got from all the rest of this team. All of you knew I was next in line to be promoted, and I work my ass off for this company. And every friggin' one of you guys who I bent over backward for all treated me like I didn't exist this week!"

"Hang on, Mal. It wasn't about you. It was about Samantha Gary pulling rank on our department without even discussing it or including us in the decision. It was poorly handled on her part, and all we saw was her fucking exercising her authority and rubbing it in our faces."

"What? That's stupid!"

"Mal, the proper procedure would have been for Frank Gary to come down here, have a short meeting with Richard, John, and Ben, and brief them on your new position, only it came from his sister, and she included half the guys who shouldn't have even been in there, including me. I had no business in that meeting. Okay, so they opened up a new position. Big deal. Mallory, that was a show, and that was Samantha Gary pissing on all of us. It had nothing to do with you."

Oh... oh... oh... oh... "Well, why are you guys treating me like shit then?"

"It's just how it's coming out; that's all. Believe me; something isn't right with the way this was done. We may find out why, or we may never know."

Damn it. Why did he have to tell me all this? Now, I was just confused. And I felt bad. Everything Ned said made sense. "I hadn't realized all this. Look, let's just move forward from here, okay?"

"Okay, Mal. I really am proud of you. I told Sean. He also said to congratulate you."

I glanced at my phone to check the time. "Thanks, Ned. I have to go."

"Big plans tonight to celebrate, I bet."

I cleared my throat. "Exactly."

"Be safe tonight. Call me if you get into trouble. You know you can always do that even if I am a dick to you," Ned smirked.

"Thanks, Ned."

He opened the door, exiting first. I collected my bags again and walked out, shutting my door behind me.

My non-boyfriend was right on time. His greeting was a lot quicker — one kiss, and he was stripping me as fast as he could while removing his own clothes as well. "Sorry, babe. I am aching for you... so badly, it hurts."

That's all he said as he guided me right on the floor and sunk his mouth into my sex. The hums and groans coming from him were sheer eroticism. I lasted longer than I thought I would, maybe fifty seconds as the frenzy of pleasure seized my center, shattering me once again uncontrollably to where only Todd could take me. He lapped and sucked, making me squirm away. It was too much, too much to take.

Then he lifted my legs, rolled on a condom, and penetrated me. This man was confident when it came to sex, much more than I was. Here we were, on my kitchen floor, with the lights on, fully exposed, and his body was every bit Viking. I lost control, climaxing again. He, on the other hand, lasted longer, and on one final thrust, he pulled out, removed the condom, and stroked himself, releasing his juices all over my stomach.

Now, at first, I was confused about what he was doing, and it took a second for me to register. I have never seen a guy do that, and once the shock wore off, it was kind of sexy. I could not stop looking at him, pleasuring himself while knowing I was watching. That was actually really hot.

I was fascinated. He was just so masculine... the look on his face was both victory and relief. I was open to watching him do that again. That was the first time I had seen a guy get himself off.

He looked down at me. "Woman, I had to jerk off Wednesday in a stall at work because you looked so good and I couldn't touch you."

I chuckled. "Really?"

"Yes, really. I know what this pussy feels like now, and I want it."

He kissed my ankle and released my legs. "Stay here. I'll get a cloth and clean you up." I sat up on my elbows as he returned with a few damp paper towels. I watched as he wiped the warm towels in circles, picking up his release. Todd was very focused and thorough.

He sensed me watching, suddenly meeting my eyes with a quick glance and a click sound from the corner of his mouth, making me grin. This was quite an adorable side to him.

When he was done, he extended a hand and lifted both of us to our feet. He kissed me for several moments, making sure I knew this was more than just sex. I knew it was more, and I knew we were together now as a couple without him saying a word.

Then he actually voiced that he had missed me this week, adding a stroke from his thumb that caressed my cheekbone as his hand gently rested on my neck. That instantly gave me a feeling of being weightless as I melted into his hand.

We dressed, then sat at the table; this was our talking time. My everyday phone rang, and it was Angela. I let it go to voicemail as he watched.

Then he asked, "You two are pretty close, aren't you?"

I smiled. "Yeah, we are, so you need to get used to her because she's going to be around a lot."

Todd sat back in the seat. "Thanks for the warning," he replied with a look of concentration.

"Do you want something to drink?" He cracked the corner of his mouth, baring a slight grin. "No, thank you. I had my fill of liquid for the night."

Oh, my gosh. He was referring to me. "Seriously?"

He turned it into a sinister grin. "Very seriously, babe."

His eyes glanced to his watch, so I asked, "How long do I have you for?"

He was already predicting my disappointment. "Well, I hate to eat and run, but I have to go."

What? That was quick. He gauged my facial reaction, and then he added, "I'll be at the gym tomorrow morning at seven-thirty."

I was confused. "Yeah... and?"

He went straight-faced, standing and pulling me to my feet. There was playfulness in his gaze. "Well, if you manage to get this beautiful ass up and there for seven-thirty, I'll be willing to personally train this body some more."

Oh! The way he talked sent shivers through me. He kissed my lips while smoothing my hair. "Get some rest, beautiful. You're going to need it for what I have planned for you in the morning... if you dare?"

Todd searched my eyes. He kissed me again, lingering this time. "Please keep in mind this is just temporary, Mallory. This will all change sooner rather than later. Just give me time. I will have it sorted."

He was leaving right now. I sighed as I walked him to the door. He attempted to placate me with one final reassuring kiss.

He whispered into my lips that he looked forward to being with me again as he separated from me, leaving me with mixed emotions. All I could do was watch him drive away again. I sighed.

Todd Duvall had just entered me here on my kitchen floor, and the sex was over the top again. Amazing... I wanted more of him. I wanted a lot more of him. I reached over to the phone he had given me, and I was about to try it out again and send him a message when my main cell phone started buzzing. I picked it up, placing the bat phone down on my table. It was Angela, of course. She was demanding to meet me for drinks.

When she threatened to come over, I agreed to meet her downtown. I needed to visualize everywhere Todd and I had been without her or anyone sitting there or ruining my memory, at least until the morning.

Thomas texted as well, wanting time to celebrate. Damn it. I ignored the text. And if I happened to see him tomorrow, I would introduce Todd to him.

I didn't owe Thomas anything. When I arrived at where I was meeting Angela, it turned out to be her plus a few friends of ours. She was throwing me a celebration for my promotion without inviting Thomas.

This was not what I was expecting at all, but here was my friend, making the effort to celebrate me.

My frame of mind was elsewhere as I tried to pull off normal behavior. Angela announced to me that her family was having a cookout Sunday afternoon, and I was invited. Well, invited was the intention, but expected was implied. I didn't commit, but I knew it would be good for me to go.

She assumed my behavior was because I had my new responsibilities on my mind, and she assured me that I was going to ace this position.

The evening out with the girls was a good decision — just the distraction I needed. While I said goodnight to everyone, Angela walked me arm in arm to my car.

She wanted the scoop on Todd and promised me she would force it out on Sunday. To her, it was actually girl gossip and fun between us.

To me, it was serious business, and there was no way I was going to that cookout, now that I had just slept with him twice, and I was carrying a bat phone in my pocket just in case he contacted me.

In bed, I stared at my bat phone. It was almost ten in the evening already, and I thought, *Oh, what the hell. He said any time, day or night*, time to test this theory.

I texted him: *Thanks for coming over. I needed that just as much as you did, I think. Angela took me out to celebrate after you left.*

I looked it over for spelling errors then sent it.

Todd's response was immediate: *I enjoyed my unfortunately brief but effective time with you also. We need to talk about Angela. Get some sleep, babe. I'll see you at 7:30.*

Wow, this bat phone worked well. Just as promised, there he was, leaning against the entrance-area counter and talking to the female with a huge grin on her face.

He looked over at me and left her immediately, greeting me with a kiss that could clearly lead to sex. I was left breathing fast as he released me and took my bag, guiding me to check in.

That woman no longer wore the smile she was giving him; she was sizing me up. I could have cared less as Todd took my membership card, handed it to her to scan, then she handed it back to him.

He gave me back my bag and tapped my ass, telling me to hurry up as he sent me into my locker room.

Todd Duvall was in charge of my fitness this morning, and he took his job very seriously. After an hour and a half of pure torture, he told me not to shower and said that we were going back to my house.

His words were something like, "I need to fuck you hard in bed."

Again, Todd had that white car and was following me home. I kept glancing in the rearview mirror at him.

Several times, he was on the phone, and when we were almost to my condo, my bat phone rang, startling me.

He asked to park in my garage. Okay... That was odd, but I didn't see an issue with it. When we were inside, he dropped our bags and lifted me, kissing me just like the kiss he'd greeted me with this morning.

He guided my legs around his waist and asked where my bedroom was. I pointed for him, and he carried me up the stairs with zero effort right to my bed.

We moved as a unit; he positioned me on my bed as he continued to kiss me. He released his assault on my mouth. Of course, this Viking knew exactly how to kiss. Now he was removing my clothes and pulling his off just as carelessly.

They were in the way of what needed to happen. Again, our garments were in a heap on the floor. This was our third time having intercourse. Just as the previous two times before, he went straight to my sex, lapping like he couldn't get enough. I was powerless as the orgasm tore through me.

I could not get past this. I think I lasted a tiny bit longer than last night, but I wasn't sure.

I tried to squirm away from his oral assault. He let up, then hovered over me, positioning himself and telling me he was going to fuck me now. No condom was between us as I felt him pushing in with sustained force.

My legs were pinned under him. There was no finesse right now, as he thrust in and out with determination. Now he was upright, grabbing my hips and spreading my legs apart as he worked his cock, pulsing with a rhythm that was satisfying him. I opened my eyes, and he was looking at himself thrusting in and out. Then he glanced at me.

"Your body is so damn sexy... I'm going to cum." He dropped my hips and pulled out of me, stroking himself and releasing his juices on my belly again. Holy smokes... this man was born to breed.

I assumed it was over, but he was still hard as he positioned himself back in. I was confused for a moment until he was really working me.

I threw out the fact that I already had an orgasm, and he grinned. "Good, now you're going to have another."

What? That was impossible. It was not possible for me to have another. He rubbed and worked on me, and just as I was about to throw in the towel and say I'd had enough, he touched a spot on my clit with his finger, and that was it. I exploded inside, exhausted and vulnerable. My body was over-heightened with sensitivity as he said out loud, "That's right, babe. Cum again; I can feel you."

I was done and trying to squirm away; he stopped and pulled out, still erect, as he lay down beside me. I fell asleep deeply in the warmth of his body next to mine.

Next thing I realized, he was waking me up with the backs of his fingers tracing my upper body as goosebumps appeared down my arm, causing me to shiver. He leaned in to kiss me.

I opened my eyes. "Hi." I turned toward him. He had clothes on and not his gym clothes.

"Hi yourself, how long have I been asleep?"

He held a slight grin. "I already showered. How about you get up and get this lovely ass in and cleaned up? I have my computer here. I just need your Wi-Fi password. I'll do some work downstairs while you get ready, then I was thinking we could make breakfast together."

He was staying. Oh... Todd was staying! I had to ask through my excitement, "How long do I have you for?"

"Two hours if that's okay."

"Yes, I'm good with that."

Todd angled his head to the side, studying me, then announced, "We need to go over some things."

Oh. "Like what? Is it work-related?" I asked as he traced his finger around my shoulders.

"Some, but we need to have a clearer understanding of what our relationship is now."

Whoa! What the hell is this about? I sat up in a quick jerk. "Maybe we should start that conversation right now."

He casually sat up. "Hang on, Mallory. Maybe that came out too strong."

"Ya think?"

"But you are right. Now is as good a time as any. Let's get you dressed, so there are no distractions because you naked is a huge distraction."

Well, I would give him that as I wrapped my blanket around me. He smoothed that over quickly. The questions were starting to surface in my mind now as well. What did I want to establish out of this conversation? What was this relationship?

He took it down a notch, speaking casually, "We have to be very careful at work. You completely earned your promotion. Do not question that at all, okay?"

I didn't like where this was going. "Okay?"

He continued, "I pushed your promotion. We needed you to be my level of status in the company. I'm working on modifying the dating policy so that equal levels can date. This policy is ridiculous, to begin with. I should have read it more carefully when I started. But then again, I had no idea you could actually become mine, and we would be together. It was generated from a revengeful girl with a really exceptional lawyer. I get why it's there, but it's now fifteen years later. But here we are, cockblocked by it."

I laughed. Did he really just phrase it like that? I reiterated, "Cockblocked?"

A sign of amusement crossed his face, and he came at me, pushing me back onto my bed, and saying seductively against my lips, "Yes, Miss Kennedy. Cockblocked."

He kissed me for a minute, and then climbed off me, resuming his speech. "Angela is another concern. I know you are close. Keep me out of conversations."

I cleared my throat. "Those baseball tickets... I took her, and they told us it was the Duvall table. We also found out it was a corporate table. Is it yours?"

It was plain as day that he didn't expect this question. He weighed his immediate answer and remarked, "I own that table. Best investment I have made so far. Many deals have been successfully negotiated at that table."

"Okay, I get that. Why is it the Duvall Corporate table? Do you have a separate company from SBS?"

Again, the answer was quick and minimal. "Yes."

I immediately responded, "What is it, and why?"

He hesitated in answering, "That concerns the other issues I'm working on to bring us together."

The Dating Policy

Well, wasn't this just ducky? I was in a situation of I tell you everything while you tell me nothing. I went for it. "Todd, this is bullshit... You realize this, right?"

He sighed. "One hundred and eighty days. That's what I need, and I will be all yours."

I was very confused. He put a day count on his total availability... Why? What did this mean? He quickly switched back to work. He was caressing me again. "The most difficult part of my day from now on... is not being able to touch you during all the moments we'll be interacting. Also, you should know that I'll be picturing sliding my cock inside you."

Wow, like that was not a distraction. My tummy growled. He moved down me, opening my blanket, and exposing my stomach to kiss it.

"Get into the shower, babe. I'll start breakfast."

And he cooks! My corporate Viking cooked! I did as I was told, and when I joined him for breakfast, there were two omelets with homemade home fries... seriously thinking of keeping him now.

What was a measly hundred and eighty days when I had this to look forward to? Again, I told him about Thomas and Brian, and that Brian was married to Jessica from work, and Brian saw us kiss a week ago at the gym.

This did not concern Todd at all. It was me making a bigger deal out of it than I needed to. I was glad I told him again, though.

My not-yet boyfriend left at noon. I had the whole morning with him, regardless of what his situation was.

I looked for my laptop and checked all my bills. I stared at my bank balance. It was only on Monday that I had signed my new HR papers, and my check was doubled in my account. I jumped up and did a happy dance.

My afternoon was going to consist of a shopping spree. I would allow myself to spend this check; then I'd figure out how to save and invest the ones from here on out. Carole did offer her help. I would go back and see what SBS offered for investments.

When I finally got home that evening, I realized that I have been so money conscious most of my life that spending money, especially my new money, was harder than I thought it would be. I came home with two bags. One had a few outfits for work, and the other had the new briefcase-looking computer bag I wanted to buy. I pulled everything out and organized it.

I heard a ding on my phone that I'd received a text. I picked it up to find out it was my bat phone. I instantly smiled.

Todd was texting me: *Morning workout?*

I grinned and replied: *Sure, what time?*

Then he texted: *7 a.m. your bed?*

The sudden heat I felt as I stared at his words. My body was now programmed to my new lover as I typed *Yes*.

Well, it was sex with my Corporate Viking in the morning again. I walked over to the fridge and pulled out my half-emptied bottle of wine and grabbed the fancy champagne glass Todd had left for me.

Sex three days in a row; wow, that was a record for me. I was used to three times a month with any man from my past.

I swallowed a healthy sip, and my thoughts were now focused on "his issues." I pulled out my laptop and fired it up. Again, I searched for anything I could on Todd, and nothing came from it. I tried with his first initial, his full name... and nothing. This man was such a mystery.

I wonder what his other corporation was. I typed in Duvall Corporation... and nothing. I gave up. I was going to see him in eleven hours. I would just have to ask.

I woke up early to the bat phone and an incoming text: *On my way, gorgeous.* I smiled. I was already up. I was all showered and on my first cup of coffee.

I think he texted me from around the corner because the next thing I realized, my doorbell was ringing.

I greeted him in my exotic silk bathrobe that my brother brought back for me about ten years ago from a country that we were not allowed to talk about. It was over the top pretty, but I very seldom wore it.

I opened the door for him. And wow... we both took in what the other was wearing. Todd showed up in loose linen pants and a casual white linen cabana shirt. He looked like the poster child for a Caribbean getaway.

He walked in and shut the door behind him.

"Damn, woman." He came at me and kissed me hard.

At some point, his hand had found its way through the overlapping material of my robe and right to my satin panties.

He stopped kissing me and backed up, now pulling each end of my robe open to reveal what I was wearing. He looked down, and then he looked into my eyes. "I need to remove these with my teeth," he stated, and he scooped me up over his shoulder.

Being carried up my stairs by Todd Duvall for the second time this weekend was something I would never get bored of. I was very scared, though, of being over his shoulder like this. With each step he took, I couldn't help but think if he dropped me or lost his balance, I would be severely hurt.

I counted each step getting closer to the top with his masculine grip firmly holding my legs against his body. I let out a breath of relief when he lowered me to the floor in front of my bed. He looked at me, concerned. "Are you okay?"

I nodded, "I was afraid you would drop me."

He chuckled, "Not a chance, babe."

The Dating Policy

This man showed up this morning, looking like a tropical dream. I already knew what he felt like inside me, and it was Sunday morning and our third straight day of sex. I wanted him, and I wanted him now.

We were still vertical as he began with the kissing then the disrobing. I was in front of him wearing just my panties. He moaned into my mouth while his hand caressed and massaged my buttocks.

He pulled back. "I have never wanted a woman as I want you... ready?"

I looked at him, nearly panting, yet confused. He lifted me and tossed me on my bed. I half screamed-half laughed as he proceeded to rub my sex through the material layer that separated skin on skin.

"Mallory Kennedy. You started out as a plan, and now you are my only mission." Oh, I was a mission now. I was available. How was I a mission? I was free for the taking, and now I needed him to take me... take me hard.

He did exactly what he said he would do, and my panties were removed by him dragging them down with his teeth. The look in his eyes was pure need. As he cleared my feet, he bunched them up, put them against his nose, and inhaled like that was his last breath. When he was done, he looked right into my eyes. "These are coming with me." And he tucked them into his pocket.

Todd was still dressed, but he changed that quickly. He took a step back and was naked in seconds. Sunday morning, there was no oral sex involved. He looked at my body, spread my legs, positioned himself, and penetrated. He let out a battle cry when he fully entered. "Mallory, my dick craves you." After a few pumps, he stopped, both of us at the edge of desire.

"I need to ask. Are you on any type of birth control?" I looked at him, knowing this was something we should have talked about before. "Yes, for the past thirteen years."

That was it. He sealed his mouth back to mine. When he let me take another breath, he announced, "I am going to cum in you," like this was his mission from the first time we engaged in intercourse. My Viking worked his body, and he wasn't holding back. Maybe he was a little reserved the last few times, but not now. He was on a mission.

It took my hands wrapped around his ass, pulling him in, that made me climax into orgasm. That was a trigger for him as well. He pulled out to the tip of his cock, then pushed back in, and he released every bit of essence of himself inside of me.

There was something different, knowing he'd just released in me. He stayed in his plank position on top of me until he was breathing normally again. He turned his head, so he was looking right down at me. "I can't wait to do that again." And he kissed me gently, pulled out, and took the spot to my right.

I turned to cuddle into him as my fantasy man placed his arm around me, pulling me tight against his body, basking me in his scent and warmth. I was exhausted and fell asleep.

It wasn't long enough; Todd was announcing he had to go. With a swift kiss and sudden removal of his body heat, I moaned a complaint. I could hear his chuckle as he flipped my blanket over me to cover me. "I'll text you in a little while, babe. Get some rest."

I stretched out as I replied lazily, "Okay, bye." I heard him exit as I fell back asleep. My morning may have started with Todd Duvall, but it was not going to end with him.

I picked up my regular phone and saw that Thomas had left a text message asking if he had done something wrong. What I should have done was tell him I was in a relationship, but I didn't.

I wasn't sure how to handle this. I was going to ask Angela later. Then I picked up the bat phone. Was I being too needy to think that him stating *I was now a mission* when there were no obstacles on my behalf outside of the dating clause at work was actually a line just to get in my pants? Sure, there was this bat phone. I picked it up and texted him: *I'm up. Were you just a dream this morning or were you actually here?*

Not even a minute went by; he answered: *I left evidence inside you.* Ummm... well then, I think I should stop overthinking.

* * *

Angela was sending me a warning text on my main phone: *Just wait till you see all the food. I think the gym might be a good idea this morning. Are you up for it?*

Yes, I think I was up for it, and I confirmed. It was only ten in the morning, and we met there just about the same time. It was all business. We found two empty elliptical machines, and fifteen minutes into our workout, she started asking all kinds of questions about what it was like having to work with Todd since she knew about my interest in him. Well, she actually called it a crush. I hated that expression even in high school.

Just as I was about to tell her, she leaned in. "You are not going to believe this, but there is your boyfriend at two o'clock, and he's heading this way. Oh, and look, Thomas and Brian are over there."

"What?"

I fell forward on my machine, but she was right. Here was my not-yet boyfriend heading right for us. I don't think Thomas had seen us yet.

Todd hopped onto the platform, dripping with sweat. My heart raced as I felt dizzy. I gulped some water down, looking for a distraction.

"Well, hello, ladies. Starting the day with a good workout, I see."

He was looking right at me, sporting a half-smile on his face. Why didn't he stay with me this morning? He left, and I assumed it was because of his "issues," but no... it was to come here, and apparently, I was not invited.

Angela commented, "I didn't know you were a member here, Todd." She automatically called him by his first name.

There were no interactions she would ever have with him as far as SBS. She was too far down the chain.

He turned to her. "Been a member here for a while, Miss Deprima."

She laughed. "You don't have to be so formal. You can call me Angela."

He turned back to me. "You look full of energy. You must have gotten some good sleep, Miss Kennedy."

I cleared my throat because, right now, you could probably see my heart beating against my chest.

Todd grinned; he knew he was torturing me.

Angela was mustering all her small talk to keep him here for my sake, but I wanted him gone. She asked him if he was done with his workout or just starting.

Again, he glanced over at me. "This is the end of my second workout this morning."

I wanted to die. And the bastard knew he was taunting me.

Angela commented, "Two, oh, boy. We'll be lucky to finish this one."

He stepped down. "Oh, I don't know about that; you ladies look quite fit, especially you, Kennedy. I bet you could keep up with me."

I had to slow down and drink more water because now I was blushing. I could feel the heat surge in my cheeks.

Angela tried one last time to keep him here, and I was going to have to kill her later. She was thanking him for the baseball ticket, and then she asked if that was his table or his family's table as she explained that they said it was the Duvall table. He turned to her and simply answered yes.

Angela now being Angela commented that it must cost a fortune; she didn't know SBS paid that well.

He cut her off. "I must be going now, ladies. Enjoy the rest of your day."

Angela tried to tell him about her family cookout, but he was already walking away. She leaned in. "Well, how did I do? I tried to keep him here. He still has a stick up his ass, but if you like that type... then that's fine. Who am I to judge who is best suited for you? My family could pry his history out of him. They are really good at collecting information. When are you going to make a move on him so you can bring him over?"

"You know there was a dating policy at work. We can't date. SBS forbids it."

"What? What do you mean you can't date him? How is it any of their business?"

"If you look in the employee handbook, it's in the back with company policies and procedures."

"Seriously, Mal? I threw that damn thing out the day I brought it home. SBS has no business telling me who I can hook up with or not. Besides, I know of a few married couples there. I bet they met through working there at the same time."

"You are correct. There are six married couples at work who all met at SBS."

"See? Why should you and Todd not be able to date then?"

"Because also, in that timeline, a manager was dating a salesgirl, and she sued the company for a half million, and that is the reason why I cannot date Todd."

"Well, don't tell them. It's none of their business anyway."

"If we got caught, it is instant grounds for dismissal."

"Look, Mal. He was certainly paying attention to you. I'm just saying. He could have cared less if I was here or not. He was mostly into you."

I choked on my water as she scrunched her brows together, "You okay, Mal?"

I nodded and swiped my forearm across my mouth. "We have to work together on occasion, so we have to be cordial."

She slowed down. "Now, if you were to feed that line of bullshit to the person on your other side, it just may have worked, but it's me, Mal. My BS detector is working just fine. Now, you want to tell me what's really going on, or do I have to torture you all afternoon about it?"

Again, I knew better. "Okay, I really do like him, and this dating policy has me in a bind. I've been waiting a year, working on myself to change, and finally, Todd and I are talking and interested in one another, only work says, 'Nope, no can do. Date each other, and you're fired.'" I caught my breath, "This beyond sucks for me and I have to work with him directly now, and it's bugging me. There are times we are walking and talking that I want to push him against the wall and kiss him."

Angela laughed. "Well, maybe that's the real reason there's a dating policy in effect. Maybe too many people were caught canoodling instead of working." She went on, "I don't think there is anyone I would want to date at work."

Great, she put another thought in my head now just as Thomas and Brain spotted us. I saw Brian grab Thomas's shoulder. I could tell he was saying something negative about me. Thomas rolled Brian's hand off as Angela asked me if I wanted her to handle this.

I did. I so wanted Angela to handle this, but I should have told Thomas myself that there was another guy.

I declined her offer and did what I thought was right. Thomas made his way over, wiping the sweat from his hairline. "Well, here are my friends; how's it going, girls?"

Angela spoke first to break the ice. "Hi, Thomas, how are you?"

He looked at me, "I'm feeling left out to tell you the truth."

I glanced down, feeling bad about my behavior. "Sorry about that, Thomas; I've been busy."

Angela watched me, ready to take over. I cleared my throat, knowing I should have handled that more strongly. "Thomas, I'm sorry I've been blowing you off, but I have a lot going on in my life."

He grinned and shook his head, "Brian told me you had a boyfriend; was it the guy that just left?"

I must have turned pale as I turned my machine off. I was done with my workout. Angela took over. "Nothing personal, Thomas, but we've been busy with stuff that doesn't include you, so I think it's safe to say that it's none of your damn business what we do, when we do it, or who we do it with."

He laughed, "I was just saying, Mallory, I know I'm in the friend zone, and I don't care who you're with. I hope you don't let our connection go because of a boyfriend."

I could only say, "Thanks for understanding."

And I grabbed Angela's hand before she threw down her real Italian temper. All I heard in the locker room was, "Fuck him; don't you dare fall for his bullshit. He's up to something. I'm telling you, Mal; that was not a normal conversation, and honestly, it was a little creepy. Does he know where you live?"

I answered, "No."

Then I remembered him asking me a lot. My address would be easy to find on a search, so that really didn't matter. Besides, I lived in a gated community. At the same time, it did matter suddenly, and I picked up the bat phone to text the best ghost I knew to let him know what happened.

Todd inquired what Thomas's name was. I answered Thomas Randolph. It took two minutes for his reply. Todd was texting: *Kris will be waiting outside the ladies' locker room in five minutes to escort you and your friend out.* I began to tremble while Angela was now repeating her, "What's going on?" question. I texted back: *Is that really necessary?*

Todd was calling, and I answered like I didn't know who it was. "Mallory, just let Kris escort you out. I don't know who this idiot is, but I can't turn around to do it myself." Angela wanted an answer as I held up my index finger.

She crossed her arms and tapped her foot in an irritated fashion. I gave in and said, "I texted Todd, and that was him calling me. I was going to ask him to wait around and walk us out, but apparently, he left. But he knows the staff here, and someone is going to walk us out."

"To tell you the truth, Mal, we really don't know who Thomas is. I mean his brother married Jessica. That should send up red flags right there."

We burst out laughing. I scurried to gather all my stuff, and Angela reminded me just to play it cool. She went over our game plan and said that we should walk out like we've known this staff member forever and this person was a friend just walking us out. Angela played this so much better than I did. I'm sure I looked like I was up to something.

She made up for my awkwardness when Kris greeted us at the entrance of the ladies' locker room. Kris was one of the guys I had admired my first day here. He stood tall. He was a personal trainer here, and his shirt advertised precisely that. He also had the deepest voice I had ever heard on a man.

Right when Angela and I cleared the door, he guided us with a hand gesture to walk in front of him as he followed. Angela grinned, looking over her shoulder, spotting Thomas. "We think that guy over there might be a creeper."

Kris walked with a big sway in his gait from his legs being so muscular. "We'll keep an eye on him."

Angela smiled and turned, "I like you, Kris; are you single?"

He grinned, "My wife says no."

She laughed, "Now that's how you train a husband."

* * *

Three hours later, I was back with Angela and her family. I bought a few bottles of wine for my contribution to the Deprima family cookout. She wasn't kidding about the food. Angela greeted me, "Good idea we went to the gym, right? Well, up until the ending. Come on; you need a drink, and we need a plan."

She took the bag of wine from me and jerked her head for me to follow. She laughed as she walked by all the food, "Look at all this?"

I managed to crack a smile. "It looks like a typical Italian cookout to me?" I said, and we opened a bottle.

At Angela's family cookouts, there was no existence of the word diet. We ate, we laughed, and we drank, making all thoughts of Thomas slip away. One conversation flowed into the next; Momma Deprima asked me about my fella. Angela stated that we saw him at the gym this morning.

Her brother-in-law, Richie, butted in instantly, playing Mob Boss, saying, "If he does anything to hurt you, we will take care of him." Funny thing was, I have actually thought Angela's two brothers-in-law were in organized crime.

I really never knew what they did. Years ago, when I asked about what they did for a living, I got the reply, "Management."

Angela's sister Karen, who had big hair and a big mouth, asked what my fella's name was while Angela freely told her. I was mortified as Karen looked him up on the Internet and got nothing. I was kind of grateful he was a ghost on the Internet.

She stated right away, "Well, he's not very important then. There isn't anything here about him. Angela, did I spell his name right?"

Her words oozed in a nasally spoken city girl accent, and she accentuated every third word. Angela took her phone. "Yeah, that's the way you spell it."

The Dating Policy

Karen was crazy about the entertainment business, stalking the society pages, reality television, and any celebrity gossip she could get her hands on.

She knew everything about everyone from celebrities to the spoiled rich. Her husband Richie often poked fun at her, announcing that if there were ever a TV game show like *Jeopardy* and the only topics were reality shows, celebrities, and the wealthy, he was going to stick her on there, and they would be an easy win.

Karen always fired back that her knowledge had helped him out a few times, so he should not berate her social interest in keeping up with society pages and who's who.

This was a very amusing family to observe. By my second glass of wine, I was enjoying myself here, especially being away from all the crap I had on my plate. Angela was the most normal of the group. Karen went on and on, "Ya know, his name does sound familiar." Angela brought up the ball game again and reminded her sister that it was his table where we sat.

I was definitely going to kill my best friend later. Chester stood up and poured me another glass of wine. Apparently, I looked as I was feeling... mortified. "Don't worry, Mal. They'll be on to another topic in just a minute, and your fella will be a memory." He gave me a wink and a click from the side of his mouth.

I took another big gulp. I picked up my bat phone and texted Todd where I was and said that I was in the safest company in this entire city. His answer seemed satisfied. Just as Chester sat back down, the girls were talking about the kids and some kind of mishap at one of their schools.

By five o'clock, I was ready to head home. I was exhausted from all the events of today.

Mrs. Deprima packed me a "to go" plate, and how could I refuse? All my favorite foods were there. I hugged her, and she held me for a second longer. "Don't you worry, Mallory. You're gonna get your fella. You are such a beautiful girl on the inside and out. Just be patient; men need that in a woman."

"Thank you. I have all the time in the world. Thanks for the plate."

She now asked, "Will we see you for family dinner Wednesday?"

I looked disappointed as much as I could. "Sorry, I won't be doing those for a while. I have a new position with the company, and it is keeping me pretty busy."

"Yes, Angela told me all about it. Congratulations."

"Thank you. Again, thanks for including me. I love your cookouts."

"You're always welcome here. You know that."

"I do, and thank you."

Angela took my plate from me. "Come on, Mal. I'll walk you out. Be right back, Ma."

We left. I pulled out my bat phone and texted him: *Hi.*

He was instantaneous: *Hi, miss me already?*

I answered: *Kind of.*

He replied: *Don't tell me I picked one of those needy women who is always calling or texting when their boyfriend isn't around?*

I had to read his reply twice because my first response would not have been nice, but I could now see the sarcastic undertone in his message. I typed: *Sort of.*

He responded: *Good.*

Good? That threw me for a curve.

I typed: *Do you want me to be needy?*

He replied: *Kind of.*

I laughed: *See you in the morning, Duvall.*

He answered: *I hope so, but no promises. Let me know if he tries to contact you.*

I texted: *Okay, I will. He hasn't done anything to make me feel threatened.*

Just be aware of your surroundings more, babe. That's all I am asking.

That was it. Todd just asked me to be more cautious. I will do that, and I told him goodnight.

What a difference a weekend made. It seemed that the shock of my new position was over and accepted now. Richard even said good morning to me like he used to on occasion.

Ned came right into my office and sat, asking me how my weekend was. These guys were so confusing... stupid office politics.

Then he asked me if I had lost some weight because I was looking good. Coming from Ned, that was a compliment.

Even though he was no longer in the service, he still kept in top shape.

My day was filled with learning a new computer program. I hated this stuff, but IT told me it would cut out a good hour of nonsense from the old program.

I had four pages of notes by the end of the day.

Angela knocked on my door at five. "Hey, want to hit the gym?"

"Yes!"

That was just what I needed to clear my head right now. No Todd today, but I pulled out the bat phone to text him that Angela and I were hitting the gym.

He texted me back that he had some matters to take care of this evening, and the gym was out for him.

Angela commented on how aggressive I was during step class. I shared about the program I had to learn today, and she pitied me with empathy.

Thank goodness, Mother Deprima packed a plate because it was my dinner tonight. I was home for ten minutes, and Todd texted me: *Are you home yet?*

That was odd.

I replied: *Yes, just heating up some food.*

There was a knock on my door, and I jumped. I looked through the peephole, and there he was.

I opened the door with a big grin. "Well, well, well. I should be more careful about giving my code out."

He laughed and came at me, hooking his foot to shut the door. This man kissed so well, and I still couldn't believe he was mine.

He stopped his assault. "Have a good workout, babe?"

Catching my breath, I cleared my throat. "Yes, I did. I needed it after learning the new IT program."

"Do you need help with it? I know it very well."

"I might. Keep the bat phone close."

He pulled it from his pocket and placed it on my table. "Always do."

"So, what brings you to my neck of the city?"

"My appointments are done, and I wanted to see you before I headed home."

Home? Hmmm... now that was an interesting topic. "I'm a lucky woman to have such attention from a man; where is home, Mr. Duvall?"

"Wherever I hang my hat."

I rolled my eyes. "Seriously, where do you live, Duvall?"

"I live downtown." His phone started ringing. He looked at it, then stepped away from me. "Excuse me; I have to take this."

He walked deeper into my living room. I tried to give him privacy and continued with my food prep.

I heard bits of what he was saying like "when" and "which car."

A few seconds later, he hung up and came at me with a complete mood change, now very serious.

"I have to go. Sorry, babe. I'll be in touch."

He kissed me swiftly, and he went out the door.

I couldn't even get an "Is everything okay?" out because he left so suddenly.

So, I picked up the bat phone and texted it to him instead. No response. Now, I was concerned.

This stupid device was supposed to work around the clock, day or night, no limit on time. It just failed the test. Midnight, he left me a message that he was finally back, but he said he would not be in tomorrow. He had to take care of some personal business.

I texted him back that I hoped everything would be okay.

That was it — no return message.

I thought, and I stewed, and I thought. It turned out it was a lie from the man who said: "Anytime, day or night." I had not heard from Todd, and now we were into Wednesday.

I didn't know if he was here at the office or still out.

Angela poked her head in. "I know you've been busy, but it's family dinner night, and we would love to have you. Free meal and entertainment anyway," she said with an exaggerated cheesy smile on her face.

This may be just the distraction I needed.

"Yes. I will be there."

She clapped her hands. "Ma will be thrilled. Dinner is at six-thirty in case you forgot."

I chuckled. "No, I didn't forget. See you a little after six."

I brought wine again. After supper was when Karen started with her celebrity gossip updates. This was a very busy week in the news, and she took it very seriously.

She couldn't wait to tell us about what happened to Odessa Williams this week. She was beside herself, unforgiving of Odessa's recent actions. I didn't know who she was.

Apparently, we had our very own multimillion-dollar heiress in town, and she was a bad girl — bad decisions, bad crowd, bad reputation. No wonder I didn't pay attention: a spoiled, rich, attention-seeking female who probably never worked a day in her life. Yeah, I was good at not knowing her details.

Karen went on, "She's a bit of an alcoholic as I know it, has a drug dependency too. You know they all do those designer drugs these days."

Richie spoke up. "Well, maybe we should start dealing drugs, Karen. That could be a job for you. Hang out with all your people, provide a service, bring home some money."

She gave him the eye. "Not in front of the kids, Richie. Don't even joke about something like that. Next thing you know, they'll be going to school and telling all their friends that their mother deals drugs."

He laughed. We all laughed, and then she went on, "Well, that's how all these rumors start, don't you know? They hear it in conversation, and they believe it. Then they tell all their little friends."

"Yeah, Richie. Shut it," Angela said playfully.

He laughed a little more. Karen continued about how Odessa's behavior had been out of control lately. Angela asked to see a picture.

Karen brought her images up on her phone and handed it to Angela. Karen filled us in some more. "She is quite exotic looking and still a year from thirty yet. I bet she can afford all types of beauty treatments to keep her looking young forever."

Angela went through the pictures. "Yeah, she does look familiar. I've seen her before." Angela was swiping through the photos. She stopped at one and said, "Oh, fuck! That's Todd!"

I tried to grab the phone from her hands as Karen scrambled for it as well, saying, "Let me see him."

The Dating Policy

I reached it first. There was my not-yet boyfriend, holding her by the arm, and it looked like he was escorting her somewhere... maybe away from the cameras. She, on the other hand, had a big grin on her face.

She was the woman next to him at the Mexican restaurant. All at once, I felt dizzy, mad, betrayed, and sick.

Karen took her phone back, looking at the photo and announcing. "Oh, that's her husband. He's a handsome guy, isn't he?"

"WHAT?"

I stood so fast, mustering everything I had to keep it together, but I knocked my chair over backward to the floor. Our family dinner night went silent. Even the kids watched as I grabbed my wine and chugged the rest down while Angela explained that was the guy I liked at work.

I got a lot of, "Ohs."

Chester stood up, walked over to me, and poured another glass with sympathy. "Here, Mal. This one's on me. If it makes any difference, I can take care of this for you."

"What?" I gasped. "No! I just need a minute."

Karen sneered. "You are not her solution, Chester. Sit back down."

Then Karen said to me, "I would move on, sweetie. There's no way he'll ever divorce her. Why would he want to leave that kind of money?"

I needed air.

I excused myself as Angela gave me a minute. I think she was explaining to the family about Todd and me.

She came out with my wine glass a few minutes later. "Here, Mal. Well, it's lucky there is a 'no dating' policy at work. And thank God you didn't sleep with him. That could have been a disaster."

I wanted to cry, but I knocked back the drink instead. "You're right, Angela. He is an asshole. You pegged that right from the start. I should have listened to you."

"Aw, Mal. I'm sorry it turned out like this. There are plenty of guys out there. Mr. Right will fall into place, and you won't have to worry about work policies or wives or anything else interfering. No more Thomas; no more shit. I think dating is only complicated because we get the guys with baggage, those not yet committed, and the ones who still only want to have fun."

She laughed, trying to make light of it. "Hey, give yourself a few days and hope you don't have to work with him. I mean it, Mallory. Like Barbara says, 'Trust your instincts.'" She blew me a kiss. "I'm here if you need me."

I nodded, but it was time for me to leave. I went back in, and as much as the family tried to keep me there to work through it, I needed to be alone. I didn't work like her family did, and this was a private matter.

The only one I trusted was myself.

I stopped at the liquor store and grabbed another bottle of wine. At home, I looked up Odessa Williams on my laptop, and there were hundreds of photos of her. I could only find two with her and Todd.

Well, his "situation" was a wife... Isn't that just great? Never would I have pegged him for being married. I looked at the bat phone... Should I? Or shouldn't I? I just stared at it. Then, to make up for my anger and betrayal, I poured another glass of wine.

The more I looked at her, the more I hated her. I found all the dirt I could on Odessa Williams. What the hell kind of woman names their kid Odessa? I rolled it over in my mouth — Odessa, Odessa, Odessa.

Her name was stupid. What does that name even mean? I looked it up. Argh! Now I wished I had never gone that far. It was introduced by Russia's Catherine the Great, and she was inspired by Homer's *Odyssey*.

Then I looked up the USA Odessa name registry and damn it! It's one of the top one thousand names from the 1800s, and I was pleased for only a moment by this fact: "rarely used today."

I hated that stupid name, "Odessa." After I finished stalking the Odessa Williams family fortune with her family history and the money and businesses they sat on, I started digging deep... which took me about an hour and another glass of wine. I had the courage and picked up the bat phone, and then I typed: *Marriage is not an "issue." It's a commitment.*

I was happy with the way it looked, and I hit send. Well, my phone lit up instantly. I didn't answer. There was no way I was prepared to speak to him. It went to voicemail. I didn't expect him to call. I expected a text. I left it alone.

The fifth call was coming in now, and I set it to vibrate. I dumped the rest of my wine down the sink and placed the bottle in the fridge. I ignored everything and went to bed. I left the bat phone on my table, and I went upstairs.

Chapter Eight

My Thursday started by not looking at the bat phone and leaving it at home. That turned out to be a curse rather than a blessing. I was also hungover from too much wine.

Ned came in. "You look a little dehydrated, Mal. What did you do last night?"

"Angela's family night. Too much wine."

"I hope you didn't drive home. You have to watch your reputation here now that you made rank."

I hadn't thought about that. "Thanks for the heads up. I will keep that in mind in the future."

Ned tapped my desk. "We have a manager meeting after lunch in the boardroom." "Okay, I'm just seeing that, Ned." It was popping up on my daily announcements.

Ned hung around for a second as I was unpacking my briefcase, and then he said something I automatically answered, and he left.

All morning, I was dreading the meeting, thinking that Todd was going to be there. I lucked out; it was only for our department.

No sign of Todd all day until I arrived home. There was a note stuck on my door; my name was handwritten on the outside.

I yanked it off and brought it in. Curiosity got the better of me. I picked up the bat phone, and there were seventeen text messages, eighteen missed calls, and two voicemails... plus one handwritten note. I regarded it as trash.

I started with the voice messages. They were him commanding me to, "Answer the goddamn phone." I deleted them.

Then I read all the text messages. They also backed up his voice message to answer the damn phone.

Finally, the note: Mallory will you please call me or text me; just do something to communicate with me. I want to explain. It's not what you think. Let me make it clearer for you.

I dropped the note. "Make it clearer for me... You're married! I think that's pretty clear."

I picked up the bat phone and texted him: *I'm home. You may come over and explain.*

He replied, *20 minutes.*

I reached for the rest of my wine and poured it in a pub glass to calm my nerves.

Todd was right on time, knocking on my door. I downed another gulp and went for it. I opened the door.

This was not a passionate conclave. He didn't even try to kiss me. This was all business. I closed the door with more force than intended behind him as he ignored my mood and went right to the kitchen table.

"Mallory, please sit."

He pulled out a chair for me, and he noticed the wine on my counter. He reached for it and placed it in front of me. "Yes, my 'unresolved issue' is that I am married, but we are separated."

I huffed out a deep breath. There was hope. I tried to ask a question, but Todd informed me that he wanted to finish first. I could ask anything I wanted after.

Okay, I would give him that. I sat back and picked up my wine, wrapping my hand securely around the lower part of the glass, and positioning it close to my chest. "Go on then," I said to get the upper hand.

He sat. "I met her when I was in college. I interned for one of her father's businesses. We were both attending the same college, but I didn't know her. I was too busy with school, my internship, and work to have any sort of normal college life. It was not a priority, nor could I have been bothered to do the social thing. One day on the job, her father was touring his companies. He liked to check in and have a look for himself. Edward Wallace ran the company I worked for, and he took me with a few of the other interns down to meet Nicholas Williams. Nicholas took a liking to me right away. He liked the way I presented myself and had heard about my work ethic. He even said he liked the look of me. He already knew what my GPA and major and minor were; he asked if I knew his kid. Well, I didn't, and then he asked me to go to lunch with him."

I took another large sip of my wine, then started to relax, listening to the backstory of my current non-boyfriend.

Todd read my new mood and made a mental note of it and continued, "It was at lunch when he propositioned me to watch out for his daughter. He knew I was paying my own way in college, and he proceeded to dangle the carrot in front of the carriage horse that his company would absorb all my student loans if I kept her out of trouble. I was in my third year, and my bill was pretty hefty. I was thinking of all the classes I still wanted to take but couldn't afford. He went one step deeper and sweetened the deal by guaranteeing me a good position in one of his companies when I graduated. I was highly motivated at the time; I saw this as a major advantage, and I took it. How hard could it be watching out for a chick? Then he shook my hand, and that was that. I became her guardian. Mind you, at the time, I didn't know what she looked like or what her personality was. All she was to me was my ticket to financial freedom for the next year and a half. He had us meet the next day."

I tensed up again because now I knew what she looked like. "Well, I assume you've seen a picture of her by now, correct?"

The Dating Policy

"Correct." One word — that's all I could give him.

"I'm going to skip some stuff if you don't mind and fast forward a bit."

I nodded. I didn't think I could handle, "the college years with Odessa Williams."

"I graduated the third most accomplished student in my school. I spent so much time under Nicholas's wing that the top two placed ahead of me because of their dedication to college. I was dedicated to my career so much... so I married his daughter, and her dad gave us his blessing. Shortly after marriage, I was earning my spot that was given to me. The wife became bored and chose her social life and social status over me. I actually think she pushed for the marriage so she could leave school. She grew up spoiled and doing whatever she wanted. She knew this money game much better than my recent exposure, as it had already started to wear on me. Another year went by; she did anything she wanted when she wanted, and being a wife quickly faded from her interest."

He paused to check my expression from his pacing, sharing his history, clearly telling me things that made even himself uncomfortable. I watched him evaluate my current state as he became satisfied to continue. "Night after night, she went to parties or social events. She would fly off for weeks at a time. I didn't know where she was; I got sick of it, so I completely focused on the career I'd worked so hard to achieve, and I let her go. It wasn't even six months later that Nicholas had a sit-down meeting with me.

Apparently, she was making a fool of herself in the media. He asked me what was going on, and I told him. He was stuck. I was doing an exceptional job for his company, and his daughter had dumped me to go off partying. I immediately offered to file for divorce. I thought that was a clean, easy way out of this shit for me. He refused the idea. He and I negotiated again that afternoon and worked out another deal. I got what I have today because of that mediation, which includes my table at the ballpark, plus job security. There is a lot involved, Mallory. It's all mine. He cannot take it back. I have six months left until the end of our 'agreement.' Six more months to play this charade, unless he allows me to revisit and revise the plan." Todd was finished with his explination.

I had to give him credit. Not once did he say her name. He even referred to her as "the wife."

"Can I ask questions now?"

He studied me, then repeated, dead serious, "There may be questions I cannot answer. I do have a nondisclosure agreement in effect."

"Okay, so you said you are separated from her, but I saw you together a few weeks ago. So, what's with that?"

"Mallory, I am her caretaker. I'm babysitting for the most part. She is a spoiled brat. All the attention must be on her. If the money wasn't there, there would be nothing."

"How are you able to work and watch over her at the same time?"

"Her father has hired another agency 'babysitter' during the day, and work is flexible."

"How is work flexible?"

"Nicholas Williams."

"What does he have to do with SBS?"

There was silence. He didn't say anything. This must have been one of the things he couldn't tell me. I wasn't getting it, though. "Mallory, this is the safest way to answer what you want to know right now. I am married 'on paper' to this multibillion-dollar tycoon's daughter. It looks good on one's resume."

Oh, I became amused and even grinned a little. "So, you weren't hired on merit."

He cracked a smile too. "I was hired specifically on merit, by the way."

"So, how's this going to go now, Todd? You're married for another six months, and then you're free of all this. Because to me, it doesn't sound like it's going to be that easy. This sounds like years of more BS."

"I am approaching ten years with her. The prenuptial agreement will expire, and I can go after her for so much more. Nicholas and I have an agreement, and he will take charge of her again in six months, releasing me of any obligations."

"I don't get it."

"Mallory, please just bear with me. You are the first woman I have actually wanted to be with in a long, long time. No, I take that back... You are the only woman I have ever wanted to be with by my own choosing."

He struck my heart with that statement, which made me reevaluate my priorities about what I wanted and needed to hear from him regarding our current situation. "But how will this work in the meantime? I mean, we can't go out. We can't date with work policies. What is it going to be like for the next six months for me?"

"The work thing is taken care of. It just has to be looked over by the corporate attorneys. Another month tops and a new policy should be in effect."

I sat up straighter. "Really?"

"Really," he mimicked me. I could tell he wanted to kiss me. This conversation about his "unresolved issues" had gone better than I expected, and I was sure he felt the same way, but I wasn't done yet. "So, you have to drag your wife around and pretend you're married for another six months?"

"Believe me; it's harder than you think. I've even tried to set her up with a few men. That backfired because she was only with them overnight and not out in public."

I gasped at the idea. "Do you know how messed up that is?"

He didn't reply quick enough, so I asked, "Last Monday night, what happened? I assume, now that I know about your wife, that it was because of her that you had to rush out of here."

The Dating Policy

"Correct, and I am sorry about that. The stupid cow went out drinking and smashed her car."

I was shocked that he had just put her down like that. "You really shouldn't call your wife a stupid cow. It may put a strain on your marriage." He shook his head.

And I added, "Besides, she's more like a cash cow anyway. How did she go out drinking? Didn't she have her babysitter with her?"

"Sometimes, she pays them to leave her alone."

"What if something serious happened to her during the time she paid them off? Does that come back to bite you?"

"You don't know her, Mal, and I hope you will never have to meet her. That was the biggest thing I negotiated with her father. If she does that, then it will not come back on me. I can only do so much, and there is only so much I am willing to do."

"Do you have to be there every night? Do you live with her?"

"Yes, I have to be there every night. No, we live separately but across from each other. When she is around, she goes with me on business trips. Two separate suites, so don't even go there." Good. I was just about to ask him the sleeping arrangements as my blood started to boil.

"What about the gym? Why are you free to be open with me there?"

"I have a few places that are just mine; she is restricted from going to them. I need my sanity too. The gym is one of those places."

"What are the others?"

"The baseball park."

"Oh? Um... how about work?"

"That's not on the list. I would like to add this address, though." I panicked. "WHAT? Why would you bring attention to me like that?"

"Because I need a life too... If I can't take you out in public, then I should be able to come here without interference."

"Todd, they'll know. They'll know you have some side action going on."

He grinned and cocked his head slightly. "Side action?" He repeated it a few more times, very amused with my word choice. "Well, if that's the situation, I haven't had any side action in a few days, and I think we need to resolve that."

"Hold that thought right there, mister. I'm not through with this conversation." He grinned and stretched back, unbuttoning his cuffs and rolling them up a bit. I took a gentle sip of my wine, watching him making himself more at home as he pulled his tie through his shirt collar. I knew what he was doing, and the fucker was doing it well. "So, what would happen if the wife found out about me?"

"I really don't know, Mallory, nor do I care. She has her life, and I have mine. Besides, it's all winding down, and the lawyers have already started the paperwork."

I studied him, and I had to ask, "Have you ever had a relationship with anyone before me?" I held my breath.

"No relationship. You are the only one."

I exhaled in relief, but I really think he didn't answer that fully. So, I approached it differently. "Todd, I am not prying, but okay, so you didn't have a relationship, but have you had sex with anyone between when you were with her and when you've been with me?"

I knew that look, and I already had my answer as he took in a deep breath. "I have had a few indiscretions. They meant nothing to me, and I used protection."

I needed to know this stuff, and now my brain was screaming at me, you dummy! "When was the last time you slept with your wife?" Damn. This was so messed up, even saying that out loud didn't make me feel the full effect that I was with a married man.

He stepped back, studying me. "Do you really want to know that, Mallory? This is the stuff that is going to eat away at you."

"I need to know, Todd. This is going to eat away, no matter what. With how you just answered that I need to know even more now."

"Okay, there may have been some slip-ups a few times over the past six years."

"Slip-ups? Just how does one's penis land in a vagina accidentally?"

He lowered his head in fake defeat, adjusting to give me a glimpse of his smug grin as he admitted. "One bottle of great whiskey, that's how."

"Oh."

"I didn't know you back then, and sex was just an act for several years. This is different, babe... We are different. I want to be with you, only you. I want to make love to just you."

He made his move toward me, extending his hand to lift me out of my seat, then tilted up my chin. He looked into my eyes. "I know it sounds bad, but when you really look at the whole picture and know the backstory, it doesn't sound so bad, right?"

"I suppose, but you are still married, and everyone sees you as a married man... to her."

I choked out the word her. He caressed my cheek and looked into my eyes. "Do you have any more questions? Because I would really like to rip those clothes off you right now and plant some more evidence inside you to make sure you know I am yours." That was a mood changer. He triggered motivational sex. He already knew what to say to me and just how to say it. I tried to stay on track and keep sex out of this.

I scrambled to think. "Give me a minute. I'm thinking." He began to unbutton his shirt very slowly, keeping eye contact with me. My eyes now focused and followed what his hands were doing. All my concentration went to what he was doing, and he knew it. "You are not playing fair, Todd."

"No, Mallory, I am not playing fair. You know what it's like between us now. When it comes to you, I will play hard and dirty. I will do everything I can to make sure you know I want you. It is only you, Mallory. I just want you, babe."

He stood taller, removing his shirt. He watched me closely and took a few steps back. He lifted my hands to place them around his bare waist.

My hands were acting of their own free will. His aroma filled my nostrils. I slowly inhaled as it triggered euphoria throughout my body.

Automatically, I gravitated to kiss the bare skin between where I was holding. Todd cupped the back of my head gently. I could feel his body stretch, and he let out a hungry moan, triggering me slick with wetness, ready to take him in. In one easy lift, he had me off my feet and at his mouth.

I was giddy, realizing that he could pick my weight up so easily. "You will be mine, and everyone will know," he stated as he kissed me with heat, placing me back down.

Todd took my right hand, cupping it on the bulge in the front of his pants. He let my mouth go. "This is what I have to control every time I see you now. I want you to touch me. I want you to stroke me."

He moved slightly back to undo his belt and zipper. He took both my hands in his, and we pulled down his pants together, freeing his hard cock. He held my right hand again and wrapped it around him, closing his hand over mine. Together, we stroked him as he closed his eyes for a moment, savoring the feeling.

I watched him and watched our hands working him. I wanted to lick him. I dropped to my knees and swirled my tongue on him, teasing him. He worked his hand on mine as he groaned in pleasure.

His hand let go. "Suck me, babe. Take as much as you can. I want your lips around me." I granted his request as I held the base of him, taking as much in as I could. I was getting into a rhythm when he pulled out suddenly. I looked up to see what the matter was.

Again, he lifted me to my feet. Off went my shirt and bra as he assaulted my breast. My pants were next. He backed me against the wall and spread my legs. Todd slid his fingers around my sex, and at the same time, he entered my mouth with his tongue nearly mimicking the actions of his fingers. He paused, whispering into my mouth, "Ready, babe?"

He positioned himself and slowly entered. Never in my life had I had sex standing straight up with anyone except Todd. This was our second time, and right now, I was becoming a huge fan. He clasped his hand in mine and raised them just above his shoulders as he worked himself in me. I was going to cum, and I told him so as he thrust with more force at a faster pace.

There were only a few moments of the constant rubbing from the angle he was entering me. That's all it took. I exploded into orgasm, with his release following. He let go of our hands to cup my butt, giving me more support.

I rested my hands on his shoulders as he leaned his forehead against mine. "Don't give up on me."

I nodded. "Okay."

Todd stayed until midnight just to reassure my uneasy feelings, trying to show me that I was his goal.

He picked up the bat phone, placed it in my hand, told me never to leave it at home again, and then kissed me goodnight.

That was kind of cute. I liked that he did that. The one guy who I have ever felt such a strong attraction to had to be married... just my luck.

He had explained himself, though, so that gave me an incentive to wait it out.

* * *

I was in a great mood Friday morning. Angela poked her head in during her first break. "Hey, you free for lunch?" I thought for a moment. I was caught up, and I missed having lunch with her. "Yes. Let's go across town to Piper's."

"That new southwest bistro?"

"I got a copy of their menu. Everything looks delicious, and I have been dying to go there."

"Piper's it is." She winked and left. I decided I needed Angela to be more a part of my relationship, not just Odessa, Todd, and me for the next six months.

Angela would be able to handle this better than me, and so now I was going to get her on board. We only had an hour. The food was served buffet style. We each filled our plates with what we wanted and sat right down.

She got right into it. "How are you with this whole Todd thing? Are you okay? I know you really liked him."

Well, we only had an hour. I took a big clean breath and exhaled. "Swear on your mother's grave that you will never tell a soul."

She had not expected that. Angela was as superstitious as they came, and she was taken aback by my request. "Why do I need to do that? What's going on, Mal?"

"Swear it, or you will never find out."

Oh, she did not like this one bit. "This better be good, Mallory. I don't like this one bit. Okay, I swear."

She made the sign of the cross on her chest. I leaned in and spoke quietly. "So, here's the thing about Todd. We have slept together."

Angela gasped. "What?"

"And last night, he came over and explained everything."

"Explained that he was married?" Her eyebrows crunched, and the straight line of her mouth that set her jaw forward was a look I knew on Angela.

I saw that nothing good would come from me explaining his situation, as I could see her struggling internally as she tried not to take it personally for my sake. Then I gave her the condensed version.

Angela listened more openly than I expected; she actually felt bad for Todd. While she was fully absorbing what I revealed, I told her she was the only one who knew outside of Todd and me, but I needed to get it out, and she was the only one I could trust. I also told her that the next six months were going to be difficult, and I needed to confide in her to help me when or if I was not dealing with it well.

She reached over with her beautifully manicured nails and cupped my hand. "I've got your back, Mal. I won't tell anyone, especially Karen, and I will make sure she shuts her mouth about Todd and the idiot he has to deal with. Mallory, I have to tell you, now that you say all this, he makes much more sense to me. I mean... the poor guy." She shook her head as she gave me genuine sympathetic eyes.

I loved her as I have always loved this woman through all our tough times. She was always going to be there for me. This was something I'd never had in my life, and I needed to welcome it.

Lunch was delicious. This was going to be a new favorite for us when we could eat together. I had just gotten back when I opened my office door to see a beautiful bouquet of spring flowers with a small note. Instantly, I lit up. I opened the note. It was in Todd's writing: You have proved this was the right decision. Keep up the good work. That was it. No signature... nothing. I almost laughed, and then I thought he was crazy.

How sloppy of my not-yet boyfriend to send me flowers. Every other manager had better have gotten flowers when they were promoted. I knew that card meant more than my work here too.

The flowers were lovely, and I appreciated them. Ned was in within twenty minutes. He must have known I had flowers delivered.

He peeked in. "Hey, Mal. How's it going? Flowers? Well, you must have an admirer." He was fishing again. "No, just appreciation and encouragement. See, it's the little things that count. A gesture like this will make it easier for me to gladly take work home instead of pushing it off until Monday."

"Really? That's what you're going with?"

"Why would it be anything else, Ned? What are you thinking?"

He shook his head. "Women get flowers for three reasons. One is to impress them, the other is out of obligation for a birthday, or the last is he fucked up."

I narrowed my eyes at him. "Your poor wife, maybe you should send her flowers just to say, 'Hey, you're doing a great job raising our kids and keeping the house in order.'"

Oh... Ned never thought about doing that. "See, Ned. It's the little simple things that help us go the extra mile," I said, even though he was absolutely correct in assuming it was those reasons why men give flowers.

He changed the subject to ask what I was doing this weekend. I smiled. "Catching up on what I was going to put off until Monday."

He shook his head again. "Well, have fun with that."

I grinned and moved my flowers, so they were in between my two computers. Angela gushed over the arrangement and took it from me to help carry it out. She asked if I had any plans tonight or tomorrow night. I didn't know, and I asked her if I could call her when I got home.

She smiled and understood. Then she put in a request for another baseball game. I laughed, but that wasn't a half-bad idea. My not-yet boyfriend came with perks, and I should utilize them.

When I arrived home, I spotted them on my small deck before I pulled into my driveway. When I approached my door, there was a full bouquet of white long-stemmed roses. They were beautiful.

Then there was an office-sized file box next to it, sealed with another note. I brought all my flowers inside first, and then I retrieved the box. It was kind of heavy.

I opened the first note: Call or text me when you get home. I texted him: *Home.* I started to open the box and his reply: *Can I come over?* came through.

I looked at it. Um, Yes!

He replied: *On my way. I'm cooking tonight.*

I grinned and opened the box — one nicely packed meal for two. Everything was in separate containers and fresh.

This was like a cooler. There were skewers of vacuum-packed seasoned shrimp, cubed sirloin, diced vegetables, and wild grain rice, along with a very pretty bottle of white wine.

Todd was scoring major points here. I moved to the card on the roses. "To new beginnings."

Well, he could not have worded that more perfectly. My not-yet boyfriend arrived with a leather travel bag.

He immediately kissed me. "Well, hello to you too. What's with the bag?"

He grinned. "Well, after I feed you, I was hoping I could spend the night."

I wanted him to, but I had to ask, "How is this possible?"

He looked at me, confused for a moment. "On my part or yours?"

"Oh, sorry. Yes, I want you to, but how can you?"

"She flew to Canada with a group. She needed to 'recover' from the car accident."

"But doesn't that mean you have to go?"

"No, babe. That does not mean I have to go. That means we can spend the weekend together if you want. I mean, I am inviting myself, so it's okay if you have other plans."

"My plans, my plans, let's see... locked up in my condo with you or anything else I want to do... hmmm, tough choice. Well, since you are here, I choose... you."

He laughed. "Babe, we are not locked up here. We have the gym and the ballpark. It just so happens that there's a game Sunday afternoon. Would you like to go?"

I really tried to act impervious, only the stupid grin on my face gave it away. "Okay, should I call Angela? I mean, the last time you offered, you gave me the tickets."

He grinned and kissed me. "No Angela. I am taking you this time."

"Really? Hmm, I don't know? Angela was a fun date. I'm not sure you can top her."

He cocked his head to the side, pulled me in, and rubbed my ass. "Let me show you just how fun I can be."

He gave me a swift kiss, then let me go and moved around me to pull the food out. He asked, "Hungry?"

Actually, I was. "A little." He handed me his bag. "I'll work on dinner, gorgeous. Can you take my bag up to the bedroom for me?"

So, it was now "the bedroom" and no longer my bedroom. I let out a little laugh and told him, "Sure."

He kissed me again, but he held it a little longer.

My Viking was staying the weekend. This was much more than I expected, and I was elated by the fact that this was going to work out after all. When I made it back to the kitchen, he had opened the wine, and two glasses were poured. He lined up everything else next to the stove.

He announced, "I have to learn where you keep everything."

He handed me my glass. We opened all my cabinets, and he observed where everything was kept.

He approved, telling me that's the way he would have arranged things. It was my not-yet boyfriend's first night with me.

I learned he had to take a lot of phone calls. I was fine with all of them up until the one he had to take at two in the morning.

He got out of bed and went downstairs for that one, and I swear I heard a female voice call him "honey."

When he returned, he tried to be quiet, but I asked who it was. His reply was honest, even though I didn't really want to know.

He said, "It was her. She's drunk and high. I'm sorry, babe, but this is what I deal with all the time. She is nothing to me, and her time is going to expire with us soon."

This was going to be the hardest part... to let go and not take this stuff personally. Todd pulled me against him, wrapped his arm around me, and whispered, "Sleep, baby," and I let it go.

Saturday morning was, without a doubt, much better with Todd being here. For the first time, I was a passenger on the way to our gym. Every time I glanced over at him driving, I was rewarded with a squeeze of his hand holding mine.

We were in his blacked-out BMW. I was thinking of the obvious reasons people could not see in.

It was halfway through our workout that I looked at him. I think for the first time in my adult life, I was actually falling in love. I felt stupid, vulnerable, exposed, jealous, over the moon joyous, like he was my next breath, and then the worst emotion to hit was possessiveness.

I wanted to protect him, especially from her. He looked at his phone again. I knew from the expression on his face it was her.

He shot an aggravated glance to me, and I knew he had to answer it. I nodded as he walked away. This was the downside to having my not-yet boyfriend for a whole weekend. That bitch got to call and take priority at any moment.

Suddenly, I realized what a blessing it had been that I didn't know he was married when I didn't know what was going on.

I jumped on the treadmill to burn off some of the irritation. He was gone for fifteen minutes, and by the time he got back, I was too tired to say anything sarcastic because I ran that whole time. He came over, straight-faced, "We have to go. I need to go straighten something out, and I need to take you home."

"Is everything okay?" I asked, but obviously, it wasn't; otherwise, he would not have to take me home. "More bullshit I have to deal with. I shouldn't be more than four hours."

I hopped off the treadmill, now very glad that I had worn myself out; otherwise, I was sure my other mood would have been ready to battle. Todd carried both our bags in and dropped them inside my door.

I think he did that to improve my attitude, to show he was coming back, and his action actually satisfied me. He kissed me softly with underlying passion. I could feel him sealing my body to his, leaving me with a sudden unquestionable hope that he was mine. "Relax for a bit. I will be back as soon as I can."

I kissed him back with more reserve from my creeping jealous mood swing than I intended. "Don't keep me waiting," I sarcastically bit out.

He ignored my intent. He liked that I said that out loud as he smacked my butt playfully. I gasped at the smack as he kissed me again before he exited.

This was stupid. The whole situation was bleak, so instead of moping around and watching the clock, I went back to bed.

The Dating Policy

The bat phone chirped with updates as I sleepily replied. After his second attempt to have somewhat of a text conversation, I gave up on any thoughts of rest and dragged my butt into the shower.

I forgot what it was like to be in a relationship, especially learning to be the third party in one. I had a whole new set of rules to learn and adapt to. The first rule I learned was less sleep.

I started my Saturday household chores and texted my non-boyfriend that the door was unlocked. Todd arrived while I was vacuuming the second floor, the final stage of my domestic duties.

My location was easily found as he just watched me with his arms folded and an air of contentment about him. When I finally noticed him, I half screamed, forgetting I told him the door was unlocked.

He had done very well, holding the laugh, keeping his amusement in check. For the first time, I was seeing my not-yet boyfriend in a normal, everyday setting. Although there was nothing typical about Todd, he looked relaxed. He was still far superior to any guy I knew — the way he carried himself was with strength, determination, and confidence.

I liked my relaxed Todd as he made his way toward me, "Now all I need is you in one of those French maid outfits, and you will have covered all my domestic female fantasies."

I laughed. "Watch out. I might put a cleaning cloth in your hand to cover my male domestic fantasies."

He had just closed the distance to me. "Any time, love. By the way, I know exactly what I will clean first."

He wiped his hand against my crotch. It was lucky we were already upstairs because my bed was sixteen steps back. I counted those when I woke in the middle of the night, having to use the bathroom.

My condo had an amazing walk-in closet instead of breaking the space between the bathroom and closet. It was only me here anyway. I never minded the extra steps because I thought a huge closet was much more important when I bought this place.

My non-boyfriend picked up where he left off with a kiss and the promise that he was going to make sure I was going to feel where he had been. I forgot to ask any questions on where he had to go, what he had to do, or anything I could have used as leverage to make what I know less or maybe more complicated.

None of this could ever be any good information. I needed to decide right now what I needed to know and what I needed to stay away from to make it through this insane scenario for the next six months.

The next thing I felt was Todd's hands around my waist, and there was suddenly no carpet under my feet as Todd launched me onto my bed. "Your turn," he announced, pulling my pants off and kissing from my ankle upwards.

He protested a little, "You showered."

I nodded. Just as he reached my sex, he looked at me. "I like you sweaty. Your scent goes straight to my dick." Then he started licking in long slow strokes. There was no way I was going to last.

I think he felt me as he stopped. He moved up. "Oh, no, you don't. Not yet, babe."

He positioned next to my body now, kissing and exploring the dips and curves of my female anatomy with his fingers. I was so close. Whatever he was doing, I was going to become unglued at any moment.

He stopped, and all I could do was breathe deep from the now lack of his exploration. "Mallory?"

I took a few more breaths, then opened my eyes. There was the same grin on his face as he had worn that first nice day he had when Angela and I were at the park. He continued talking, "I want you to get on top of me and fuck me."

What? It was clear to both of us that he was much more experienced with sex than I was. I was a good student all my life, and I was willing to learn, especially with Todd guiding. He had seen the apprehension, and he softened. "Don't worry. I'll show you what to do, babe. I think you'll like it."

I sat up, and he rolled on his back. "Swing this leg over like you are going to sit on me."

Well, I wasn't that stupid. I just didn't have a lot of sex in this position. "I know what to do. I'm just a little rusty at this."

He looked serious and waited. He lined himself up, and I took him all the way in. His moan said it all.

I pumped him up and down, setting a soft, smooth rhythm. "That's it, babe. You feel so good. My cock is so hard."

His phone went off, and I tried to stop as he threw his phone on the ground. "No, don't stop. Keep going, baby."

He now took ahold of my hips and set the new pace he wanted me to follow. Thank goodness I had been working out. I could feel this in my thighs. No sooner had I mastered this than he pulled me down harder on him. "Just like this, babe. I'm not going to last."

He removed one of his hands from my hips and started to manipulate my clitoris. No one had ever done it the way he was touching me. That was it. I lost myself in pure ecstasy. I heard him grunting as he held my hips to him. He climaxed, and I needed to lay down.

I moved to his side again as he praised me. We were there, cuddled into each other for a minute, and his phone went off again.

This time, I noticed it was programmed with a different ringtone. I knew this tone, but I couldn't put my finger on where I had heard it. Whoever it was, Todd was letting me go and moving quickly to retrieve it.

He answered the phone and walked out of the room away from me. I cleaned up and got dressed.

Todd was jogging up the stairs. "I'm sorry, Mallory. I have to go. She is flying back per Nicholas's orders. She has an escort, and I have to take custody at the airport. I know this puts a major inconvenience with my plans and you."

He carefully watched my expression. "Hey, come here." He reached for me. "The next few months are going to be hard on both of us. But there is an expiration date. Everything will be done. All ties will be severed."

I was looking right into his eyes. He believed what he was saying. The confidence that he carried assured me that this was temporary. He added, "Yes, this is the 'adapt and regroup' story of my life with this woman. I am still taking you to that game tomorrow. I will pick you up and drop you back."

I sighed. "How the hell are you going to be able to do that? I'll just meet you there."

He readjusted his posture, and I could see the transformation. "Like hell you will. I will pick you up. This is the end of the logistics discussion for game day."

How could I protest? He was naked, being every bit the Todd Duvall I knew at work, only standing here gloriously nude in front of me. I kissed him quickly. That was my sneak attack.

I always fantasized trying that if I ever ended up in one of his ass-chewing interrogations. He smacked my butt hard, and I jumped as it brought up a bad memory, he grinned. Okay, this was how confusing my non-boyfriend was.

Everything he brought over, he left here. He walked out wearing the outfit of the day. That was it. Everything else stayed.

This man was beyond unpredictable as I picked up the bat phone and texted: *You forgot your bag...* I received an immediate response: *I did not forget; I am hoping you can find a place for those things in your house. I would like to keep a few more clothing items in case I sleep there on a work night. What are your thoughts?*

He was asking me what my thoughts were. He wanted someplace in my home to keep his stuff while this was all going on. I looked at his bag and thought. As much as I wanted to fling it out the door, I wanted to sleep with it all next to me.

That afternoon, I created a space for my not-yet boyfriend to keep stuff here. Damn it! I was falling for him big time, and he was married... Todd called a few hours later to see how I was.

I had never had to compete with another woman, but on that same note, my former relationships just sort of happened, and when they were broken off, it was never a big deal. But now, I knew there was no competition, but it still bothered me.

I proceeded to call Angela. By the end of her listening, she informed me we were going out dancing tonight and for me to get all dolled up. We were meeting downtown, starting with dinner at one of the more upscale restaurants. I hesitated, then remembered I had just got a huge raise. I agreed and proceeded to do as Angela ordered me to prepare and primp myself to look pretty. This was just what I needed — a little boost to distract me from my current situation.

Chapter Nine

Angela was already in the bar with some very handsome young professional man talking to her. She spotted me right away and waved me over. I arrived as the guy was watching me walk toward them. Angela introduced us. Apparently, he worked with her brother-in-law. He was a good-looking guy... his name was Johnny.

He stuck around and announced that he felt the need to escort us, two beautiful ladies, this evening just in case someone got out of hand tonight. Angela laughed and said it was okay with her.

I shrugged; I didn't mind if he tagged along. I pulled out the bat phone and texted my not-yet boyfriend that I was meeting Angela for dinner, then we were going out dancing, but not to worry... we had an escort.

My phone immediately lit up. Todd was calling. I held up my finger to excuse myself as I walked away, answering it.

Todd started right in with, "What escort? Where are you? Where are you going dancing? Who is the guy?"

Geez! I would never have expected this from him. I started to answer his questions about where we were right now, and most likely, we were going on the new club right down the street.

Then he started grilling me about who the guy was. The way he talked to me struck a nerve. I was getting irritated. Who was he to question me? He was the one who was still married and home with the wife right now when he should be with me.

I tolerated only a few more seconds of "Todd-like attitude," directed at me, grilling me. I hung up, putting an end to that attitude. I had seen him act out so many times at the office. Besides, he was really pissing me off. I glanced around and there, approaching me, was Thomas; I stepped back out of caution, remembering the last creepy time I had seen him at the gym.

He was sporting one big grin on his face, walking right up to me and asked what I was doing here with great enthusiasm. I told him I was with Angela for a drink as he took hold of my waist, redirecting me into the bar.

Johnny clearly said something to my gal pal because she turned to see who I was with. "Thomas? What are you doing here?" she asked out of pure suspicion as if he had been following us all along.

He chuckled, extremely amused by her false accusations. "Meeting a few coworkers, this doesn't seem like the type of place you would hang out in Angela. What are you doing here?"

Oh, my gosh! Did he actually answer her like that? Johnny straightened up as Thomas signaled a stop with his hand, "Relax, Rocky; if she is going to dish it out, she had better be able to take it."

My phone was going off. Thomas looked and pointed at it, "Do you need to answer that?"

I shook my head.

"You're an ass, Thomas; we don't need your company tonight." She went straight for the kill.

Thomas grinned, "I'm not here for your company, but I must say what a delight it is bumping into Mallory. You are the icing on my cake. By the way, you look beautiful."

He was now standing on the other side of me, ordering a gin and tonic. I gulped, looking from him to Angela. My phone was lighting up again as Thomas watched. I tucked it into my bag as Angela now watched. Both of them were wondering, and knowing at the same time, who it was blowing up my phone.

She leaned in, "Maybe you should answer that?"

I glared back, "Nope."

Johnny stood there, relaxed, chewing on the bare toothpick from his already eaten olive garnish of his Bloody Mary.

He was more interested in Thomas than what was going on with my phone. Angela also pointed to what I was doing. "Then, if that's how you are handling it, you're going to have to fill me in later."

The restaurant was filling up as she announced, "Oh, I didn't make a reservation." Johnny winked at her, touching her shoulder. "Don't worry about it, Ange. I'll be right back." He sauntered into the restaurant.

Quickly, I leaned in and told her about Todd's blow up as I felt my phone vibrate inside my bag. Screw him! I ignored it again, and I swapped the attention from me to her, asking her about Johnny.

Thomas's first friend was now entering the bar. He introduced me but not Angela, and I thought this was just going downhill fast. I told Thomas it was nice seeing him, but I had to get back to my own company tonight, signaling him to move on.

He was not insulted as he touched my shoulder, telling me we need to keep in touch, and it was great seeing me while he moved to the other end of the bar with a now third friend joining them.

Angela rolled her eyes, "Block his number. There is just something not right about him." I laughed as my phone finally stopped all the vibrating.

Apparently, Angela knew Johnny better than I realized. Her sister had been trying to set them up for the last couple of years. Angela wasn't feeling it, and he was already too much a part of Karen's family.

I tried to convince her otherwise as she laughed. Johnny was back, retrieving us with the announcement that our table was ready. He had us walking in front of him, then pulled out both of our seats and sat himself to the right of Angela. I observed him monitoring the restaurant traffic.

I checked my phone — five missed calls and seven text messages telling me to answer the damn phone. I stuck it back in my bag and left it. There was no way I was going to let him ruin the rest of my night out.

Just as our meals were coming out, Johnny was very focused on someone. Angela noticed and looked in the direction he was staring. "Oh, my God, it's Todd!" she pointed as I turned around in complete dismay.

Johnny spread back wider in his seat, extending himself to his best advantage. His words were calculated as he tried to figure out what was going to happen next. "You know this guy?"

Angela nodded. "The guy from work who has the hots for Mal and the one she has not been answering for the last half hour."

Johnny took it all in as Todd spotted me. I turned back to the table, nearly panicked. Johnny openly said, while keeping an eye on Todd approaching, "Want me to get rid of him?"

I waved my hands over each other, more panicked about what Johnny just said as I explained, "No, no, no, it's okay."

Todd ended his hunt at our table and stood cold as ice in a suit that screamed power. Johnny openly looked him over as they sized one another up.

Todd started with a hello to Angela and then to me. He had no idea how much I told Angela or that Angela even knew about us, and right now, he clearly didn't give a rat's ass what anyone knew.

"Mallory, can I talk to you a minute?"

Our waiter was setting up the tray stand. Angela was announcing the arrival of our food. She acknowledged Todd standing at the end of our table, saying hello and introducing Johnny.

Todd repeated a greeting to Angela while both men gave a very slight nod of acknowledgment.

He reached for my arm and secured a hold as he directed the apology to Angela and Johnny. "Excuse us. This will just take a moment."

I was guided right out of my seat. It was clear he had done this a few times in his life. Angela gave me the Is everything okay? look, and I nodded yes, still in disbelief that he was here in front of me.

Todd escorted me out of the restaurant, and his car was parked right in front. He requested that I get in. I looked around for potential escape routes.

There was no way I was leaving Angela here. We had plans for an enjoyable night. This was crap. "No!" I protested, turning around to walk back into the restaurant.

He reasoned with me, trying to reach a compromise, "Mallory, I just want to talk to you. I promise."

I stopped and turned toward him, still fuming from the phone conversation. "What is your problem?"

He calmed down now and asked me politely to just get in the car for a minute.

I sighed. I knew we were starting to create a scene.

"Okay," I answered, and I let him open the door. The first thing said was a big compliment about how beautiful I looked. The second was him apologizing for the first phone conversation.

He explained that my not picking up the phone drove him insane, and I had promised him that I would not do that anymore.

I was not expecting the next thing at all. He asked if he could join me tonight. I froze, dumbfounded. "But we are out in a very public place. What about work? What about your wife?"

"Fuck 'em, all of them. I want to be with you tonight."

I went to say something, and I stopped, then went to say something else, and I stopped, still bewildered. He picked up my hand and kissed the back of it. "How about it, Kennedy? Can I be the one to escort you this evening?"

I nodded as a smile started to spread across my face. "Todd, you are the only one I want escorting me everywhere." He lowered his head with some degree of relief. He looked good in his steel-gray suit. He came around and opened my door, tossing the valet his keys. "Thanks, Justin. We'll be about an hour."

"Just text me, Mr. Duvall. I'll have her waiting."

I flexed an eyebrow, "Her?"

He pulled my ear to his mouth, "Every great tangible known to man is female."

I did a double-take to what Todd was professing. The valet tipped his hat and made his way to the driver's seat.

I leaned in as Todd put his arm around my waist. It was official. We were a couple. I whispered. "You know the valet by name?"

Todd answered, "Yes."

I snapped my head straight ahead and watched for people's reactions. "Oh, this can't be a good thing."

Next, I heard a voice behind me, "Mallory, are you okay?"

It was the voice of Thomas. Oh, shit, I didn't tell Todd that Thomas was here. Todd, clearly feeling confident, answered for me. "My girlfriend is fine. Who are you?"

The Dating Policy

I stood between them and answered for Thomas. "Todd, this is Thomas. He coincidently is meeting with friends in the bar tonight. I haven't seen him forever."

Todd moved me away from Thomas and slightly in front of him as he replied, "Best be getting back to them."

We were about ten feet away from Thomas, now making our way back to the table. I apologized right away for not saying anything in the car. Todd gave a cool, calm response that we would talk about Thomas later.

Angela and Johnny had their eyes on us coming back. She motioned to my plate. "I had them leave the cover on to keep your meal hot."

Now, Angela watched Todd pull my chair out, and he took the seat next to me. "Oh, you're staying?"

Todd replied with a sarcastic tone from his grin. "Yes. I am staying."

I offered to share my food with my now-boyfriend in this very public place. He assured me that he was all set and flagged down a waiter, who did not hesitate to greet him, "Mr. Duvall, nice to see you this evening. What can I bring for you, sir?"

He picked up my wine glass and took a sip. Then announced, "Derek, please bring us a bottle of the Savoy."

Todd looked over to Angela. "Angela, what are you both drinking?" She pointed to her martini and said, "Apple," and then to Johnny's glass as she said, "Bloody."

The waiter nodded. Angela smiled. "Thank you, Todd. You didn't have to do that."

"You are welcome, Angela."

Johnny sat back. "So, you're Todd Duvall. I know your name from somewhere."

Angela kicked Johnny under the table as Johnny reacted, "Ouch!" and looked over at her as she gave him the shut-your-mouth face.

He looked from her to Todd to me. I stuffed my face with another slice of my prime rib. I offered Todd a bite, and he took my hand, guided it to his mouth, and ate it right from my fork. Holy smokes! That was sexy as all hell, and this was the complete opposite of a low profile. This screamed that we were clearly together.

Angela grinned, giving me a wink, pleased he was claiming me. She couldn't help herself. "You know, Todd, this would clearly be frowned upon at work."

He agreed. "You're right, Angela, and what would they say about this?"

His hand caressed my jaw, coaxing my head to turn, now aligned with his. He held me still, leaning forward, pressing his lips softly against mine.

Angela half laughed, lifting her martini with a toasting gesture. "Well, look at you, Mr. Duvall. Aren't you full of surprises?"

She brought the glass to her lips and finished off the last sip. The alcohol Todd ordered arrived, allowing me the possibility to peek around nervously and judge if there were shocked looks on any of the patrons, or even worse, if anyone we knew from work was possibly dining here tonight.

I was the one in this new relationship having a panic attack, even though Todd was finally acting as I thought he should, and this was exactly what I wanted.

My boyfriend was proving he didn't care who saw us together tonight. This was completely throwing me off-center. I downed what was left of my wine, hoping it would act as an instant sedative while they poured a new glass from the chilled bottle. He observed my action as I set down my glass.

He leaned into me again, causing the hairs on the back of my neck to rise as the alcohol made its way through my body. His voice lowered to a murmur. "Are you okay, babe?"

I turned my head slightly, chin tilted down in his direction, and muttered through clenched teeth, "No."

Todd laughed. He actually laughed. It caught Angela's attention because she had never heard Todd laugh, but there was my boyfriend, leaned back in his chair, one arm around the back of my chair, picking his wine glass up without a damn care in the world. I leaned into him and quietly asked, "Are you on something?"

He turned his head to look right at me. "I will have this conversation in the car with you, but that answer is not anything from a chemical compound. By the way, I am very against any mood-altering drugs unless you truly have an injury, and it is medically necessary for pain management."

I agreed with him and had to state this right now, "Of course, I feel the same way. I am against recreational drugs. Shoot, I don't even like taking Ibuprofen, but sometimes when I work out with this new guy at the gym... I may just have to on occasion."

Todd liked that answer so much that he winked at me, rubbed my shoulder, and I earned another kiss in public! I finished my food, and we were all talking when suddenly a very well-dressed man approached the table.

He addressed Johnny first, "Mr. Cambonelli, I hope you were pleased with your table this evening."

Angela watched Johnny as he relaxed further in his seat, replying to this stranger, "Yes, and I appreciate you fitting my ladies in. This is Angela."

He looked down and acknowledged Angela with an approving nod, now asking her, "How did you enjoy your meal?"

Angela replied, "The shrimp was divine. I enjoyed every bite. Thank you."

He grinned. "I am so happy to hear that. I hope we made an impression and that you will join us again... soon. As a guest of Mr. Cambonelli, you are always welcome."

Angela picked up her cocktail and raised her glass to him. "This is the best apple martini I have ever tasted. I will be back."

The Dating Policy

He smiled sincerely at her. "I will personally make your next one. It is my family's recipe as well as our lemon. I am going to let you in on a secret; it is not on the menu but ask for 'The Grapes.' We only make this for a few customers."

Everyone at the table was intrigued, except Todd. He knew the code word for sure. Angela toasted to him. "I will."

Johnny felt in control of the table and introduced me as Mallory, Angela's friend. He looked down at me with Todd's arm still around the back of my chair in his relaxed seating position.

The well-dressed man was now addressing me, but he kept looking over at Todd. "And you ordered the prime, my dear. How was your meal?"

I laughed. "Well, there are no leftovers. It was delicious."

He chuckled. "I adore a woman who is not afraid to eat."

Johnny went on to introduce Todd, but the nicely dressed businessman cut him off.

"Mr. Duvall does not need an introduction here. I know his family intimately."

I wanted to run... run far away. This was a mistake. How could anything good come from this? This guy knew Todd, his wife, and whoever the fuck else was in the cards.

If I could have removed Todd's arm right now, I would have. Todd did it instead, but only to shake hands with Sergio. "Good to see you, my friend. Let me introduce my girlfriend, Mallory," Todd stated proudly.

If I could have fainted, I would have. I was a deer in headlights. My heart was pounding so hard in my chest; I thought it was actually moving the outline of my clothing. I felt a flat line tone in my ears while this man grinned and said something to me.

It was as if he was speaking another language. Sergio smiled, reaching for my hand, and kissing the back of it as if I was delicate and valuable. All I could do was watch my hand in his and nod.

The pounding of my heart echoed in my ears, fading out the flat line tone, and I couldn't hear a thing around me. I glanced over to Angela, who looked very impressed and raised her drink toward me.

Good idea. I scurried to pick up my wine and drank as Todd rested his hand back around my shoulder again.

I didn't know why, but Johnny was too intent on everything Todd was saying. It was like he was studying him. Todd tapped my outside right shoulder with his thumb. Sergio was saying something directly to me. I turned my head to Todd's thumb and then quickly up to Sergio's happy expression as he slightly bowed again, taking my hand in his.

"Miss. Kennedy, I look forward to seeing you again... soon, I hope. Remember... when you join us, ask for me directly upon arriving.

He kissed the back of my hand again. "Such a beautiful woman you are."

Todd nodded, and Sergio disappeared. I looked over at Todd, who displayed a very proud attitude and who also felt the need to kiss me again in public.

I drank. This was my solution to get my nerves under control. Todd moved the bottle away when I finished this glass. So, I immediately started with my water glass. Desserts came around, but Angela still wanted to go dancing.

The men were game, but I just wanted to go home. This evening was already more than I could handle. Angela took another minute to finish her drink. Todd stated that I was riding with him to the club.

His car was still parked right out front, but Johnny had to wait as he handed the valet his ticket.

Todd turned to me in the BMW, amused at first. "Were you able to take in anything Sergio said?"

I shook my head with a definite no.

He picked up my hand. "You are welcome there with or without me. I am banking on the 'with' part... but if you and the girls want a night out, you will sit at my table."

My eyes widened as his grin spread to "the clause."

"As long as there are no men, especially that fucker Johnny or that other meatball Thomas, the meals and drinks will be on me."

I stared. Never have I had this experience in my life. I wanted to rip Todd's clothes off. I wanted to climb him now. And now he was admitting to me that he had never felt so jealous in his life as when I announced that Angela and I had an escort for the night.

That was why he showed up here. Then my stream of consciousness surfaced, remembering everything that had played out tonight so far. There were no phone calls interrupting us so far, making me wonder about the wife. I wanted to ask what was going on with... her, but I didn't want to burst my own happy bubble.

I had my adoring boyfriend, who was quickly changing to be a complete boyfriend, and we had one more part of the evening in public to get through.

This round, I was going to handle much freer and accept it. We arrived. I really could not remember this type of club setting. I was a little older, but it seemed a lot different from ten years ago.

To start with, this was a more expensively dressed set of people. Angela and Johnny were behind us as Todd walked right to the front of the line. The bouncer undid the rope as Todd flashed three fingers. The bouncer nodded as he fended off sneering comments from the patrons standing in line.

I thought I heard him say, "He owns the place." I had no time to turn to see if I heard that correctly while Todd held my hand, pulling me toward the body-moving vibrations resonating from the speakers.

The Dating Policy

He walked all of us upstairs into a separate section. It was not the VIP area. It was smaller and overlooked the dance floor. The bouncer here must have been in the World Wrestling Federation. I had never seen muscles like his, not even at the gym. He moved another rope for us to pass. He asked Angela and Johnny their names so he could personally address them as they walked in. Me... Oh, I was ignored. He had seen Todd holding my hand, so I think that's all he needed to know about me.

Angela was even more impressed. "You know, I have been here once before, not with Mal but with a few other gal pals. Usually, I have to drag Mal out. She is such a homebody." Todd was satisfied with that one statement and kissed the side of my head.

Angela grinned. "So, when I was here, I never even knew this section existed."

Johnny agreed, "Me too, but now that I know where it is, can I use it?"

Todd looked Johnny straight in the eye and pulled the disciplinary Todd I knew out of his hat. "No," was Todd's answer.

Angela kicked Johnny again and whispered something to him. They went to the dance floor. Todd pulled me to him. "May I have this dance, Mallory Kennedy?"

That was so damn cute. I smiled and nodded, dropping my purse on the couch. He led me to the dance floor. Well, lo and behold, why was I surprised that Todd knew how to dance?

There were a lot of people staring at me. Not at Todd, but me.

A very trendy expensive-looking girl approached Todd, beautiful makeup, probably a size two or maybe even a zero, must have been a few years younger than me, she was openly looking me up and down, then leaned into him, saying something.

He laughed and shooed her away while she shook her head disapprovingly, still watching me.

I needed a break. This was getting weird. We arrived back to the exclusive lounge area, with drinks already set out for us.

I picked up mine and scooted next to Todd in the love seat. We had a full aerial view of the crowd down below; it was amazing. I also noticed the ice bucket filled with premium water bottles.

I was feeling elated as Todd kissed the side of my head then over to my ear as he announced, "I should not have waited this long. I have spent this last year miserable, babysitting a spoiled brat when I could have been with you."

Just as I turned to kiss him, giddy with confirmation that I was his choice, I glanced to a body in motion heading toward us. It was a petite brunette owning my newly claimed space.

It was Odessa. She stood there in front of Todd with a smug grin on her face.

He didn't make any changes. I, on the other hand, separated from him with some distance between us now. "There's my husband."

She leaned down to kiss him but stopped right in front of his face. They were a couple. I could picture it. I saw that they had absolutely been married for the past nearly ten years. Todd grabbed my hand because I think he could sense I was going to run.

She stopped right in front of his lips. She looked down at our hands joined, then right at me.

Her hand combed his hair as she said, "Mixing things up, I see. I like this choice better than the last one for us."

She turned back to look at him. "I miss you, baby."

She went to kiss him as he let go of my hand to stop her dead in her attempt. I wanted to jump up and run down that set of stairs that had brought me up to this blind balcony. I clenched the non-giving couch material so tightly my knuckles ached.

Then I heard the venom extracted in every word Todd spoke, "Listen up, you fucking human waste. You have one chance to understand this. We are finished. In less than six months, it will be final. You come within twenty feet of her, and I will make your life hell. You are nothing to me. If you think your games here tonight are going to stop us, you — as always — lose. Go drink your bottle of vodka and smoke your crack or pop your pills. I am done. You are no longer my obligation."

Unfazed, she looked at him as a grin crept along her mouth line. "Baby, we will never be done. I like her. This is going to be fun."

What the hell did that mean? She glared at me. "He always had great taste in women. I look forward to sharing you soon."

She went to touch me, and Todd violently stopped her hand motion. "Get the fuck out of here. I own this club solely and control the riff-raff I want to keep out, and you Ms. Williams, are no longer welcome here."

Todd summoned Jesse. "Please escort Ms. Williams and her party off the premises. I heard they brought illegal drugs in and distributed them in my VIP lounge. Call Curtis down at police headquarters and have him fill out another report."

Jesse waved his hand for her to follow as she laughed. She turned for a second. "Those drugs attract your crowd as do I. She's cute, baby, but you will be nothing without me. See you at home later. I'll keep our bed warm." She sneered at me. "You're temporary, just like all the others. Get used to it."

The only thing that I was registering now was that she never took his name. Todd even referred to her as Ms. Williams. If there was any hope I was holding onto, it was the fact that she never took his name. Todd was fed up with her, and I think he was defending me as best he could with her. "You're the one that's temporary. Go back to Canada, you drug-addicted drunken whore."

The Dating Policy

I officially wanted out of this toxic web of disaster. She was way more than I wanted to deal with as far as an ex goes. I knew nothing about this sort of animosity since I was still friendly and cordial with all my past boyfriends.

Angela was texting me: *Why are we not allowed up?*

I texted back, shaking: *The wife is up here and being escorted off the premises. You'll see her in a few seconds.*

Yup, here she is, she answered.

Just hang tight for a minute, I replied.

Got ya back, sista, she texted.

Todd poured wine into the glass that was in front of me. He turned in my direction, worried about what I just went through as he touched my clenched hand, soothing it as he encouraged me to release my grip and trust him.

I saw the value of trust written all over his expression while he guided my hand to support the alcohol, he was holding for me.

It was a minimal peace offering and more of an understanding of what I had just witnessed.

He looked so concerned. "I am sorry for that repulsive display. First, I will tell you. Never have I brought another woman into play. That was all an act on her part. Maybe that's what she does when she is out partying. I don't even care. Nor has she known of the few times I've ventured away. That was also an act. I thought marriage was going to be different. It was a big disappointment, but not a mistake. I benefitted a great deal from it businesswise."

He put his hand over mine and took his own sip from our now communal glass of wine. He offered me a sip, but I was too rattled.

I softly spoke, feeling the internal battle of leaving on my own or seeing this through tonight, "No, thank you."

I was still in a battle with my own thoughts.

Then he went on, "Let's just start now, ignore what just happened for a moment, and let's start fresh right now... I haven't said this for a very long, long time. We can't erase what just happened, and this is probably not the best time to say this, but... I love you, Mallory." He looked intently at me.

I now controlled the glass and took a gulp of wine. I froze and looked from him to the glass because I didn't know why I did that. I excused myself for doing it because I thought that was probably rude of me.

He smiled. "Hey, if you downed the glass, I would have understood."

I shook my head. "Todd, no... I just need to say this right. I think, for the first time in my life, that I am in love too... with you. When you leave me, I feel empty and can't wait to see you again. I want you in bed. I want to spend as much time as I can with you, and it is frustrating as hell. My emotions are all over the map.

Sometimes, I don't even remember my ride home because I am preoccupied with thinking about you."

He lowered his head, then raised it. "Can I be with you tonight? I mean sleep over tonight?"

This was again... a whole new can of worms. He had just declared his love to me, and I found my way to finally say those words to someone I did love. That I was falling in love with, that came with some unresolved issues. Oh, God... the wife! We were going to have a big conversation about her very soon.

His saving grace was how he handled her in front of me. I knew he was done with the marriage. "Mallory? If you're not comfortable, I understand."

"Oh, I'm sorry, Todd. Of course, I want you to sleep over. Yes, I would like that very much."

He grinned. "If I stay work is going to be a challenge unless you let me bring more clothes."

I managed to chuckle. What the hell were we going to do about work? "I think we need to make a plan for work."

"I don't see work being an issue other than me not having enough suits at your house."

"Really? Because I see work as being a huge issue! It's my job, Todd, my only source of income."

"I'll let you in on something, babe. Nicholas Williams bought SBS."

I shot up and off the sofa. "What?" I needed cold air. "This is a fucking disaster!" I took a few water bottles out of the ice bucket and rested them against my neck. Todd was studying me.

"Mallory, this isn't a bad thing. It's a good thing... let me explain. Please, come here and sit back down."

I cracked open one of the bottles and drank half of it down. Oh, that felt so much better. He took ahold of my elbow and gently guided me back to the couch. "I know this is a lot of information and a lot to deal with after the scene that just happened."

He looked at his phone and answered it, "Give us ten more minutes. Introduce them around the VIP."

"Who was that?" I asked

"Jesse, about Angela and the prick she's with."

"Oh, my God, I forgot they were waiting to come up." I quickly picked up my phone to two missed texts.

"Don't worry. I have them all set up. I want to talk to you for a minute." I finished the other half of the water bottle. "Nicholas has been looking for a supply house for some time. He is getting into tract housing."

"What is that?"

"Housing developments in which multiple similar homes are built on a tract of land then subdivided into individual small lots."

"Oh, I know what that is. I just never heard that term you called it."

He nodded. "I have been working with Nicholas for the past twenty months on this. There was a reason I was hired at SBS. Old man Frank wants to retire, and I was sent in to see if this was a strong enough acquisition for Williams Enterprises. Papers were just signed. It will be announced in another month or so as everything starts to transition."

"Do I still have a job?"

Todd finally relaxed, acknowledging my disposition, and grinned. "It will still hold the SBS name, and everyone has their jobs. You were the final recommendation for the success of the company. After you were moved to management, it was a done deal."

"What? Did you give me that job?" Now, he went all serious on me because as soon as I said it, I remembered this conversation was already done and resolved.

Todd was angry... "No, I did not give you that job. You earned that job all on your own. You are an asset to that sales department, and everyone knows it. Your position was created with a goal this company was lacking, and the decision to put you in charge was decided by the whole board of new owners and present owners."

I felt a new sinking feeling. "So, Nicholas Williams has seen my work stats?" Todd laughed with joy. "Yes, and he's very impressed with you."

"Yeah, well, I'm screwed. Just wait until he finds out I'm sleeping with his daughter's husband."

A grin of satisfaction morphed into place on Todd's face, and he announced with pride, "He likes me better than his daughter. I make him money. She makes him lose money."

"And I am the tramp in between." Nothing could explain my position better. He found a positive twist and laughed. "Yeah, but you're my tramp that I happen to love."

He reconfirmed that he loved me, then sealed my lips in a kiss. "It's going to be all right, love. Oh, and that dating policy you are worried about is gone. We just have to lay low until the announcement." He was not going to let me overthink this.

I challenged him, "And is sleeping over at my house lying low?" Todd was clearly debating how to answer me.

"Well, you don't live next to the office. I don't see why it wouldn't be. I mean, you can sleep at my place, but I don't think you'd like my neighbor very much." I laughed.

He was so right. His quick wit was refreshing, and something I relied on to keep me on my toes. I knew his neighbor was the psycho soon-to-be ex whom I just unfortunately met. "So, now that Odessa knows what I look like… what do we do now?"

"What do you mean?"

"Todd, she knows what I look like." He raised an eyebrow and remarked. "Don't let her kiss you. I'll be pissed."

"What? What kind of answer is that!"

He laughed, clearly amused. "Well, apparently, she insinuated that she wants to fuck you."

"Seriously? That is not funny!" He was such an ass. He laughed even harder; he was amused, thinking of what had transpired.

"Sorry, babe. I thought that was kind of funny. You don't have to do anything. She is nothing. Are you good now?"

I opened the other water bottle and took a few sips. "Yeah, I'm fine… Angela, damn it. How long have we been talking?"

"Relax, babe; she's having a great time. She is happily socializing with Alex Bradley."

"Who is he?"

"Catcher for the game we're watching tomorrow."

"Oh, are we still going?"

"Oh, hell yeah." I liked how he answered that. "Come on, woman. Let's go get your friend."

"Okay, but I have to tell you; I'm actually ready to go."

"Are you sure?"

"Yes, I'm sure. Angela is right. I am a homebody. This whole evening was a little too much for one date in public." He moved a strand of hair off my face.

"I know, and I apologize again. By the way, I love that you are low-key."

I compromised, "How about we go meet Angela and stay for one drink, then go home?"

"Whatever you want, Mallory; I just want to be wherever you are tonight."

Todd was correct. Angela was very happy talking to Alex. She introduced us to Alex, who was very into anything Angela was doing and saying. He said hello to Todd and asked him directly, like old friends, why he hadn't met Angela before.

Todd introduced me as his girlfriend, and as I saw that Alex knew Todd better than I thought, he moved his curious attention to us. Just as promised, we stayed for one drink, picked up my car, and then went back to my place.

This whole day wore me out. Todd and I went to bed; he must have read how exhausted and drained I felt. I think my phone vibrated on the nightstand, but I was too far gone to check. A text from Thomas came through that stated: *Your boyfriend is married. At least I can give you a clean slate.*

The Dating Policy

I drifted as I felt Todd texting and communicating with several devices. His warmth and scent filled so many satisfactions, soothing my soul, and creating total bliss; he pulled me against him and kissed the top of my head.

I didn't even remember falling asleep. I did remember waking up... there was no goodnight sex. As soon as I moved, he was on me. "Good morning, gorgeous," he started, spreading my legs. "My dick is throbbing for you, your scent, and your touch. I am so fucking attracted to you."

He scooted down between my legs and dove right in with the licking. Then he added moaning and longer licks with soft suckling. That was it. I tried to pry his head away as I shattered into an orgasm. Todd straightened up, pulled me down a little by my hips, hovered over me, and penetrated. He was talking sex as he angled deeper into me. This man was on a mission — describing what he was feeling by working himself in me. This was not just sex; this was a sexual experience. I've never had anything like this before, especially to his level.

I had a blip signal my brain; I thought that this was a little unfair. He was doing all the work, and I was just lying there not being a team player. I changed my strategy. I went for it, and I began to work with him on the same page. I pushed up against him, giving him more thrusting action. He looked into my eyes. "That is so good, baby. I can feel you riding my dick." He lowered almost on top of me, and now I was able to hold his very firm ass. I pulled him deeper and held him there as he pushed with smaller pulses. I did not think this was possible.

It has only happened once before with him, but I was going to come again, and he knew it. "That's right, babe. I am going to blow my load inside of you. Cum for me, gorgeous. Same time..." That was enough to set me off, and we climaxed together. Todd was such a powerhouse. I felt as if I was the luckiest woman on this planet... that was until his phone went off.

Again, I knew that song but couldn't place it. He pulled out and kissed me quickly, apologizing that he needed to take the call. He leaped out of bed, grabbed his phone, and turned into the all-business Todd. He even closed the bedroom door as he exited it. I wanted to care and be concerned, but I had just had not one, but two... shattering orgasms, leaving me beyond mellow, happy, and very relaxed. So relaxed, I pulled the blanket back over me and settled on the spot he slept in because his scent still lingered, then I closed my eyes.

For the second time this morning, I had not realized I had fallen asleep until I felt him caress my face and kiss the top of my head. I sleepily opened my eyes, feeling like my prince had finally arrived.

Todd had showered, dressed, and complimented me on how beautiful I looked. Well, that caught my attention; I sat up to him explaining that he had to go, but he reassured me that we were still going to the ball game this afternoon.

He referred to his new issue as "a situation," and said he would keep in touch. He made sure I had my bat phone, kissed me, and left. There was no time for questioning or an explanation. It all happened that fast. It had to have been because of "the wife."

I really can't stand his "situation!" Just as all the confusion settled and I was deciding how I was going to approach this, a text appeared on the bat phone: *I told you how beautiful you were this morning; let me add... I love you.*

Okay then... he just texted that. I now had it in writing. I didn't care what the fuck she was up to. I was good, and I would leave him to deal with her without overthinking it.

I texted back: *I love you too... looking forward to our afternoon.*

He immediately answered: *I will make it special.*

I smiled because I felt so good about seeing him this afternoon and texted: *Just spending time together is special enough.*

I received one more text: *Can I sleep over tonight? We have work tomorrow... so you decide.*

I took a deep breath and replied: *Yes.*

He made a smiley face and answered: *I'm bringing more clothes...*

Okay, that was a reality. This morning, I had to figure out more of the closet logistics... what was I willing to give up in space?

I was single... It had been well over a year since I had lived with anyone. I surveyed the area, rolled up my sleeves, and began.

Todd called for the fourth time, clearly annoyed, and apologized. He was sending a driver to pick me up. Now, I was wondering what the hell was going on.

My new boyfriend sent a car and driver to pick me up. My driver's name was Bill, an older yet very personable man. He kept me engaged in conversation from the moment of picking me up to dropping me in the underground garage where another attendant opened my door and addressed me by my name. It was a little intimidating, to say the least. I was not used to this treatment at all. This was the kind of thing my mother fed on, and I was not sure I was a fan.

We arrived at the deck, and there was Todd, leaning over the rail, dressed in jeans and a cream linen shirt, wearing a baseball cap backward. He was on the phone with someone but turned in our direction as my escort presented me to him.

Chapter Ten

Todd was ending the call as he reached out and shook my escort's hand, thanking him. Todd stepped closer to me with a big hello kiss. I liked this look on Todd. He almost blended in as a regular guy. Right into it, not wasting a moment, he tried to apologize for this morning, and as much as I wanted to get into it with him, I decided I didn't want the burden of knowing right now.

That could ruin this afternoon for us. I simply gave him a soft kiss and said we would talk about it later and we needed to have a good afternoon. He brushed some strands of hair off my face and kissed me again, completely understanding. He took my hand into his and said, "Okay, babe. Come on; I want you to meet a couple of friends of mine."

What? I was not ready for this! No... no additional people! I just wanted it to be the two of us, to talk and have a semi-normal date.

He led me to his "Duvall table," and there were two couples seated. Everyone watched us approach, and I feared that they had all known Odessa for years.

I looked up at him; there was a proud grin on Todd's face as he introduced me to one of his longtime friends from college, Joe Whitman, and his wife Amanda, and then Mark Riel and his wife, Louise.

I was introduced as, "This is my girlfriend, Mallory." I wanted to curl up and disappear. I now knew they had all lived through the Odessa years and knew "the wife" very intimately, and that he was still married to her. The men exchanged a warm welcome with me; the wives were... expressionless but polite.

That was fine with me; they were nothing to me. I had Todd, and he was now really trying to bring me into his world. I felt much better about this relationship. I wasn't the mistress anymore. I had crossed over to being the girlfriend.

Todd's familiar bucket was already on the table, and the seated wives had already helped themselves to all the limoncello, with the empty carafe placed between them. Todd kissed the side of my head, asking what I wanted. I scanned the contents of the bucket, too nervous to ask for more of that lemon beverage and offered a compromise. "How about the Chardonnay, is there one left?"

Louise poked through, casually and slowly, pulling a single size bottle up encased in ice, chilling her fingers, and stating, "This is too much work," looking over at Amanda as she agreed with her.

Todd stopped Louise from any further action. "Hell, no! That won't do for my woman." He glanced around and spotted Holly, waving her over. She dropped what she was doing, wiping her hands on her long apron, smiling as she came to us.

"Hello, Mr. Duvall." She scanned all of us, singling me out, "Oh, I remember you, sweetheart. You and your girlfriend were here. It's lovely to see you again."

"Holly, this is my girlfriend, Mallory; get used to seeing her. We're going to be spending a lot of time here this season." Todd paused to wink at me. "Can you bring us a bottle of La Crema and two stemless glasses, please?"

I was not aware of my jaw dropping as Todd gave it a gentle touch with the tips of his fingers, setting my mouth shut and kissing me right on the lips in front of everyone. "Certainly, Mr. Duvall," she scanned the table. "Anything else?"

Before anyone could answer, he said, "That will be all for now. Thank you, Holly."

Louise rested the wine on top of the ice and started talking to Amanda again, ignoring the rest of us.

Todd pulled my chair closer to him and rested his arm on my back. Joe and Mark engaged in conversation about the land that Williams Construction had just purchased. I learned that Mark was a contractor. I asked him who he bought his supplies from, and it was from our company. I was surprised I had never heard his name.

Apparently, he was one of Ned and Bill's shared clients. He was handled by management since he was an over three-million-dollar purchaser and paid his bills on time. He had two construction companies. One, he managed through Williams Enterprises, and the other one sounded like a property management company.

Mark looked like he was trying to understand something.

Todd confessed, "Mallory works in sales there. She's the newest member of the management team."

Mark glanced from me to Todd and back. "Mallory... Kennedy?"

"Yes," I said, curious that he knew my last name. Then a mischievous little-boy grin spread across his face as he was really trying not to show any emotion.

He looked at Todd, who was sporting a similar grin as Mark said, "You old hound dog," right to Todd.

Joe grinned too.

"Okay, fellas. What did I miss?" I just put it out there in the middle of their man-cave moment. I knew my brother, and I knew his buddies and could recognize when some secret code thing was going on.

Joe spoke up. "Nothing, Mallory, it's good to meet you finally." Oh... okay... Obviously, they knew about me before I knew about Todd and our relationship coming to fruition. I saw this as a good sign that he had buddies, and he talked to them about me.

I heard Amanda tell Louise that Odessa wanted to have lunch with them this week. I could tell that everyone else heard that too.

My boyfriend briefly clenched his hands, then leaped into action, kissing my forehead and excusing himself. "Amanda, I need your assistance a moment." We all watched Todd getting up, then striding right to Amanda, who was trying to figure out what was going on. He took control and grasped Amanda's arm while he spoke to me. "I'll be right back, love." Joe looked confused as to what he should do.

If no one got that damn message loud and clear, then they were just stupid. He walked up the stairs with Amanda to the top deck. Beers were grabbed all at once from the bucket and opened. Louise even pulled the wine resting on top and cracked it and poured it into her glass. She looked a little shaken.

Mark leaned into her, saying something as she focused on Amanda's empty seat and nodded in agreement. Mark then turned to me and went for a distraction technique and asked who else I knew in construction. When I listed my clientele, he actually broke out in laughter, in sympathy. This opened up a whole new comfort level, at least with him and me. Joe was the real estate guy, and his dealings with some of my customers also intertwined us as a group.

Todd was not gone long, but it was clear he had words with Amanda. She remained silent when she arrived back to the table. Joe turned his head toward his wife and whispered something in her ear. She shook her head and stated, "I will stay."

Our wine arrived, and my boyfriend kissed me right on the lips while he held my chin, then released it. He assured me that I was going to like this brand, and we were going to enjoy our night together. He added, saying a little louder than he usually spoke, that he was driving us home, so there were no worries. If I noticed that, everyone noticed that.

I was watching both of the other couples. Joe was the real-estate point man. He was expendable. Any realtor could take over for him, provided nothing was signed. I knew Mark had a stake in Williams Enterprises. He scheduled the jobs from start to finish, but he also had his own business, so I wondered if he was allowed to bid separately. I was going to do some research on Mark because I was curious now how this all worked.

Many of my clients explained how they won their bids, and I sometimes even knew whom they were bidding against. A crazy racket this was. I always remained neutral. I understood the bidding wars and the bidding fixing wars.

I suddenly saw Mark's position in this whole scheme of things. That was when Louise started to engage in a conversation with me. This was becoming more interesting. I loved the wine. I loved Todd's attention, and I had figured out the playing field among the men.

I decided to trump Odessa tonight. I owned this table right now. I was the future, and my boyfriend had my back. This was my launch. "To SBS and the future of the company. Hopefully, we will be profitable all around. I'll do what I can to make our partnership stronger." Todd gloated like a proud partner. That was the only validation I needed. All four adults were watching me. The husbands gave their approval as the wives had seen what and where I was coming from. The rest of the night, the conversations were only between the men and me.

The wives drank from the bucket or ate their meals with minimal interaction. I noticed that they texted a lot... probably where their conversion continued. Screw them... they were nothing to me. My poor boyfriend had arranged a social "get to know my friends" get together, and it was becoming a flop.

He was my first goal. I straddled him, ignoring our table, and I told him I loved him, and I loved that he had done this for us. I then told him that women could be self-goal-oriented, and I would work on fixing this so all of us would be more comfortable. He insisted it was not necessary, but I assured him it was to maintain a smooth environment among all of us. He actually rolled his eyes at me. I laughed enough that he had to support me, straddling his lap.

Todd and I were a team. I truly felt like his girlfriend, and we had each other's best interest at heart. Wow, to be in love and have this... I couldn't help but kiss him like it was our last. Oops, too much for this crowd. My boyfriend preened, basking in the attention from me and completely approving it.

It wasn't until I saw Angela's picture on the big screen that I actually realized we were almost at the end of our game. Todd laughed and said she was in the wives and girlfriends' section for the players. He filled my glass with two innings left, and we excused ourselves. I could not wait to get to her. Todd held my hand and led me down. No-one stopped us or questioned us.

We reached Angela, and she screamed, jumping up to hug me first, then Todd, which caught him by surprise. He invited her back to the deck with us. She didn't know what she should do since Alex had asked her to attend.

That was it. Todd walked to the fence and called for Alex. He walked over, and they were talking. He gave Angela the thumbs up with a wink. Todd returned and told Angela we were taking custody of her.

Alex was going to meet us in the garage at the after-party. After-party? We returned to the Duvall table with one more female to level out the odds. Amanda and Louise were nothing against my gorgeous little Italian powerhouse. Todd sat her right between himself and Amanda's husband. Joe and Mark were very interested in talking to Angela for the rest of the game.

I was quite sure that Todd had a reason for this strategy, and I was going to bring it up as well when we got home. I grinned, thinking about that. My life living with this success-driven, passionate, loving, possessive, delicious-smelling sexual god... Where do I sign my life away? I want a pen.

The Dating Policy

My darling Angela was a hit with the men but not with the wives. He proved his point. Good, good boyfriend! We delivered Angela back to her date, Alex. There was something there... Angela was into him.

Todd and I drove home as several texts appeared from Thomas. Todd was very curious while I halfheartedly read the first. He asked openly who was texting me. I told him it was Thomas while rolling my eyes from boredom. He asked if he could see.

I willingly handed over my phone, not caring who called or texted me tonight. This satisfied Todd with a whole new level of security between us. He retrieved several suits in garment carriers from the trunk of his car, then asked me to grab his duffel bag. I did and laughed at how heavy it was. He intercepted my keys from me to open my door; he asked what it took to earn the privilege of possessing one of these.

I replied, "A divorce."

He retaliated, "Already in order. And what if I exchanged one of mine for one of yours?"

I agreed. That was a fair trade. My boyfriend wrote his address and the security combinations and kissed me as he handed me a key to his place that was across from his soon-to-be ex-wife's. I opened a cabinet that held all my spare keys. I pulled out my second front door key, grabbed the spare garage door remote, and kissed him, handing them over. For a nanosecond, I saw relief in his expression.

That brought me satisfaction. I led him upstairs and dropped his duffel bag where his new "space" was assigned. I had even cleaned out a drawer in my bathroom cabinet for him, plus a dresser drawer.

While he unpacked, I listened to the trouble that Odessa was capable of and what he had to deal with today right up to his private conversation with Amanda when he summoned her away from the table. Todd was more forthcoming than I ever expected, which put a huge value on him in my perspective. Tonight, was all about the cuddle. He made no advances as I quietly fell asleep, wrapped in his arms. My new boyfriend wakes up at five in the morning on a workday. Ugh! I gave him what he needed... sex.

What I did not expect was he told me to pack some clothes. Tonight, we were spending the night at his place. We took separate cars. I was having major anxiety. His place was right across from his still legally married wife!

We arrived at work at the same time and parked next to each other. Todd got out and kissed me before we headed to the door. Then I remembered the work policy and no one knowing about the takeover.

"Hey, cool it on public displays of affection at work... remember?"

He chuckled. "I don't give a shit about that anymore. Listen, though. I have a busy day... not likely we'll cross paths today, so you be a good girl while you're away from me, okay?"

I grinned. "I will try to stay out of trouble." He slapped my ass. "Hey," I pointed at him. "That is not appropriate work behavior, Mr. Duvall. Hands to yourself, please."

He just narrowed his eyes and cocked his brows at me with a slight grin. "Be ready for me tonight. I am going to fuck you hard in my bed."

I blushed. "And that is definitely not a proper exchange while at work." He smiled as we reached the door. He opened it for me.

"You know how to contact me, babe, if you need me."

"Yup." I badly wanted to kiss him, and it felt like I was being denied. He nodded.

"You are going to have to wait — work hours... remember?" He was such a damn tease. He opened the door to my department, then nodded. "Talk to you later, babe."

"Okey-doke, roommate." He grinned as he turned back to me.

"I like that. I think that's how I'll introduce you from now on."

I gasped and turned to him as the door closed. There were a few people here and, just as I was turning, Ned was walking in. He looked stern.

"Good morning, Mallory."

"Oh, hi, Ned. How was your weekend?"

"Fine, can I talk to you for a moment?"

"Um... sure. Just let me put my things in my office."

"Okay."

Now, Jessica was sneering at me. "Can you just stop leading Thomas on!"

"What!" Oh, my gosh? Where was this coming from? That's all I could manage to say in reaction to this fucked up conversation.

"Thomas says you keep breaking your dates with him."

WHAT!! I could not have been more confused "I have not made a date with him, Jessica!"

She rolled her eyes. "Okay, Mallory, keep him on standby; just see where that gets you!"

I couldn't deal with this crazy-ass woman right now as I stormed away from her, fuming all the way to my office. Wow, Ned watched me with a scowl on his face and called my name in an irritated manner. Clearly, he too had a problem with me this Monday morning. I made him wait while I dumped my bags on my office chair, closing my door partially behind me, then squared my shoulders for whatever he could possibly have to say. I walked in confidently, not confrontationally, and he directed me to have a seat. He closed the door behind me, then sat on the edge of his desk in front of me. I had no idea what this was about, and suddenly, I became suspicious. He drew it out, not knowing how to move forward. "Is it Sean?" I panicked at the idea, for a moment completely changing my mood.

"No, sorry, no, Sean is fine. I'm concerned about you."

"Me?" I let out a breath of relief. "I'm good, Ned. Why are you worried about me?"

He looked me sternly in the eyes. "What is your relationship with Todd Duvall?"

Whoa! "Why are you asking me that?"

"Because you arrived together, he came over and kissed you, then slapped your ass as you were walking in."

I knew from the sudden adrenalin rush of body heat that we had been caught, and I was blushing. It wasn't very professional of me to give away my emotions like this. I cleared my throat as my heart rate pounded rapidly in my chest. "It's none of your business," I was able to chirp out.

"Mallory, I care about you as if you were my own little sister. Stay away from him. He is trouble."

"Don't tell me what to do. You do not have that authority, Ned. I don't care who you are. My personal life is my personal life."

"Mallory, he's married! And believe me, he is well taken care of with her family, and he will never leave her for you."

"Fuck you, Ned. You don't know anything about him." I was mad as hell that he said that to me. He had just stated that I was of lower value than money and Todd would never choose me. Karen did that too. I was beside myself with anger. They didn't know us, his situation, but they both pointed out I was not worth it.

"Mallory, the last company he worked for, he was let go because he had fucked an employee, and she brought up sexual harassment charges against him."

I gasped and looked right into Ned's eyes. Everything in me just shattered. My life just stopped. I judged that he was telling me the truth as tears started to swell in my eyes. I did not know anything about that. I wanted to puke, faint, and cry all at the same time. I think my heart actually stopped as a tightening feeling encased my neck. Ned softened. "I am sorry, Mallory. I just don't want to see you get hurt."

I needed to leave... right now. There was no way I could get through work today. I ran out of his office and grabbed my bags, then grabbed my door and shut it harder than I wanted to. Ned was coming after me as he tried to approach me again. "Mallory, stay; don't run."

I choked back the tears that were ready to stream down my face. "Fuck you, Ned. Tell them I'm going home sick." I left as quickly as I could. I looked at Todd's car parked next to mine, and I wanted to kick it. Do something malicious to leave a mark just as his life was leaving a mark on me right now.

I couldn't hold the tears back any longer, and they were now streaming down my face as more and more people were arriving for work. I held it together as best I could on my drive home, wiping my face every few seconds.

How could I have been so stupid? I was a pattern in his married life. I was just the "next" girl. I bet Odessa was right and I was the next plaything. Ned and Karen were right. Why would he leave me when he could have anyone?

I felt numb when I arrived home. I dropped my bags on my table, went up to my bedroom, climbed into bed, and curled up in a ball. I had nothing left in me. His pillow still carried his scent from last night and, as it hit my nostrils, I grabbed ahold of something I was never going to have and started bawling uncontrollably.

A text was coming through: *How you ended up content with dating a married man, I will never figure out. Consider a single guy as your best choice.* Thomas only made me cry. How did I let this happen? At some point, I fell asleep.

"Mallory, Mallory, what happened? Babe, wake up." I opened my eye. I wasn't sure where I was or what was going on. I turned, looking back around, registering my bedroom and knew I was laying down in bed and that I was home. Todd waited at the edge of my bed. "Hey, what happened? You're not answering the phone. I found out you left because you got sick today, but your makeup proves you've been crying. What is going on?"

I managed to sit up and looked him over. He was in the suit he left my house in this morning. Well, I started crying again. He tried to soothe me, but I didn't want anything to do with him. When he realized I was pushing him away, he asked, "Okay, what the fuck is going on? What happened?" He was pissed now, and so was I.

I thought the fair thing to do was see if he could explain. I wiped my eyes and told him what happened in Ned's office. He transformed to the Todd who became judge and jury when he needed to find out exactly who had fucked up... he was seething mad. He flexed his hands a few times, closed his eyes, controlled his breathing for a minute, and I think he was trying to count internally because the slight movements from the different shapes of his mouth permitted a hint of a possible anger control technique.

I was a little scared. When he opened his eyes, he spoke clearly and articulately in low tones. "Do not believe everything people tell you," was his first statement. Then he tried to soften, unsuccessfully. "Ned was out of line telling you that. He needs to check his facts. That is not what happened at all. I was working at another one of Nicholas's companies. I work wherever Nicholas sends me. There were problems in the company. I was there for a year and came up with the solution. It was two years ago, by the way, and in New York City. It was New Year's Eve, and I went to a charity event party that was a very high-status social evening. The wife had to make an appearance, of course. She was on pills and mixed her vodka with them. I was furious, but that is who she is. I had to send her home and stay on to make the rounds that Nicholas expected me to meet at this event; we were in the middle of a large acquisition, and I was expected to play nice with certain key management. Later in the night, when all my obligations were done, this woman came up to me, very friendly, very willing, and very eager to get laid. I told you I had a couple of one-night stands. She was one of them. I didn't know who she was, and I ended up with her in the coatroom. That was it. 'Wham Bam, thank you, ma'am,' and we went our separate ways. I didn't even know her name."

I leaned back, bracing myself, horrified that he was disclosing this to me. "I hope you used a damn condom!"

He softened. "Of course, I did, and believe me, I am not enjoying disclosing this to you at all, but that fucker Ned has set this in motion, and you will hear me out, damn it!" Todd took a breath and continued. "About a month later, when I was wrapping up my job there, I found out the company was being sued because of me and a sexual harassment case that was filed. I was obviously unaware. I found out that the woman who came onto me that night at the event worked at the company. I had never seen her a day that I was there. Anyway, long story short, I was set up. It was proven it was a setup. The facility at the charity where it was hosted had surveillance, and we used the video footage.

We found footage at work that showed she was stalking me, going through my desk after hours. I ended up getting a restraining order on her, and it was thrown out of court. She will never be able to work for one of Nicholas's companies ever again, in lieu of me not pressing charges. I tell you, that was, in itself, a hard pill for me to swallow. Nicholas insisted on that ruling, and I haven't figured out why to this day. I was able to take a summer off for having to deal with that shit. Then, SBS came on the radar. We worked out the strategy for six months before I was positioned. I came on board, and I took one look at you, and I knew you were going to be trouble. You were a genuine distraction, and I also knew if I detected any signal from you that there could possibly be an interest in me, you were going to be mine. I wanted you, and that day you collided into me, I knew you were mine."

I was crying again. I was also feeling like an ass for letting Ned get into my head. Todd pulled me over and kissed the top of my head. "New rule between us, Mallory. Do not believe what people tell you, and if you are in doubt, always ask me. I will tell you everything, whether I want to or not. I will never lie to you, and I hope you will never lie to me. I want our word to be the strongest bond we have between each other, okay?"

I latched onto him. I felt like an idiot. Never have I acted like this with any guy. He wrapped his arms around me just as hard, kissing the top of my head... confirming that I was the only woman he wanted, loved, and wanted a future with.

Well, it was three-thirty. Todd told me to pack for his place. So, I grabbed his duffel bag and loaded some of my stuff into it.

He informed me that my car was staying here. He had another car I could use if I needed to do anything on my own. He then warned me he had two stops to make on our way to his place. I refreshed my zombie-looking tear-stained makeup to look smarter and sharper. I was a woman who let a man take me down. This was not going to happen again. I needed to toughen up being with Todd. Of course, people didn't like him; trying to break us up was going to be a mission with certain people.

I had to trust him and be confident in our relationship, to know and feel he had my best interests at heart always. He remarked that I looked much better now. I was beautiful. He took his duffel packed with my clothes as I grabbed my work bags, then off we went. I did not expect the first stop to be a jewelry store.

He took my hand, and we were greeted right away. "Mr. Duvall, how nice to see you today. What can I do for you?"

"Hello, Victoria. This is my girlfriend, Mallory. I want to buy her a ring." I must have looked shocked because she smiled. Then I thought... how many times has he been in here that she knows him personally and who the heck else is he buying jewelry for?

"What kind of ring did you have in mind?"

"Something very sparkly that everyone will see."

She lightly laughed pleasantly. "I can certainly help you with that." She extended her hand to me. "Come this way, my dear. What are your preferences?"

"I don't wear jewelry. I have no clue."

She smiled. "Well, it looks like your boyfriend is going to change that situation." She brought me over to a mixed diamond and precious stone collection. I loved them all, suddenly feeling like I was picking out something foreign to me, and it was. I never even looked at jewelry.

Todd wrapped his arm around my waist. "See anything you like?"

"All of them. But how does Victoria know you by name?" I asked a little defensively.

He chuckled. "I have a bit of a cufflink addiction. It's better I get that out now before you find out on your own."

He made Victoria laugh. "The cat's out of the bag now, Mr. Duvall. You might have just lost her."

I looked at him, very amused, "Seriously? You are such a pretty boy."

He shrugged. "It's all in the details. But enough about my secrets; let's get back to why we are here today."

Victoria pulled out a sapphire-and-diamond mixed setting. It was beautiful. She asked, "Which finger are we dressing up?"

Todd answered, "Right hand, middle finger. My girl needs a power ring for when assholes try and throw her off-target; she will have something to remind her to keep strong and on task as she flips them off."

I burst out laughing. That was the most hilarious, most amazing thing I ever heard. He was dead serious, and I loved him for that as I turned around to kiss him. Victoria laughed as well. "Well, this is a new concept. I might just have to use this for future marketing."

Within twenty minutes, Todd and I had picked out my new power ring. I wore it out of the store, my brain dancing on cloud nine. He opened my door. "Show me, baby." I flipped him off as he admired and grinned. "Perfect." I kissed him swiftly and smiled like an idiot to our next stop. We pulled up to the valet in front of a huge glass skyscraper. Todd took my hand and pulled me from my seat and into the building. He dropped my hand once inside and moved it to my lower back to guide me along. People knew him in here. He was being nodded at in greeting, and a lot of people were noticing me. We went right to the very last elevator, and Todd slid a credit card into a slot. At least it looked like a credit card.

"What is that?"

He tucked it back in his pocket. "My 'get out of jail free' card."

"Your what?" He just smirked as the doors opened, and he guided me inside. "Todd, what is this place?"

"Northeast headquarters."

"Northeast headquarters to what?"

"Williams Enterprises."

I braced myself against the wall. "WHAT?"

"I want you to meet Nicholas."

"No... no, no, no, no. This is not a good idea. No, no, I can't!" Oh, now I wanted to throw up.

"It's fine, Mallory. He knows we're together."

"WHAT? This is not good. No, not good at all. I can't do this, Todd."

He cocked his head slightly, looking at me. "I've got you, babe. It's fine. Besides, I am taking you to a corporate event this weekend. So, it's better you meet him now."

"WHAT? I can't do this." The elevator stopped, and I was frozen, still bracing myself to the wall. Todd pried my hands from the wall and started to pull me.

"Mallory, you are being ridiculous. Stop this right now." I let him lead me. People were staring. I must have had a huge red-letter A all over me. I was the girlfriend of the owner's daughter's husband. I was petrified while Todd guided me by my backside. We walked to the very end of the hall, and he opened the door to another reception area. A very polished older woman looked up. "I don't have you on the schedule, Todd. What can I help you with?"

"I just want Nicholas to meet Mallory." He was as cool as a cucumber. I was physically shaking. He took a mint from the bowl and unwrapped it for me. "Here, babe. This will help." Before he put it in my mouth, my hand started to function, so I grasped it from him, recovering some dignity with this wakened nightmare unfolding second by second here at Williams Enterprises. He grinned quite amused, while ever so slightly shaking his head side to side. Mrs. Benoit put the phone down and asked us to wait over there, pointing to the seating area.

"Mr. Williams will be out in a minute," she announced. Well, my very bad boyfriend could not do as he was told and started some small talk with Mrs. Benoit. I was stuck standing there as he conversed. Todd was so good about including me that he made me answer when I wanted just to die right here, right now. Mrs. Benoit was very polite in engaging in Todd's conversation until a door opened behind her. Out walked a very fit, fair-skinned, above average height, mature man.

Odessa's facial outline was the spitting image of her father, only the petite version. She had all his features, but her skin was olive-colored, and now I really wanted to die. Nicholas Williams grinned immediately, seeing Todd. "My boy," was how he greeted him.

Then he looked at me with an equally big greeting. "Mallory Kennedy." He came at me with his hand extended. "I've heard a lot about you, my dear. Please, come in."

Nicholas snarked at Todd, "Good for you, son." He gave Todd a hearty pat on his shoulder. We walked in, and his office had a wall of pictures of his family.

It looked like Nicholas had four children. His wife was an exotic beauty, very Egyptian-looking. I was fixated on the photos, especially of the one of Odessa which was staring at me in her father's office. Todd called my name as I tore my eye from hers in the photo.

He and Nicholas were talking over a very large-scale development model. I turned, and there was the whole miniature version of what the developments would look like with the tract housing. It was beautiful; there must have been a thousand units here. Nicholas looked up at me. "Do you think you can handle this, Mallory?" I looked down. I spread my hands out over it.

"All of this?"

Todd answered, "It's a ten-year plan, babe. You'll be fine." He just called me babe in front of his father-in-law. Bad... bad... boyfriend!

Nicholas was watching me. "Mallory, please relax. My daughter and Todd are not together. The marriage... I was hoping it could last, but I cannot continue to put my son through the pain and agony my daughter inflicts on all of us. She is an addict. We've tried everything. The only thing I can do now is to try and keep her safe. I'm not going to lose Todd because of this. He is everything I hoped for from a son. Just to be clear on what I am about to say, he is divorcing my daughter, not me. I will be

The Dating Policy

family to him always. By the way, I am very impressed with your records and background, and I give my blessing to you both. Work hard and become part of our family, Mallory. I want you to represent not only my son but this industry we are building. You are going to be part of the bigger picture and help bring success for the future to all of us. Are you onboard, Mallory?"

I was a deer in headlights again. This man was so passionate; there was so much strength in his delivery. He had a mission, and it was for success. I answered weakly, "Yes, sir."

He grinned. "You can do better than that, Mallory."

I cleared my throat. "I can handle all of this." I waved my hands over the model again.

Nicholas was pleased. "I know you can. If Todd has faith in you... then, so do I. Welcome aboard, Miss Kennedy." I looked at Todd and sighed.

"I have your back, love." He winked and gave me a playful cluck from the side of his mouth. What? No... no... no... bad! Bad! Bad boyfriend! No endearments! "Just so you know, Nicholas, I've been staying over at Mal's the past few nights, and she's going to be staying with me tonight." I gasped. I wanted to pick up a house from this model and throw it at him. Nicholas nodded, appreciating the warning.

"I'll see about sending her to Paris. Gretchen is at the flat on break. It will be good for her to spend some time with her sister. Endure a few more months, and this will be over."

Todd looked at me but spoke to Nicholas. "I know we agreed, Nicholas. But is there any way we can make this divorce happen next week?" I gasped again.

Nicholas rubbed his chin. "Mallory, would you excuse us for a minute?"

He didn't have to ask me twice. I said sure and bolted out the door. I closed it a little too hard behind me.

"Mrs. Benoit, is there any water around here?" She moved her chair slightly, and there was a built-in refrigerator to the left of her. She handed me a bottle, and then I asked, "And a bathroom?" She pointed around the corner.

"To the left, dear." I stuck my hands under the cold water and suddenly noticed my new ring. What the hell did I get myself into? Everything Todd was doing was exactly what I hoped he would do and so much more, except for meeting his wife's father. I could have been spared that right now. I liked Mr. Williams, though. Actually, I really liked him and how he responded to including me in the big picture. Besides, he was my company's new owner now. He was my Boss! There was a knock at the bathroom door.

"Mal? Are you okay, babe?" Argh! I gritted my teeth.

"Stop calling me that in your father-in-law's office."

I could hear the amusement in his tone. "Are you okay?"

"Yes, be out in a minute."

"Okay, I'll wait right here." I wiped my hands and opened the door. He was leaning against the wall, grinning. Todd announced, "Nicholas says you need to take care of me. I'm his favorite." I looked at him.

"Seriously?"

He laughed. "Yup. He had a conference call coming in. That's why he can't say goodbye properly." Todd took my hand and walked me down the hall back to the elevators. When we were alone inside, he pulled me into him. "Looks like I will be divorced next week, beautiful."

"I can't believe you asked him that in front of me and called me babe and love and baby. What is wrong with you?"

He grinned. "I love you. You are my babe and my baby."

"But not in front of your father-in-law!"

"You are that to me in front of whoever the fuck is around."

"It wasn't very professional."

He laughed. "Let's go home, babe. I want to show you your new second home."

I shook my head. "I already don't like your neighbors."

He pulled me into him. "Then we can sell it and find somewhere we both like."

"Todd, do you know this is the kind of conversation you have after years together? Not days."

He shrugged. "I march to my own beat. I think outside of the box. I make my own paths. I —"

"Okay. I get it..." Todd reached for my hand as we made our way to his car.

Chapter Eleven

I was petrified from the moment we turned into the massive parking garage that I would be confronted by "the wife" all the way until we were safely on the other side of his door inside his home. His place was huge. This was not a unit; this was a penthouse. He stared down at his phone that was now in his hand. "Honey, I have to take this. Walk around. Get used to your new place; make yourself at home."

And off to the right, he went. That was his office. This place was an open-floor concept. I liked the setup. His bedroom was at the end, and the view of the city was incredible. What surprised me was there was no second floor, and there was only one bedroom. I supposed the office could be another bedroom; it had its own full bathroom attached. Then there was another half bathroom in the middle. I did just what he said and made myself at home. I found the wine, and after a long day, I opened a bottle, poured two glasses, and brought him one. He nodded, and I came over to him, placing his drink in front of him.

"George, hold on a moment." He held the phone down. "Do you want to go out for dinner? Order in? Or make our own?" I smiled.

"Can I cook?"

He grinned. "I would love it if you did." I kissed him and made my way back to the kitchen.

After poking around, I remembered he was right. His kitchen was set up just like mine. It felt like I had already arranged everything the way I liked it. I decided on lemon pepper chicken. Forty minutes later, he came out of the office. "That smells good. I am suddenly a huge fan of having a roommate."

I grinned as I pulled the roasted potatoes from the oven. "I love your kitchen."

"Good because it's yours now too." He picked up my right hand and looked at my new ring, then kissed it. He pulled me into him and kissed me gently at first, then a mission started. I was breathing heavily as we separated. "I want my dick in you. Can dinner wait?"

I looked around. All the heat elements were off, and covers were on, keeping everything warm. "Yes." He scooped me up like a bride and carried me to the bedroom. Todd undressed me carefully, fully concentrating on the task.

As I stood there naked, he studied me as he undressed. "You are so beautiful," he stated as he pulled my body into his. The intensity of his kiss was like nothing I have ever felt before. Todd reached between my legs and touched me, sliding his fingers against my folds, rubbing me. I spread my legs apart to accommodate him, and then I wrapped my hands around the base of his maleness. He moaned into my mouth. He liked that. He leaned back and pumped himself into my hand a few times. "I love your hands around my shaft." I started holding him firmer and stroked with the rhythm he just set for me. He stood there, eyes closed and softly moaning. I was going to cum if he kept that up. I stopped. He looked down at me with heavy eyelids.

I admitted, "You're going to make me have an orgasm just listening to you." He grinned slightly, lifted me on the bed, and spread my legs.

"I need to be inside you," was all he explained as he lined himself up, then penetrated me. I was an equal player this time. I had been making mental notes and was onboard with complete participation from here forward. Todd really liked this. Several times, he had to stop and tell me not to move as he got himself back under control.

His body was so magnificent. I was feeling around him, and he started pumping himself into me again. He built himself a rhythm, thrusting as I worked to push down on him for deeper penetration. It was him saying, "Come for me, baby," that I obeyed at the moment, calling out his name and grabbing ahold of him. He released, pumping his juices into me, gritting out that he fucking loved me. Todd collapsed beside me on the bed announcing, "Welcome home, girlfriend." I giggled again.

Dinner was delicious. We cleaned up together, and then he had more work to do. I missed a good day of work all because Ned tried to interfere with my life. I asked Todd if I could work in his office with him. He looked around, sizing up a potential spot for me. "I am going to buy you a desk tomorrow. Pick one out, babe. Also, you need your own computer."

I held up my laptop to show that it wasn't necessary. "No, my girl will have her own proper computer. How about we set you up over there?" He pointed to the opposite corner of his desk. "That way, I can see you and think dirty thoughts while I'm talking to our contacts."

I laughed. "Just as long as you don't say anything dirty to them while you're ogling me, that will be fine."

"Ogling you... I like that. I want to ogle you again." He came at me, nuzzling into my neck. That was so ticklish. I was trying to swat him away as his phone rang. He stood, stopped, and walked in the direction of his desk. He called back to me, "That did not save you, Miss. Kennedy. There will be more ogling later." I smiled while he answered and winked at me.

I took in my newly assigned space and started moving things as he watched and talked to whoever was on the other end. I moved a chair to where I thought my desk might be, and then I searched around the penthouse. I found a small desk and chair in the bedroom. That would be perfect for me. We didn't need to buy me a desk.

I went to Todd, who was still on the phone. I walked right up to him. He placed the person on hold. "What's up, beautiful?"

"Sorry to interrupt, but what about the smaller desk and chair in the bedroom? Those are perfect for me, and we don't have to buy anything else."

Todd confirmed that he would call right back and hung the phone up for a moment. He thought for a second, then commented, "What if I have to get up in the middle of the night and work?" I grinned.

"Then you get up, come in here, and don't wake my ass up."

He narrowed his eyes. "But what if it was my intention to wake your ass up to begin with?"

"Well, if that is the intention, then I think you can do a much better job than turning on a computer. You have succeeded many times on your exploration adventures."

He grinned, conceding. "Desk and chair are all yours. I look forward to late-night adventures."

I kissed him and started rearranging the furniture. Within an hour, I was set up, opposite him in our office. I had a great new view in my corner office — him. In the spot where I had taken the desk, I replaced it with a comfortable chair and an end table, so there was somewhere else to sit in our bedroom besides the bed. When Todd's call ended, I took his hand and led him in the bedroom so he could see. He loved me leading him, and he liked the changes I made. He was sitting in the chair with me across his lap when the doorbell sounded. He patted my butt.

"Come on, babe. Let's see who is summoning us." I instantly thought it was his neighbor. Turns out, it wasn't... It was Amanda. I was pouring myself another glass of wine while Todd answered the door. She went right into a rant, forcing her way in and backing him up to the point I knew he was letting her just so I could see the show.

"So, you have the balls to tell me not to talk about my best friend in front of your new fucking girlfriend when you spring the news on all of us without warning! Odessa is beside herself that you are parading that whore around under her nose and telling everyone she's your girlfriend. What the fuck is wrong with you? She has been calling me, crying, and you are acting like such an ass. It's pathetic."

I took a drink of my wine as Amanda turned and gasped, noticing me now leaned against the counter. I spoke before Todd did. "Don't worry, Amanda. We'll never have to pretend we're friends."

She looked at Todd. "You brought her here! Next to your wife's home!"

Oh, boy. This was not going to be pretty. I had seen Todd transform as soon as she referred to me as a whore. I took another sip, and I watched my boyfriend do what he does best. "You fucking little leech, Amanda. If that cunt I married didn't have the social status she does, she would be nothing but a drunken, drug addict to you. You wouldn't be caught dead associating with her. You are a piece of shit, Amanda, to all of womankind. I will forbid Mallory to form even a pity relationship with you. My girlfriend is the brightest, kindest, brilliant, problem-solving, perfect woman I know. She is smart, sexy as all hell, and is the only one who has an opportunity for a future with me. That spoiled rotten cow next door is history." I watched him pause. I knew this was not over. "Here is the new deal, you stupid twit. If I ever invite Joe out again, you will stay home. You will have a headache, not feeling well... whatever excuse you can come up with not to attend. If you happen to think I am over this and you do decide to attend, I will make your pathetic life more miserable. You are not welcome around Mallory or me any longer. I don't care how many years I have known your husband. He is easily replaced. And I will start reminding you of that fact because by you coming here, insulting my woman, and talking to me about the trash I am removing next door... your husband has just lost the first-quarter bid. I have now decided to go with a lower bidder." She gasped. He continued, "You stupid girl, kiss that million-dollar profit goodbye."

She glared at me. "This is your entire goddamn fault!"

I laughed. "Amanda, you are pretty dumb. I would have defended you a minute ago but listening to Todd and him giving you simple instructions, yeah, you are no one I want in my social circle."

Todd added, "Now, Joe lost the second quarter. Go home and explain what you did before he loses the other half of the contract. Baby, show Amanda what I bought you this afternoon."

I looked down at my new ring. I fucking loved my boyfriend as I flipped her off. "He's so good to me... isn't it pretty?"

She huffed, then stormed out, slamming the door as hard as she could.

He came at me, smiling. "You did that very well, love. I am sorry you had to hear that."

I hugged him. "I love my new ring. It's perfect. You are brilliant for thinking that up. Tomorrow, I am going to show Ned and anyone else who gets in our way."

"Good girl. Promise me not to let anyone get in your head, trying to come between us."

I nodded. "You proved that to me today. I won't let them get to me. I promise." Both of us worked in the office until ten. He stretched, yawning, and I saw that as a signal to shut it down for the night. I asked him about the gym this week.

He grinned. "We can go tomorrow after work." I kissed him.

"I forgot to bring gym clothes."

He stopped our forward motion. "I have to go in early tomorrow. Which car do you want?"

"What do you mean which car?"

"Black, white, or green?"

"Green? What is the green car?" I asked, laughing.

"The Lambo..."

"You have a Lamborghini?"

"Yes, doesn't every successful entrepreneur have one?"

"I will take the white if that's okay? I wouldn't know how to drive the green. Or you can drop me to my car in the morning."

He pulled me against him. "I am not dropping you anywhere. Take the white... Oh, and before you start with 'I have my own,' I want you to know that it brings me a great deal of satisfaction that I am taking care of you, got it?" I kissed him again.

"I am open to being taken care of as long as you let me take care of you as well."

"Woman, I know just how you can take care of me right now." I woke up to my five-in-the-morning rise-and-shine roommate, and I asked him if he wanted me to get up with him. He loved that gesture, loved the idea that I would do that for him. He loved the fact that I was in just my panties next to him. After a proper morning release, he kissed me, then covered me with the blanket.

He set my alarm. He placed the bat phone on the pillow and told me my lovely ass had to be up and moving in one hour. With my eyes still closed and my head snuggled into the pillow, he kissed me one last time.

We exchanged "I love you" as he informed me the keys to my car were on the kitchen counter and he wrote down which parking section was his.

I was now smiling up at him, watching him walk away. Todd paused at the doorway as he pointed out that I belonged in his bed, and I looked good lying there. I had the biggest stupid grin spread across my face while I tried to bury it in his pillow. There was no doubt in my mind. I was crazy in love... never felt like this before.

My boyfriend was raising the bar to eliminate any future competition, and he succeeded. I feared leaving here. I touched the handle of the front door five times before I got the courage to open it. The ex was the last thing I wanted to bump into this morning. I made it to the car without interference. I arrived at my house and gathered what I needed plus a few more outfits to bring to Todd's. I touched his hanging suits. He was the one for me... no doubt.

I wore my blue power suit to match my blue power ring. I pulled up in Todd's car. I walked with power in my steps. I opened the entrance doors, then the salesroom door with purpose. There was Jessica with a mean look in her eyes. "I heard you're dating a married man."

I faltered for a second as she couldn't wait to tell me the rest, "Seems that is the type of relationship you actually deserve."

Oh, my God, she didn't know it was with Todd. I was safe. I didn't even answer her as I turned toward my door. I walked right into my office and settled in, first squaring my shoulders to get my confidence back that just deserted me when I thought Jessica had found out I was dating Todd. I focused on work. Since I had already completed two-thirds of yesterday's work last night, my agenda was to complete the last of it this morning. I was busy making up from yesterday as Ned knocked on my door. I looked over.

He peeked his head in. "Mallory..."

"I'm a little busy here. What do you need?"

"I need to make sure you're okay." Now he was half in my office that used to be my boyfriend's ass-chewing office, and that thought was front and center in my brain.

"Come in, Ned. Close the door behind you." I finished with my customer. I addressed Ned as a professional. "What can I do for you?"

"I just wanted to see if you're okay. I'm worried about you."

"I am fine, as you see... anything else?"

He looked around. "Come on, Mal... drop the bullshit. What the fuck is going on?"

"None of your business, I assure you. And for future disclosures to me, make sure you check your facts." I flipped him my new ring. "You are an asshole... and you can leave now."

Ned observed my ring and got up. "I hope you know what you're doing, kid. Message received loud and clear; you are on your own." One down. I texted Todd and told him everything.

He replied: *I want to kiss you...* I sighed and wrote him back his same words. I kicked ass this morning, starting with Ned and finishing with Bill, all before my lunch break. What was going on between all the managers? They were cuckoo today... then I got the universal bitch slap. Todd changed the first two-quarters' pricing and now awarded them to a lower bidder.

Oh, crap, this affected Bill as well. Now, they were becoming my contracts. Ned lost them, and fellow manager Bill lost them, and since they were now being subbed out to one of my more challenging contractors, they were now my projects. Then a message flashed on both my computers and my cell phone: "Mandatory board meeting 1:30, Gary suite 307, 3rd floor."

I got a text on the bat phone: *I am not going to be there for that. The meeting is about me changing the players and my buddy Mark now having to hire a subcontractor to make money. It's all your project now, babe; do me proud. I know you can handle this, and I have your back ...roommate.*

I smiled and replied: *I will make sure everyone knows I am capable of handling this.*

Todd replied: *That's my girl. I'll be at the supply house. I'll stop in when I get back.*

I took a breath and texted: *Okay.* I immediately searched the profile of the subcontractor Mark had hired. I knew D and R Mack Construction. Dan and Ryan were my clients only because sometimes they got in over their heads or they lost a job and could not pay.

I phoned Dan first, and it was a good thing I did. He was already shopping around to buy his supplies elsewhere to keep his costs down. I told him the requirements, what the roofs needed to be, and that we were the only supply house to carry the product. I asked if I could meet him for dinner. He accepted. I skipped lunch. I was on the phone with all the parties involved, collecting the information I needed for the meeting.

It was a little awkward, walking into the elevator with five pissed off managers. I had all my notes and fresh paper to add more. I asked the men where I should sit, and John answered, "They will tell you." Okay then. I had never been in this boardroom. It contained Frank, the owner.

There he was, sitting next to Nicholas Williams. I stumbled as Samantha Gary called to me to sit next to her. The meeting began. Frank introduced Nicholas to everyone as the new partner with SBS. Ned glared at me.

I looked down at my notes. Samantha announced the change in financing with the tract housing project and said that SBS would now make a higher profit. Then she explained that the contractor hired was going to have to sub the work out, and that fell under my clientele.

I told her I was ready to present my findings. She looked down at me, surprised, and introduced me. I stood, a little shaky at first. I announced that I had already spoken with the general contractor and the subcontractor he signed with.

I followed with the information that I had already set a meeting for tonight with the subcontractor because, with the price he bid, I learned he was shopping around for lower prices. I came up with suggesting the GC hire this job out as labor only and the GC agreed to buy the products straight through us with a more lenient payback term. I could feel Samantha's wrath for doing this on my own. She was about to execute me. Nicholas was nodding, and Frank was looking through me like he was trying to figure out who the hell I was. She held her tongue, ready to take over.

Frank spoke first. "Payment terms are not your business, but I like the way you are thinking about this. We cannot have contractors shopping around. What is your name again?"

I went to answer, but Nicholas did instead. "Mallory Kennedy. Her name is Mallory Kennedy. I like the way you thought this through. It seems you know how the construction industry works."

"I do, sir, and I know the problem they are going to run into is all the AIA forms and who gets paid when, especially since this is all new construction. I know your GC will take over buying the material directly, especially if they have a little wiggle room for paying it back. I looked into their records. There has never been an issue with this company." Because it was silently owned by Williams Enterprises, which Nicholas owned.

Bill spoke up. "Because this GC is my client, and if we have the GC now in charge of buying the product, doesn't this become my client again?" Frank looked at him, then Nicholas.

Frank said, "No, Bill. Miss. Kennedy is going to keep this project. She has already resolved a potential loss. Miss Kennedy, follow through with your plan. Report to Samantha after your meeting tonight, and I want full written documentation on how this came about with the steps you took."

"Yes, Mr. Gary, I will have it all to you in the morning." The meeting was adjourned, but I was asked to wait behind. When only Frank, Nicholas, Samantha, and I were left, there was a little bit of scolding on my behalf because I hadn't let anyone know what my ideas were. But they thought I did a smart job of resolving the issue. I explained that I hadn't had time to fill them in because I was on the phone, trying to figure it out, right up to when I had to catch the elevator.

Nicholas grinned. "Next time, either let Todd in on it or Samantha. I would like a copy of your report as well." He handed me his business card. "Well done, Mallory. I know you can handle this."

* * *

Todd walked right into my office when he arrived back. I was on the phone, but that didn't stop him from leaning down to kiss me. "Hold on a moment, please," I said, and I put Frank, my client, on hold while Todd grinned and pecked me on the lips. "Bad boyfriend!" He preened and sat at the edge of my desk, tossing a baseball up and catching it while I finished Frank's order. I ended the call as he gently kicked the door closed.

"I heard my woman saved the day."

"Not exactly, I have to skip the gym. I have a dinner meeting with the subcontractor."

"Can I come with you?"

I smiled. "I don't see why not." He tossed me the ball.

"Good. I was hoping you would let me tag along."

I sat back in my chair. "Actually, it will be nice to have you there with me. Where did the baseball come from?"

Todd grinned. "Angela. She spotted me, and Alex told her to give this to me."

I looked at it, and there was a "Thank You!" written across it. "Is my friend dating a catcher?"

Todd smiled. "I believe that is a yes."

I smiled widely. "That's pretty cool."

"So, give me the rundown, babe. What happened?"

I told him everything. He listened, and every so often, he turned up the corner of his mouth. I saw a proud look on his handsomely chiseled face. "Where are we meeting your subcontractor tonight?"

"Tavern on Central next town over."

"Good choice."

"He picked it."

"That's okay, beautiful. We'll put together a list of acceptable eating establishments for you to dine with clients." I was grateful, agreeing with him.

There was no doubt that Todd and I working together was going to be successful. He got things done, and I proved I could get them done on a more creative level. We chose to go back to his place tonight. It was nine in the evening, and as we walked down the hall coming to his penthouse, my worst fear rounded the corner, dressed up very fancy. She had a half bottle of vodka in her hand and some male supermodel on her right, with two women laughing and smoking a joint behind her. Odessa's eyes were half-slits. She halted for a second, then started to come at me. "What? Now you're bringing this fucking slut home! To our home!"

Todd pulled me behind him and handed me the keys. I shook as I unlocked and opened the door. "Odessa, go to hell. You will never be half the woman Mallory is. Next week, we will be divorced. I will no longer have any obligations to you."

"What the fuck are you talking about, Todd? You are my husband for five more months!"

"Our case got moved up to next week. Good riddance, you fucking waste."

Odessa threw her bottle at him. "You are a fucking asshole! You cannot do that!" She leaped at him in an attack, and he deflected her to the side, making her stumble and fall away from him. He looked at her pathetic crew. "Go pick up your trash and get her out of here." He closed the door behind him and was more worried about me than what just happened. After he made sure I was okay and settled, he called Nicholas, explaining what had happened. I stripped down to my underwear, brushed my teeth, put my hair in a ponytail, and climbed into bed.

Todd was about twenty minutes in the office before he made his way to the bedroom. I was almost finished with my report and my notes on following through with Samantha as well as Todd attending the meeting tonight. He leaned against the doorframe, watching me. I glanced up. "I am just finished." I hit send and shut my computer down.

He shook his head. "I am the luckiest man on this planet."

Instantly, he made me smile as I wondered why he was saying this. "How so, Mr. Duvall?" I questioned in delight but with a sense of wariness as well.

"Through all the obstacles I have on my end, you still said yes, letting me tag along tonight without hesitation, and here you are in our bed, with annoying neighbors next door, looking very naked — might I add — and still working."

I shrugged. "I had to get this out tonight or in the morning."

He walked over, kicking off his shoes. I placed my laptop on the end table, and then he undressed slowly, keeping his eyes on mine the entire time. When he was fully exposed, he threw back the covers. He zeroed in on my panties. "Oh, babe. Let me have the honor of removing those with my teeth." My eyes widened because I already knew what that already felt like as he grabbed my legs to place them in front of him. He proceeded to do just as he said and removed my panties with his teeth. Sex was on the gentle side this evening. We were both tired, as he positioned himself behind me and tucked my body against his. He wrapped his arm around me, and in a bedtime storytelling voice, he stated that he wanted to do everything with me. A minute later, we cuddled into each other.

He sleepily suggested that we could live at my house for a while if I couldn't handle "dumb dumb" next door, which made me giggle a little. Just hearing "dumb dumb" used as vocabulary from him was adorable. He pulled me tighter against him and announced he hoped marriage was an option between us someday, and then he relaxed and drifted off to sleep. Now, I was wide awake with my eyes perked open. Marrying Todd... what were my choices?

Yes, I would take his last name. I was thinking kids. I would like one, with the option of a second. I thought about us keeping this place for when we were in the city but also getting a house close to work. If Todd asked me to marry him, my answer was absolutely going to be yes. I woke up to Todd moving in a slight stretch as he cursed, "Damn it, woman. I have never slept past five in seventeen years. It's 6 a.m., and I am going to be late for the first time ever to a meeting."

He leaned back over and kissed me. "That's it. You're in it for the long run, Kennedy." He jumped out of bed and into the shower. I followed him. "Can I do anything to help get you out of here?"

"Pick me out a suit, babe — underwear, socks, tie... Can you make me some coffee?"

"Absolutely!" I was on my mission. I hung his suit, and the rest was laid out on the counter. I found the coffee maker and started that. I came back into the bathroom. "How do you like your coffee?" He grabbed me, kissed me hard, and then asked me if I would take his last name. He was dead serious, and I tried not to show that my brain was doing cartwheels inside and to stop from grinning like a schoolgirl. "I like the sound of Mallory Duvall. My initials would be MD, like a doctor. I think I'm good at fixing things. Yeah, I would take your last name."

"Good. Because now that I have you... I want to make you mine."

"I am yours, Todd." He was finished dressing and held me like the many times we were about to collide.

"Not the same, Mallory. For the first time in my life, I get to choose... no deals on the counter, no negotiations. It's all my decision, and I choose you."

My inner force field shattered into a thousand tiny shooting stars. If I had questioned Todd's love for me before, he just conquered all my insecurities and self-inflicted doubt. His eyes found my soul, and I nodded, then cleared my throat. "How do you like your coffee?" He released the sides of my arms and gave me a quick wink, knowing he was on a time crunch.

"This conversation is not over... just some cream, love." I gave him a quick kiss, handed him his coffee, and sent my first-time-late boyfriend on his way. "Pack some more suits for me. We're staying at your place for the week." He leaned in this time and quickly kissed me, juggling his keys and briefcase as he walked out.

I stood on my tiptoes and waved, reinforcing, "Got it covered."

Chapter Twelve

Three quiet days went by, and we started the weekend, driving up on our Friday night to the countryside. Todd referred to it as camping. We had the Williams Enterprise Company retreat to attend. It was a massive adult project challenge recreation center that we pulled into, with cottages and all. I laughed. I hadn't been to camp in fifteen years. I hated camp; my mother sent me for entire summers just so she could be with her husband or boyfriends alone. Even though it was geared to adults, all the same rules applied — six to a cabin, separate men's and women's shower, with multiple stall bathrooms.

We checked in, and we were assigned to one of the tiny cottage's way in the back. It had a queen-size bed with a very small bathroom that included a basic shower stall, toilet, and single sink. There was clearly only room for one person at a time in there. Curiously, I asked. "How did we get a cabin?"

He dropped our bags on the floor. "I know the owner, besides I told you I am not sleeping away from you ever again."

"Never?"

"Only in an emergency, that's it."

I grinned. "But I make you late."

He reached for my hand and pulled me in for a quick kiss. "Come on, babe. Let's look around, so you become familiar with these grounds. I want you to meet a few key people who are participating here this weekend. These players are important to Williams Enterprises, and they will be a good resource for you in the future."

And the first one was — oh, fuck, was he kidding me! Odessa's mother. Nope, she did not like me at all. First impressions said it all. She loathed me. Nicholas gave a warm greeting, though, and told me my report had excellent formatting. That was a little trick I learned from one of my business professors, Jerry Vargas. Best professor I ever had, I learned so many neat tricks that I apply all the time, and now I was grateful for being recognized by Nicholas for it. He wanted all reports sent like that from now on and was adopting the style for the company's procedure in submitting reports. It was clear that Todd didn't care at all about Mrs. Williams. He was polite, but he pretty much carried on like she was not here. He was very proud of me, especially that I impressed Nicholas enough to change the company's report formatting.

He playfully announced, "Well, it's a good thing I personally know the one responsible for these changes. How convenient it is that she is my new roommate because I might need some extra tutoring."

The Dating Policy

My jaw dropped. I can't believe he said that in front of his wife's mother! Nicholas did not react. I wasn't so sure he was happy with that declaration. He pointed out William and suggested that Todd introduce me to him. We walked over, and William instantly gave Todd a brotherly hard time. They were friends, but I could tell they were also rivals. It was comical listening to them spit insults at each other about who was better. I liked William as he made me laugh, telling me I was crazy for being with Todd, and I should be with a real man like himself. Todd gave William a hearty pat on his shoulder, telling him he wished, as William shook my hand again, saying it was a pleasure meeting me. As we walked along, I was very surprised to spot Mark and Louise here. Oh, gosh, I wondered if Joe and Amanda were here as well. I nudged Todd and asked. He frowned.

"No, you don't have to think about seeing Amanda again. Joe filed for divorce."

"What?"

"I'll tell you later when we're alone." Mark made his way over. The look on Louise's face was sheer bitterness. Mark didn't notice his wife's reaction as he shook Todd's hand, greeting him, then telling me what a great compromise I had figured out. He was confident this was going to work perfectly. Louise walked away while on her cell phone.

Todd picked up my hand, spotting the next person on his list. "We'll see you later. Mallory needs to meet Kirk."

"Okay, buddy." Mark turned to look around for his wife. Seventeen key players later, I was going to be lucky if I remembered four names. It was already dark out, but the place was lit up extremely well. We had all gathered down by the lake where a huge bonfire was crackling away, and our opening ceremony began, followed by a very camp-style buffet.

This weekend was not just about challenging us but also relying on others for teamwork. And, of course, there was going to be an award ceremony at the end because this was competition-based as well. After the food came the open cocktail and dessert bar. I thought this was very nice until Todd clued me in that the open bar was a test — who would show up in the morning and who would be hungover. Todd and I skipped the alcohol and hydrated with water. My very sweet boyfriend excused us for the night. We took four more water bottles, and we headed back to our cabin with his arm around me and mine around his lower back. I had never walked like this in my life; it felt really strange but good.

After he explained the Joe-Amanda relationship, I felt at ease. Apparently, she lived ridiculously outside of her means, trying to keep up with Odessa, and Joe was continually struggling to keep up with Amanda's spending. The next bomb, I did not expect. Todd requested us to be partnered up with the Mark-Louise and Edward-Abigail duos. He laughed at my horrified expression on the announcement of Louise. "Why would you do that? She fucking hates me!"

He calmed me down quickly. "Hun, you and Mark are going to be working together from here on out unless I am moved to companies further south. If that happens, you go with me. Don't give me that look, Miss. Kennedy. Your current name is temporary, and where I am, so are you, understood?"

I switched to a really stupid grin stretching across my face as I looked down at the ground to hide it. He tapped me on my back by my shoulder, throwing me off balance as I fell back on the bed. "Yes, sir." I giggled out.

"Don't worry, babe. We will deal with Louise together. Those two need us to survive. If Mark lost the Williams Enterprises position, he would be toast, and he is only there because I called in a favor from Nicholas. Mind you, he has done a good job, but there are better people for what he does.

"Remember, sexy; it's all about who holds the cards. And right now, you and I do." He kissed me... He really kissed me. Making love to my partner never felt so unified. We were together as one, and this experience was incredible. He set the alarm, stating, "Never in my life have I needed an alarm. You are just everything I want in a great night's sleep."

I giggled, then stretched in his hold. I happily announced, "Good morning, roommate."

He kissed the top of my head. "Good morning, my future ball and chain." He caressed my shoulder. "Let's skip the morning sex. I want the added aggression for our team today. You will be my reward tonight, okay?"

I nodded. "You lead. I will follow, handsome." Since he was more familiar with this course setting, I trusted his judgment, especially since he kept stressing that we were coming back here next year too. The morning announcements commenced. This was where the teams were formed. The very first team was Nicholas and his wife Yasmin, Todd and me, Mark and Louise, Edward and Abigail — twenty-two teams total, eight per team. Damn, this was going to be a challenge. I absolutely adored Abigail right from first sight. She was into this — petite little fireball, five-foot-three maybe, very fit-looking, loved being here. If they said opposites attract, that was Edward and Abigail. Edward was an accounting nerd... a soft in the middle doughboy, but he was funny right from the first meeting. I really liked them both. Mark was happy, and Nicholas was chomping at the bit.

"Let's give them a good show. We are the ones to follow!" Now, we had to come up with a team name. My mind was racing. Several lame suggestions came out, and I pulled all our first initials together. I had it.

"How about M MENTALY?" Todd laughed. "I like it, babe."

The men all liked it and joked around. Abigail loved it and sported around, sounding the M to "AM MENTALY... up for this challenge; AM MENTALY going to win this." I earned a kiss on the lips from my very proud boyfriend while two women who hated me watched. Rules were being explained. Throughout the course, no one could be paired up with a spouse or the same partner. Once you completed a challenge, you had to work with someone new in your group. There were six challenges between today and tomorrow. That meant I would work with all but one of my team members.

He gave my butt a pat. "No worries. I'll be watching out for you too."

I playfully turned into him. "As I will be watching you, handsome, do everything before me." That turned up his grin. He kissed my forehead, then released me.

He leaned down to my ear as the last team was announced. "I love you."

I turned quickly back. "I love you more." He smacked my butt again. We all started with multiple groups waiting at each of the six challenges. I didn't know how they ranked the challenges, but we started with the timber walls. There were three lanes. Each group was assigned left, right, or center lane, and that was the course you would follow through this entire challenge. We had five walls to go over. The first was five feet high, and the last was two-by-eight planks, five inches apart, screwed to trees climbing twenty feet up so that you had to scale a ten-inch width and climb back down. That one was scary to me. It was first thing in the morning, and the wood was wet with morning dew. I just hoped this was considered one of the more challenging courses. I was paired up with Mark. I really needed him the last three walls. The third wall was ten feet up — no room to climb. You couldn't even get a toe between the boards. Mark and I were last. Todd came around and watched.

Mark just said, "Ready, Mallory?"

I didn't have time to respond as he put his hand around the front of my waist and his other on my ass. He squatted and threw me up the wall. I caught the top and straddled it as he took a few steps back and launched himself, catching the top. I helped pull him up as he thanked me. Todd had the queen bee, Yasmin.

For some reason, she did not mind being around him alone. He just about carried the woman through the entire course. Today, we had the wall challenge, rope course, mud run, ditches, and ended the day with the cable course. Mark was a great partner, Edward was fantastic, and Louise was perfect for the mud. She did her thing; I did mine, and not one word or glance was exchanged.

Nicholas threw me over the longest ditch I had ever seen, praising my bravery, and now I was paired with his wife on the hardest course yet. She was equally unhappy. We were all tired and nearly broken. This one consisted of a series of thin rope cables that crossed and intertwined like a maze, starting from two feet off the ground and ending thirty feet up to a platform from which we would zipline across the lake to the last platform. Yasmin walked to her husband and said something in protest.

Oh, hubby was not changing the rules, I could tell as he led her by her elbow, slightly away from the group. I heard him telling her that she will work with me because I had a promising future with the company. Then he said to her, if she did not start accepting the idea of Todd and me, he was going to cut off Odessa's funding and make her get a job. This started a whole new muffled argument that Yasmin folded for now, clearly angered by her husband. She straightened her posture, lifted her head, walked to my side, and announced, "Let us begin."

Todd gave one last pep talk. "I know it's the end of the day, and tomorrow, our last challenge is the very easy water obstacle. So, I want you all to reflect on today and feel what we have overcome. While doing so, when each of us reaches that platform, before we take that last step to the end of this challenge... look down at the water course, see how everyone is laughing, having a good time... because that is the final obstacle, we need to complete tomorrow. By the way, I have been checking our scores. We are in first place."

Well, that was a motivational booster. Yasmin requested that she and I go last. Todd did not like this. Too many things could go wrong, and I would be stuck dealing with her. He was about to protest when Nicholas answered for the whole group. "Very fitting, my dearest, you always need the last word. Go right ahead."

Todd tried to change it as he was cut off by Nicholas. Then, he said, "Abby and I will go next to last."

Nicholas answered, "Oh, no, my boy. You two are going first so we can watch."

He muttered "fuck" under his breath. I looked at him, giving him the thumbs up that I was perfectly fine. He ignored me. Then I announced, "Mrs. Williams and I are both strong women. We have this. No worries."

He sighed. "Okay, come on, Abby. Let's show them how this is done." She was excited. They were tethered together. If one person fell, then they had the extra security of not only being tied to the cable but could also get help from their partner. Todd and Abby instantly said the wire cables were cold and slippery. Slow and steady was the pace.

As soon as they were a third of the way, Abigail commented that the cold of the steel was cramping her hands and to be careful. The next tandem set started on the wires. They would call from the first group to the second and the second to the third.

Yasmin and I were up last. I asked if she wanted to go first, and she snipped a yes like it was obviously expected. Todd had to leave the platform, and I could see he was holding out until the last second.

I stopped paying attention to him and kept talking to Yasmin about where to place her hands and how to slide her feet. She actually stopped as we were one-third of the way done. "The sound of your voice repulses me. Be silent!"

Oh, I can be silent, bitch! That message was loud and clear. The second group was on the platform, ziplining down. Now we were slowly crawling on the second part. The third group was on the platform.

That was Nicholas. He called down to me, "Mallory, I know you have this. See you on the beach." He turned and left the platform. It was Yasmin and me alone now, and this was getting trickier. She slipped four times before reaching the last section. She stopped and rested. I said nothing. She took in a breath. "Why are you coming between my daughter and her husband?"

If I could have reacted the way I wanted to, while not standing here, spread-eagle and balancing on a cable that was hurting my hands and cramping my feet, I would have answered her very differently. So, I just explained, "I was single. I work at the same company as Todd. I have been there for just over ten years. I didn't know he was married; there is nothing about him that gives off any signal that he is. No ring, no mention of his life on the computer or any connections to your family; besides, he pursued me. I tried to end it when I found out he was married. He insisted his divorce was six months away and came on like a freight train. How was I supposed to handle that?"

She understood my answer with a breathy sigh and a slight nod. "Todd is the exact husband I would have picked for her had I been given a choice. He works hard. He is dedicated, is always looking to improve himself. He is every mother's dream of what they want for their daughter. My daughter is not every mother's dream... but I always have hope. I hope this is just something she is going through, and someday, she will stop this nonsense. The reality of losing her husband is heartbreaking to her and to me. Todd has always been there for her. He has always rescued her from her careless decisions."

"Mrs. Williams, this really is none of my business. I am sorry for you and your family... what you are going through with your daughter. I believe it is very selfish of her. I have run into her on a few occasions recently, and even I can see that she doesn't care. She needs professional help. How about making her go to rehab?"

"We tried. She checks herself out and leaves. No one can make her stay. Todd is a big part of my family. I will never like seeing him with you or anyone else." Great.

Not only did she hate me, but she also just said she would always hate me. "Are we done here? My hands are cramping up, and I would really like to be done with this challenge."

Yasmin agreed and started to move again. On her second step, her foot slipped. I quickly moved to her and steadied her. "Are you okay?" She nodded. "Let's do this together, slow and steady." She nodded again.

It was an agonizing seven minutes, but she reached the platform. Then she reached out for my hand to help me up. That surprised me. I took it and thanked her. I helped her with the zipline harness and sent her down. As I was going over the lake, I looked down at the water course. That was our last challenge tomorrow, and it looked fun.

The expression on Todd's face when I finally landed on the platform was of pure relief. He kissed me as if we were alone and in our bedroom. I tried to stop him because this was inappropriate, but he was not stopping. When he finally released his kiss, he said, "I nearly ran back up that mountain. What the fuck took so long?"

"Queen Bee wanted to have a little chat with me."

He looked concerned. "Everything go okay?"

"Yeah, everything is fine." We were all tired, dirty, cold, and did we smell ripe. We had an hour and a half to get ready for dinner, so we all went our separate ways. I needed a shower badly, so Todd waited. He told me not to get dressed yet as he pulled the blankets back from the bed for me to wait there until he was done in the shower. I cannot tell you how long he was because I fell right to sleep. Suddenly, my whole body was jerked awake. I sat up, not sure where I was, and Todd stood in front of me, naked and talking.

"Damn, woman. You can snore. I have been trying to wake you up for three minutes."

I scanned my surroundings. "Well, I'm awake now."

"Come on, babe; let's get dressed and head down." I was just so tired, but I realized I loved this man beyond anything I had ever felt or known about love. Both of us were moving at a much slower pace than this morning.

I needed coffee. Everyone looked exhausted and battered at dinner. The stories were flying around about mishaps on the courses throughout the day. There were quite a few injuries that happened, and I could see how, especially with the wet boards this morning and the cable course. Abigail from our group bragged about our team. She had such a big personality. She was so cute and funny with the stories that she shared. My boyfriend radiated heat, so I was pretty much attached to him all night. I was now awake from the coffee kicking in and switched to wine. After my second glass, I was fading fast, so we headed up to the cottage. I told Todd he could go back to the group, but he insisted that lying next to me was much better time spent. I snuggled up against him, and I was asleep quickly.

* * *

Our last challenge required us in bathing suits. I put mine on this morning; Todd took it off. I guess seeing me for the first time in a bathing suit turned him on. I now put my bathing suit on for the second time, and we were good to go. This water challenge was a fun course. I finally was partnered with Abby. We splashed and tipped one another out, overreacting and embracing the juvenile spirit in most of us while loving every moment. Nicholas surprised me with a sneak attack of a water bucket dumped over my head. He was pleased that I laughed.

Yasmin just watched from the beach after we passed the finish line. It only took us an hour, but we decided to stay and hang out to watch the other teams who had to finish here as well. Todd was talking to a lot of people. I was strolling around with my solo cup filled with beer as a few people stopped me to find out where I got it. I pointed to the hut in the corner and was cheerfully thanked. This was our last day

The Dating Policy

here. The luncheon award ceremony handed out the usual medals that you wore around your neck like in the Olympics. It was all very fancy. We won first place. Nicholas spoke for our group; he addressed all of us by saying a little something personal about each of us, which was a nice touch. He made a point to introduce me as the newest member of the William Enterprise Corporation, and I received an extra round of applause. There were quite a few surprised onlookers when Todd kissed me center stage.

Oh, boy, I was the whore again; now, people that didn't know Todd brought his mistress, they knew now.

It was good to pack up and get out of there. I had a great weekend, and the purpose of its training and working through obstacles was a success, but I wanted to be back home because my body ached, and I was exhausted. I actually wanted to go back to Todd's place because he had a Jacuzzi tub, but we were at mine for a few days until Odessa settled down.

I remembered, in a few more weeks, Todd was going in front of the judge to settle his divorce. They couldn't get this week, but I was pretty sure it was a week from Friday. I jump-started with our laundry while Todd established himself on the sofa, spreading his work out on the coffee table and end table and fired up his computer.

An hour into being a normal couple, his phone made a strange ring. He looked down and grabbed it. "What? Slow down; slow down. I can't understand you… What?" He listened for a moment, then reacted, "Are you fucking kidding me? What's the address? Call the ambulance right now!" He hung up and called the police, giving them the address, and requested an ambulance. "I have to go. Odessa is down and not moving. Don't go anywhere." I started shaking a little.

"Okay, can I do anything?"

"Stay here. Just stay here." He was out the door so quickly that he didn't take anything but the phone that he had in his hand. I called Angela. I needed to talk to her. My little friend was a few states away, watching her new boyfriend catch baseballs. I was so happy for her, and listening to her was the perfect distraction.

I confessed what was happening, and she asked if I needed her to come home. This was exactly why I loved this woman. No matter what, she was going to be there for me. I assured her to stay put and said I would have lunch with her tomorrow. When she was satisfied that I was okay was when she let me end the call.

I was glued to the bat phone, willing it to ring or chirp with a text… and I got nothing. This was horrible. I didn't know what was going on. I checked to see if any messages came through, and there was nothing. The laundry was finished. I made a list of food to buy, and my phone rang with a number I did not recognize. I answered it, "Hello?"

"Mallory, it's me. Odessa overdosed. She mixed too many pills. She didn't make it. Pack up our things and go to the penthouse. I won't be there for a while, but I want you there when I arrive. I have a lot to do down here, and Nicholas is on his way. The police are over at her place now. Introduce yourself. I've already given them your name. If they need to look in the penthouse, let them do whatever they need to do with their investigation."

Tears were streaming down my face as I cleared my throat. "Are you okay?"

He sighed. "I have been expecting this moment every day for nine years. But I don't think anyone could ever really be prepared for it."

"I am so sorry, Todd."

"Thank you. Just get over to the penthouse. Call me when you arrive."

"I will."

And he hung up. I called Angela back. I was so upset. She managed to put everything into perspective for me. This was going to make me stronger for Todd to help him get through what he needed to. I programmed Todd's number into my phone. I packed our stuff up and went to his penthouse.

The place was crawling with police and news cameras outside the building. I had to show my ID several times on many levels, and they wanted to check his place. There were a lot of questions that I could not answer, like if she had a key to his penthouse. I was pretty sure that was a no. They came through with a few dogs, walked around, and cleared the place as not related to any evidence. I updated Todd, and he told me he would be home around midnight.

I have never seen so much police action. I watched through the peephole with people in full hazmat suits walking in and others walking out. There were lots of stuff in clear baggies written with a black sharpie marker with a word I could not make out. I even saw one cop toss a bag to another saying it's gotta be worth ten grand. I hated this peephole. Everything looked like you were in a bubble.

Tonight, Todd climbed into bed, wrapped his arms around me, buried his forehead into my hair at the back of my head, and never let go. The next few days were brutal with the announcement in the paper, the funeral plans, my job, and the ongoing resentment from my fellow managers; from Bill and Ned losing their clientele to me.

Todd was out because his wife had just died. No one knew about us except for Angela and Ned, and I was relieved. When I arrived at the penthouse on Wednesday, after a long day at work, Todd was in the office with someone. "Mallory, come in here, please, when you have a moment." I walked right in. There was nothing I was doing that could not wait. He motioned for me to sit. "Rich, this is my girlfriend, Mallory. Mal, this is my lawyer."

I nodded politely to the lawyer, then gave my full attention to Todd as I asked, "Lawyer for what?"

"Divorce and the estate."

I shook Rich's hand as he was summoning my attention back to him. "Technically, I am the divorce lawyer, Mallory. Todd's estate is handled by someone else in our firm."

"Oh." I had no clue why I was meeting this man.

Todd continued, "According to the State, I have now been declared a widower, and I am free to marry. The death certificate has been issued, but we will wait until after the funeral." I still wasn't getting it. He continued explaining like I was absorbing all this. "Even though all the property was being divided, she refused to sign anything, so I take over all of Odessa's assets that we originally shared."

I still wasn't getting it. Rich took over, recognizing I was clueless. "Mr. Duvall's net worth is twenty million at the moment. I have been asked to draft up a prenuptial agreement for you and him. It's nothing personal. This is just a standard agreement, but he has requested that it only have a shelf life of one year, against my better judgment. Again, Mallory, I have no vested interest in you, as cruel as that may seem. My objective is to serve Mr. Duvall. On a side note, through my own investigations, I noted that your character and integrity display strong ethical standards, leading me to see no reason to question my client's ability to make a fair judgment on this decision. This would start with the estates being completely in Mr. Duvall's name and would name you the benefactor of the entity until the year was completed from your marriage date, then naming you and Mr. Duvall as equal shareholders to all his assets."

I looked from Rich to Todd and back again. "What? Wait a minute. Wait a minute. Todd, what does this mean? Are you proposing to me?"

He half grinned. "Not yet, but soon. Are you okay with what I am setting up? I know this is not romantic, but I figure we should get the legalities out of the way before the fun stuff."

"I'm sorry; could you repeat that?"

"Rich, would you excuse us for a minute?" He stood.

"Of course."

Todd followed suit, took my hands, and stood me on my feet as well. "I have spent the last ten plus years in a relationship that was arranged for me. It came with a lot of beneficial perks and opportunities. Don't get me wrong. But it came with an emotional price as well. She was a suicide gamble every single day. Let me tell you; I have seen life and its value much clearer. I appreciated my life more. This is my lesson from the years of living with her." He paused for a moment. He was upset, then glossed it over as he continued.

"I am not lessening the fact that she has died from drug and alcohol abuse. No one could save her. That is what she alone chose, dismissing her family, me, and those who mattered. I know for a fact that she didn't question what went into her body. Her idea was: a pill, pop in mouth, wash down with vodka. She was that far gone. She put her entire family through misery without a single concern just as long as everyone paid attention to her. I will never understand that level of selfishness. Her family constantly focused their attention on making her get help and tried as much as they could every day to make sure she was safe. All she did was put them through hell, not caring, not willing to change. This part of her I will never forgive. She was the most selfish person I have ever met."

I could see in his eyes that he resented her. He was angry talking about this. Then he softened as he reached up to brush the back of his fingers from my cheekbone to my jawline.

"Mallory, you are the first woman I have ever fallen in love with, and I want you to be the last woman I ever love. This legal mumbo-jumbo will only be for a year. If anything happens to me, you will get it all. I want to be the one that takes care of you."

"What if something happens to me?"

"Goddamn it, woman! Nothing had better ever happen to you. End of story. Got it?"

I grinned a little. "Yes, Todd."

"Mallory Kennedy, will you marry me?" He said those words so confidently as he gazed into my eyes. I started tearing up, and without thinking, I automatically responded, "Yes."

He kissed me softly on the lips. "I don't have a ring yet. We'll go pick one out together. That's how I want everything to be done now. We do it all together."

I grinned. "Okay."

He stepped back. "Are your parents still alive?"

This was something we never got around to talking about. We had the conversation now. I think I surprised him a bit with the "Dad walked out on us, and my mother attached herself to any man who was wealthy in her eyes."

He frowned. "Not now, but another time, I want to hear more about your past. I think we have more in common than I realized." I was equally shocked by his response. As much as he protested my request not to attend the wake or funeral, Todd gave in and actually agreed finally to let me stay home. I took today off and, despite what Carole taught me, I used it as a personal day, and Angela was texting me, telling me that Jackie found out that I was dating Todd. Fuck! She was an instigator, and it wouldn't be long before the whole department found out.

I watched the news and saw the disaster unfolding at the funeral. It was becoming a circus show as it spun out of control. The cat was out of the bag about her long struggle with pill and alcohol addiction. They flashed several mugshots from her escapades over the years. Her drug dependency was on the front page of every paper this morning, along with pictures of her late-night partying.

I quickly checked the Internet; I found one story about "The other woman," showing Todd kissing me on the platform when I landed from the zip line at the project-challenge weekend. I was embarrassed when I texted him to let him know. The caption said that I brought Odessa to her death. I was never mentioned by name, but you could clearly see it was Todd and me. I was mortified, overthinking how this picture had surfaced or even worse... was the media spying on us all weekend? Now, I was glad I didn't attend the services.

By the time Todd arrived home to the penthouse, just minutes shy of nine in the evening, he had answers for me. Todd's investigators found out that Louise took that photo, sent it to Amanda, and Amanda sold it to a paper.

The story was now off the Internet, and Amanda was being sued. Mark was dealing with Louise but on the guidelines of Todd's lawyers. I gasped as my hands shot up, covering my mouth, realizing that Louise probably sent it to Odessa as well. "Todd, do you think her overdose was accidental?"

He hardened. "Get that God damn thought out of your head. She did not commit suicide because of a picture. Odessa was too selfish for that. She would rather be alive, causing a scene and getting the attention from being jilted. Don't you remember how she handled meeting you at the club? She thrived on being in the spotlight and playing." He reasoned with me, "She mixed too many pills, and it was an unfortunate accident."

I was not convinced. She was about to lose everything, and her friend sent her a photo of Todd and me in an intimate moment. My stomach started to ache, and I began to feel jittery. "Todd, she was losing you."

"Mallory, I understand your concern, but you didn't get to read the text conversation that followed, nor will you ever. Trust me; she did not commit suicide."

Todd was not letting any of this go unpunished. He was furious, to say the least, and Louise was now banned from attending any event or social situation with us. My heart ached for Todd. He had just lost his babysitting duties. He was freed from it, but I think he was having some internal battle on filling the gap. All I could do was support him and be patient and upbeat as much as the situation allowed. I asked him how he found out all this information that pointed to Amanda, and he quietly answered he could never give up his sources. Okay, fair enough for me. I could not believe it was Friday night. This week went by so fast.

Todd was getting a phone call. He answered, "Rich, what's up?" Then Todd walked out of the room. I was now in bed, nodding off as he walked in. "Mallory, babe... get up. No sleeping just yet. Pack your bags for an overnight. We'll buy clothes out there."

I was drained emotionally and physically. I wanted to fall asleep; into my pillow, I muttered: "What is going on?"

"The company merger is being announced on Monday."

I shot up, fully awake. "Okay. Where are we going? And why?"

He said, dead seriously, "To get married. Something is going on, and I want to be prepared for it."

I started to scramble out of bed. "How is getting married going to prepare us?"

He stopped. He turned. He came at me, scooping me up like in a dance move, and pinned me to his chest. "So, I can call you my wife now."

Well, that threw me for a loop. I was smiling too. But Odessa was just buried nine hours ago. He continued, "You asked me to wait until after the funeral. I did. I know this is probably not your fairytale wedding, but let it be mine. Let me sweep you off your feet." And he rocked me in his arms. "Carry you away into the night." He started walking me across the room. "Place you in front of an official, and we say, 'I do,' and you will be mine forever." He placed me back on my feet as I thought that was absolutely the perfect wedding for me.

I whispered into his lips, "I do."

He kissed me, smacked my ass, and said, "Good, let's get it done."

He booked three first-class tickets on the next plane flying to Vegas. We were at the airport with two small carry-on bags and his computer. I was about to ask who the third seat was for as Joe was just getting through security. Todd and I breezed through and caught up to him. He shook Todd's hand and then congratulated us. I felt awkward about everything that had happened. Joe didn't pick up on it, though.

It was just another day in the neighborhood. Surprisingly, there were quite a few people on this plane. First-class was even half-filled at eleven in the evening. Luckily, we all got to sit next to one another — Todd and I on one side and Joe in the aisle seat next to Todd. This was my first time flying first class, and it was amazing. We all ordered Bloody Mary's and toasted.

We checked into the hotel by three in the morning Vegas time. No sleep yet. Todd took us right down to the dress shop... yes, it was open twenty-four hours. I liked this simple satin and lace dress with a tiara.

They needed to make a few minor alterations, and Todd gave them our room number and said that we needed it by nine this morning.

Next stop, to a jewelry store, and yes, another open around the clock shop. I heard Vegas was the town that never slept, but this was culture shock to me. We picked out traditional simple gold wedding bands. Todd insisted mine have diamonds across the front. I liked it, and we even found an engagement ring. They called it a radiant cut. I called it beautiful. It was set in an heirloom yellow-gold setting with lots of little diamonds surrounding it.

Todd slipped that ring on me, and there it stayed. We had a few hours to sleep. The alarm went off at eight-thirty; he promptly got us out of bed and me down to the beauty salon and paid for my hair to be done however I wanted it with

The Dating Policy

professional makeup application. There he left me and told me he would be back when I was done.

Holy cow, was I tired as they poured me a glass of Champagne. I waved it away and asked for coffee. When Todd arrived, he was dressed for the wedding and turned every head in the salon.

He smiled. "There is my beautiful bride." He escorted me to our room where my dress waited. By eleven-thirty, Joe was at the chapel, dressed in his tux, and Todd was in his. He wore dark blue that looked so handsome on him. He complimented my style and handed Joe the rings.

That was it. By eleven-fifty Vegas time, Todd and I stood, exchanging wedding vows. I didn't care what we said. It was only important to me when he said, "I do," and I said, "I do."

I could have promised him anything, but the bottom line was I did, and I would forevermore, making me about the single happiest woman on the planet. I officially found cloud nine, and every emotion I had bounced joyfully from cloud to cloud, having a wonderful time. A tear escaped from the corner of my eye as Todd kissed me. We were officially Mr. and Mrs. Todd Duvall.

After a celebration meal, we went back to our rooms. Todd slipped off my dress, laid me on the bed, and started to claim every inch of my body by kissing it and saying, "This is now all mine, and this and so is this."

I was giggling from being overtired. That was until he spread my legs and kissed in between. Sex was very caring with a lot of kissing, and an "I love you" spoken several times. That late afternoon, I fell asleep, cherished by my new husband, wrapped in his arms as I dreamed... Odessa! I struggled to get away. Todd held me. He wouldn't let me up. Odessa came at me, trying to kiss me and telling Todd to share. Why wasn't he allowing me to get away? Why was he holding me down? I struggled and struggled as she was still coming at me. My eyes flew open, and I was still as could be, wrapped gently in Todd's arms. It was a dream... only a dream. I moved slightly, and he released his hold as I announced I needed to use the bathroom.

I looked in the mirror and splashed cold water on my face. Holy heck did that freak me out! It was one in the morning, and I looked down at my rings. I was married. And now I had a ghost.

Our flight back was in four hours, and we had to get up pretty soon anyway, so I decided to stay awake. I just sat there, looking at my rings and thinking. I must have fallen asleep because Todd leaning over me made me jump. I asked, "Hey, what are you doing up?"

"I'm looking for my wife."

I grinned. "Well, you found her."

"But why did I find her? Why is she not in bed with her husband?"

Suzanne Eglington

I know I had a stupid grin on my face now. My husband... I liked hearing that. "I just woke up and couldn't fall back to sleep. You were sleeping so nicely. I didn't want to wake you."

"Well, that was a fail." He took my hand. "Come on, babe. You belong in bed with me. Let me see if I can put you back to sleep for two more hours." And he did. I wish he had let me stay awake. I was crabby now from a sleep hangover. One Bloody Mary on the plane later, and I was out.

When we arrived back, Todd scooped me up again, carrying me into the penthouse. I was so exhausted. He carried me right to bed, tucked me in, kissed me, told me he would always have my back and that he loved me, then left to work in the office.

* * *

Monday morning came, and we drove to work together, same car this time. He kissed me at the door, and we went our separate ways.

I reached my office and, on my desk was a thick black-and-gold folder with the new company name in raised gold lettering across the center of it. I put my bags down and opened it. Here it was... the official announcement. I stood and peeked around. Everyone had one on their desk.

I opened mine and started to read. I went straight to the employee handbook. Right on page 12 was the "No Dating Policy." They never changed it, and I panicked.

I had to sign this, and I was shaking. I texted Todd; he told me not to worry about it. The policy was moot. At nine-thirty, I was called to report to a meeting in room 307.

Jessica spotted me walking out of my office, and she snipped, "I hear you and Todd are an item. Mr. Gary is not going to like that one bit since there is a no dating policy here. And if there wasn't, believe me, Todd would have asked me out long ago."

I looked down at my wedding rings, and I couldn't help myself; I flipped her off while making sure she saw them. "Fuck you, Jessica; I'm not dating Todd. I'm married to him."

She gasped. Well, if I was going to crash and burn from this policy, I may as well go down swinging. I went right up to the meeting.

I knocked and opened the door. There were all the Gary members. I was asked to sit at the opposite end of the table.

They pulled out the employee handbook, sliding it in front of me, and asked if I had any questions. I didn't directly know what this was about.

I took the safe route and answered no.

Samantha specifically referred to the dating policy, and I was not going there. She asked me if I understood it, and I answered yes.

Then she stated that it was a serious offense if I did not follow the policy and I could lose my job. She asked me again if I understood it. I panicked... I now knew someone must have seen that article with Todd and me kissing, or was it Jessica's big mouth?

Sure enough, Samantha was pulling out a copy of the article from the Internet.

There was a knock on the door as Todd just invited himself right in. He focused on the article laying on the table halfway between them and me as he pulled it toward him and read it, not giving a fuck what was going on.

Samantha told him this was a closed meeting. He walked to me. This was getting heated as Samantha looked from him to me. She finally ended it by firing me right here, right now.

Todd argued with her, "You can't fire her. She's not dating me. Mallory is my wife."

He placed the article to my right, looking down at me as I looked up to him. He grinned to make light of what this was as he announced to me. "That was a damn good kiss, woman."

I was feeling faint. I was nowhere near his confidence level. He tossed our marriage papers down on the table toward Samantha.

"We were married this weekend. Nicholas gave us his blessing. Oh, and this picture was at the annual corporate challenge — something you will never be invited to. We were on the same team as Nicholas and his wife. Nicholas made a formal announcement in front of all his key staff that Mallory was Williams Enterprise's newest member. You may want to rethink what you are doing. An apology might help save your job right now as well. Mallory Duvall has impressed him so much that she even influenced the way he wants all the reports handled. They must all duplicate her style. Samantha, maybe Mallory can tutor you on what he is looking for now."

They all stared. He pulled me to my unsteady feet. He told them to make another appointment if there was any other business to be conducted with me and said I was returning to my desk.

He led me out with my hand in his. "Don't worry, babe. We're in this together. They did this to try and make a peace offering to Nicholas when there is no need. Now, go to HR and change your name. Oh, and you are free to announce you are married."

I was still trembling a little but calming down. Todd had to go back to his office after he kissed me one more time.

"Remember, Mrs. Duvall; I will always have your back." The elevator doors opened, and he left.

Suzanne Eglington

High Priority: A Tiffany Chanler Novel

The Dating Policy

The Marriage Contract

The Baby Clause

Inceptions: The Kate and Robert Chronicles
You and I: The Kate and Robert Chronicles
Beckham 101: The

The Dating Policy